"Y . . . you? Why?—?" the drunk said as he recognized the face, but before he could voice the question he gave a great sigh and fell silent.

The dark figure let the dying match fall to the pavement and stood there for a moment, staring down at the dead, shocked face, then broke into an amused, satisfied chuckle. Moving quickly, the killer opened the door of the Packard and rummaged quickly through it by the light of a small flashlight. Finding nothing, the figure moved to the rear of the car and opened the trunk. The small beam of the electric light revealed nothing but a spare tire and jack.

When the figure straightened an automobile rolled up, and the passenger door swung open on silent hinges. The killer got in without a word, and the car sped off into the cool dark of the New Orleans night. The drunk's unseeing eyes were fixed impassively skyward as the faint light of a street-lamp glinted off the star-and-crescent New Orleans police badge pinned to his vest.

"Just when you thought you were weary of New Orleans as a mystery setting, here comes the first in an extremely promising Crescent City series.

—*Booklist*

"There's a pleasantly old-fashioned B-movie feeling to Skinner's first novel, set in a 1936 New Orleans so obviously well-researched . . . you believe it totally. Readers will enjoy joining Skinner to this homage to the genre's history.

—*Publisher's Weekly*

"A pretty slick presentation that . . . pushes all the right buttons."

—*Library Journal*

SKIN DEEP, BLOOD RED

Robert Skinner

k

Kensington Books
Kensington Publishing Corp.

http://www.kensingtonbooks.com

KENSINGTON BOOKS are published by

Kensington Publishing Corp.
850 Third Avenue
New York, NY 10022

First Kensington Hardcover Printing: January, 1997
First Kensington Paperback Printing: February, 1998

Printed in the United States of America
10 9 8 7 6 5 4 3 2 1

To Chris, Kelly, Esme, and Werner,
who probably wonder what it is
the old man does every day.

ACKNOWLEDGMENTS

Thanks to Lester Sullivan, Xavier University Archivist, for his advice concerning Colored Creole life in New Orleans, and to my mother, father, and grandparents whose many stories about life in the Great Depression served to make that time more real to me than the decades in which I've actually lived.

"The nature of (New Orleans) is one of contrasts, beautiful as hell and ugly as sin, one as damaging as the other to the innocent far from home. She'll kill you with kindness, then pray over your corpse. That more than anything marks New Orleans, the curious contiguity of good and evil, life and death."

—Robert Campbell, *Fat Tuesday* (1983)

"Maybe there's only one revolution, since the beginning. The good guys against the bad guys. The question is, who are the good guys?"

—Burt Lancaster, *The Professionals* (1996)

Chapter 1

The heavy downpour ended as suddenly as it had begun, leaving behind deep quiet and a multitude of glistening puddles. The newly born silence was quickly broken by the low-pitched growl of a long, dark Packard sedan that turned the corner at Washington Avenue and then headed north on Magazine Street.

The driver was feeling good. He'd just dropped seventy-five dollars on French champagne and a blond whore who looked like Jean Harlow. He'd always thought of himself as a pretty experienced man, but the beautiful whore had taught him things he never knew existed. Even now, a half hour later, he felt a contented satisfaction he'd never known before.

In the 3100 block of Magazine he pulled to the curb in front of the building where he lived and cut the engine. When he got out of the car he yawned and stretched, enjoying the cool night air. He treated himself to a drink from a hammered silver flask and bumped his hip on the front fender as he tried to walk around it too quickly on his way to the sidewalk. He grunted a curse, but the contented feelings overrode his flash of temper. He leaned against the fender, smiled foolishly, and took another long drink. He was watching the cloudy sky dreamily when a hideous scraping jarred him from his reverie. He jumped, drop-

ping the flask as he clawed under his coat for the Colt Police
Positive holstered there. He had the gun halfway out before he
saw the noise was just a dry, dead palmetto leaf, pushed along
the macadamized surface of the street by a whisper of breeze.

"Shit," he said under his breath. "Gettin' jumpy."

He shrugged his coat back over his gun and bent clumsily
to retrieve the flask. When he stood up he saw a dark figure
facing him across the hood of the Packard.

"Wha . . . ?" he began, but before he could finish a heavy
automatic in the dark figure's hand roared twice, and the
drunken man's body reeled from the impact. He fell to the wet
pavement, his fingers groping blindly for his revolver. As his
eyes searched the sky above his head, a shadow fell across
him. A match flared in the killer's hand, and for a brief instant
a face was illuminated for the dying man's eyes.

"Y . . . you? Why—?" the drunk said as he recognized the
face, but before he could voice the question he gave a great
sigh and fell silent.

The dark figure let the dying match fall to the pavement and
stood there for a moment, staring down at the dead, shocked
face, then broke into an amused, satisfied chuckle. Moving
quickly, the killer opened the door of the Packard and rummaged quickly through it by the light of a small flashlight.
Finding nothing, the figure moved to the rear of the car and
opened the trunk. The small beam of electric light revealed
nothing but a spare tire and jack.

When the figure straightened an automobile rolled up, and
the passenger door swung open on silent hinges. The killer got
in without a word, and the car sped off into the cool dark of
the New Orleans night. The drunk's unseeing eyes were fixed
impassively skyward as the faint light of a streetlamp glinted
off the star-and-crescent New Orleans police badge pinned to
his vest.

It was early afternoon as Wesley Farrell sat in his office
upstairs from the nightclub he owned on Basin Street, flipping
playing cards into an overturned hat on the floor. He was good

at it, seldom missing, but his pale gray eyes seemed to be looking at something far, far away, unaware of the hat, the cards, or even of the little wood-cabinet radio on his desk that softly played a number by Louis Armstrong and his Hot Five Combo.

A knock sounded at the door, and the eyes flicked in that direction, suddenly possessed of an intense awareness. "Yeah," he called in a smooth baritone voice.

The door swung open and a bull-necked, thick-shouldered Negro in a collarless white shirt stuck his head and torso into the room.

"A Miz Willie Mae Gautier out here to see you, boss," the black man said.

Farrell blinked and sat up, curiosity and surprise playing across the contours of his face. He and his great-aunt had exchanged less than ten words in the last ten years. He ran long, thin fingers through thick, reddish-brown hair combed straight back from his high forehead. His features were strong and aquiline, and a deep cleft divided his gently squared chin exactly in two. His skin, almost a pale gold in color, seemed to give off a warm glow.

"Tell her to come in," he said finally.

He was standing at the window when the door opened again to admit a small, elderly woman with white hair and an olive complexion. She was dressed in a white shirtwaist and black skirt, with a knitted shawl around her thin shoulders. A small silver watch was pinned to her breast by a silver clasp, and a chain ran from the clasp to a silver pince-nez perched on the bridge of her nose. Her lips were compressed into a thin, bitter line, and her shoe-button eyes were as flat and empty as two stones plucked from a running stream.

"Good afternoon, Wesley," she said in a neat, precise voice. "It's been a long time."

"Not long enough," Farrell replied. "What do you want?"

"Aren't you going to ask me to sit?" the old woman asked, unruffled by his rudeness.

"Sit or stand, it's all one to me," Farrell said as he placed a Camel cigarette in the left-hand corner of his mouth.

"Your manners are just as bad now as they were when you were a boy," she said in a voice like flint. "But then, I don't imagine you meet very many refined people in a . . . a place like this," she concluded with a sneer.

Farrell set fire to the Camel with a small, nickel-plated lighter and blew smoke into the air between them. "Don't be so rough on the place, Willie," he said. "I can think of six priests who come here every week. One of them asked me last night if he could sit in with the jazz trio. Plays a sweet clarinet, Father Jack does. As for the other people who come here, they may be whores, gamblers, and pimps, but they behave themselves and pay their bar tabs before they leave." He grinned at her with his mouth, but his pale gray eyes bored into Willie Mae's with fierce intensity.

The old woman's black eyes glittered, and she clenched her small fists convulsively at her sides. "You think you can hurt me with your evil talk, but you can't. Mine is one of the proudest names in this state; but then, a person like you can't know very much about pride."

Farrell laughed mirthlessly. "You're just playing a stupid game when you talk like that. You like to pretend that because you've got more white blood than black in your veins, it means something. You can call yourself a Creole and speak French in your own neighborhood, but once you leave it, the law says you and I are nothing but a couple of niggers, and we'll never be anything else. If you don't believe me, just go down the street to one of the other clubs and let the doorman know what you are."

Willie Mae Gautier's face paled. "You vile creature," she exclaimed in a voice gone shrill. "Don't you ever use that word in my presence again. I pray to God no one ever finds out you carry my blood."

Farrell's eyes flashed, and he threw the cigarette butt to the floor with such force that it bounced, scattering sparks in every direction. "You make a bad salesman, *tante,*" Farrell said in a thick, hard voice. "You and I both know the only reason you came here was to ask me for something, but you don't seem to know the right way to ask it. I'll make it easier for you, then. Just say what it is you want and get the hell out of my place."

Willie Mae showed no fear of his temper, drawing up her small body with regal dignity. "It's my grandson—your cousin—Marcel Aristide," she began. "I'm hearing . . . troubling things about him. He's been staying out all hours of the night, flashing around a lot of money." She paused and glanced at the small watch pinned to her bosom. "I want to know if he's involved in something that might get him in trouble. I want you to stop him before he gets in over his head."

The right corner of Farrell's mouth turned up in a derisive grin. "Why come to me?" he asked, spreading his arms in an elaborate gesture. "Does this look like a social welfare agency?"

"I'll tell you why I came," Willie Mae said, leveling a finger at him. "I came because, like it or not, we're family. Marcel doesn't even know you exist, but he's your blood cousin, just like I'm your aunt." She lowered her finger, dropped her eyes, and said in a softer voice, "Your mother would want you to help him, and you know it."

Farrell felt his neck swell with heated blood, and bright explosions of light went off behind his eyes. He put out a hand to the windowsill to steady himself, and fought to bring his temper under control. "Of all the low-down gall," he said in harsh wonder.

Willie Mae's black eyes snapped back up to meet his own. "You know what I'm saying is true, and besides," her voice dropped to a sibilant whisper, "there's no one better to look into this than you. Wherever Marcel is, you've already been there." She smiled and folded her small arms in a posture of impatient waiting.

Farrell blew breath out from between pursed lips; it seemed to have the same effect as a boiler letting off steam. "All right," he said finally. "For Mother's sake. But *not* yours, understand?"

"But of course," Willie Mae said primly. "We understand each other perfectly."

Farrell straightened, walked over to his desk, and sat on the edge. He was in control again, and he felt the tension draining from his body. "Do you know anything about where Marcel hangs out?"

"Marie-Rose Pesier's son, Ralph, told me he's seen Marcel frequenting a place called Guido's pool hall. You know it, of course."

"Of course," Farrell said, irony hanging heavy in his voice. He owned Guido's, as well as the illegal numbers drop that operated in the back room.

"Very well, then," Willie Mae Gautier said. "I'll look forward to hearing from you." She turned and walked from the room, leaving the door open behind her.

For several long moments Farrell stood there, staring at the open door. In his mind he could hear the whistle and slap of leather meeting flesh, and the sound of a boy crying for a dead mother, and a father whose face he could only imagine.

Chapter 2

The 3100 block of Magazine Street looked like a policemen's convention. Ordinarily a quiet area, now the block was filled with harness bulls chasing off morbid tourists, and plainclothesmen from the detective bureau questioning residents. Crime lab technicians swarmed over the area like cockroaches on spilled sugar, sweeping up anything that might be a clue. The lights of the police cars reflected off pools of standing water left by the rain, bathing the street in a sickly yellow glow.

Two men stood over the body with their hands in their pockets, talking quietly. Once in a while one of them would glance down at the sheet-covered form, but otherwise they might have been standing at a bar, having a quiet conversation.

"I always figured Chance would go out like this sooner or later, Frank," the larger of the two men said. He was dressed in a freshly pressed blue serge pinstripe suit, a blood-red tie, and a yellow Borsalino pulled low over his eyes. His face was big, and red with high blood pressure, and his nose a bold blade like the dorsal fin of a shark. His eyes were small and deep-set, and his mouth was a brutal gash across the lower part of his face.

"I tried talkin' to him, Captain. More than once," the other man said, with a note of tired sadness in his voice. "Even when we were in school together at Dominican, he was always takin' the long chances, just to see if he could put it over on one of the lay brothers. You couldn't scare the silly bastard. The brothers broke more than one barrel stave on him tryin'." He smiled sadly as he remembered the tough, sandy-haired kid who'd led him into so much trouble years ago.

The second plainclothesman was a wide-shouldered, heavy-set man a hair under six feet tall. He wasn't dressed as well as the captain, but he wore his plain brown suit and topcoat with a quiet dignity. He was somewhere in his middle fifties, with red hair and a mustache beginning to be shot with strands of gray. His eyes were a deep blue made for laughing, but they weren't laughing just then.

"Inspector Casey?" a crime lab man called out.

"Yeah," the red-haired cop answered, turning toward the voice.

"Got something interesting here," the technician said. "We don't see many of these." He held something out on the end of a forceps.

Casey took the forceps and held it under the beam of the technician's flashlight. It was a brass shell casing that looked like a .45, but something about it made him look closer. There was a manufacturer's name on the base. It read ELY BROS .455 WEBLEY.

"Well, well, this is something," Casey said.

"What?" the florid-faced captain asked.

"This is foreign manufacture. British, it looks like," Casey said. "Chance wasn't killed by anything homegrown. This was fired from a .455 Webley navy automatic." He handed the forceps out to the captain. "Ever seen one of those before?"

"Yeah," the captain answered. "Saw a couple of 'em when I was fighting with Lee Christmas in Central America years ago. Kinda clumsy-looking, I thought."

"Bet Chance didn't think so," the crime lab man said with a rueful note in his voice. He took back the forceps from the captain and placed the shell in a small envelope, which he sealed and dropped into his pocket before moving back to the other side of the street.

"Nobody around here's going to be using a piece like that. We got us an out-of-towner," Casey said. "Now all we gotta do is decide who among two hundred or so people decided to have Chance knocked off." He moved out of the way so the two ambulance attendants could lift the dead man onto a litter.

"Listen, Frank," the captain said as he lit a cigarette, "you wanna handle this with kid gloves, see."

Casey looked at his superior, and let his eyes and face go flat. "Why's that, skipper?" he asked in a toneless voice.

"You're right about the number of people who'd want to pick off Chance." The big man's quiet words seemed to creep from his lips and slink down the length of the cigarette in the corner of his mouth. His eyes were hooded and cagey. "We got to play this close to the vest until we can make some sense of it, get me?"

Casey caught something in the captain's voice that he didn't understand, but he nodded an assent. "Sure, skipper, I get you."

"Well," the captain said in his normal voice, "guess I'll go back to headquarters. You coming?" The cagey look had disappeared from his face, and he favored Casey with a grotesque smile.

"No," Casey said. "I'll nose around here for a while longer, see what else we can pick up from the neighborhood, skipper."

"Okay," the captain said. "I'll see you later."

Casey watched the captain cross the street and get into a smart-looking, dark blue Mercury coupé. An engine coughed into life behind him, and the red-haired detective turned to see the ambulance pull away from the curb.

"They didn't call you Chance for nothing, boy," he said under his breath. "But I could never get you to understand that the luck runs out for everybody, sooner or later." He shook his head slowly and watched the ambulance until it turned a corner and disappeared from sight.

Chapter 3

Farrell drove down St. Charles Avenue in a cream-and-red 1936 Packard roadster with the top down, the early morning sun feeling good on his face. He turned on Baronne and followed it across Canal Street into the French Quarter. He turned again at Dumaine and parked in front of a ramshackle building with a board sign reading GUIDO'S BILLIARD PARLOR hanging from a bracket out front.

To Farrell's knowledge no one had ever played billiards in there, but every other variety of pool had been.

He walked through the doorway and, from force of habit, moved quickly to the side, standing stock-still until his eyes grew accustomed to the dim interior. It was a practiced maneuver calculated to remove the advantage from anyone who might be waiting on the other side of the door to spring an unpleasant surprise.

He saw that although there were a number of people inside, only about half the tables were in use. It was too early for the better hustlers and sharks to be about their trade. A sloppy-looking man with dark, curly hair leaned across the counter, a dead cigar in his mouth, as he read the most recent issue of *Dime Detective*.

"You're gonna ruin yourself reading trash like that, Guido," Farrell said as he lit the Camel in the corner of his mouth.

The curly-haired man looked up from his magazine, a sheepish look on his face. "This Frederick Nebel writes some pretty excitin' stuff, Mr. Farrell. I just can't get enough of him."

"I hear a kid named Marcel Aristide comes in here sometimes," Farrell said, blowing smoke above Guido's head. "A quadroon, about twenty years old. Seen him lately?"

"Back there now." Guido gestured toward a table with a group of men standing around it. "He's been cleanin' Jack Fontaine out. That young nigger can sure shoot," he said, chuckling juicily.

Farrell looked at Guido for a moment, his face full of nothing, then touched two fingers to the brim of his pearl gray Stetson and sauntered back. Even though he'd passed for white for more than twenty years, the word *nigger* had never lost the power to shock him. Because he moved in a shadowy world between the races, he had trained himself not to react to any of the words white men used to demean and humiliate black ones, but he was always conscious of playing a meticulously concocted role, and like any actor he was careful to say and do nothing that would appear out of character.

The snick of billiard balls was all that disturbed the reverential quiet. A slim youngster with wavy, light brown hair was bent over the table, fierce concentration on his almost childish face. He was wearing the pants and vest of a stylish brown gabardine suit. The collar of his pale yellow shirt was open at the neck, and his blue tie hung askew.

As Farrell watched, the youngster thrust his cue viciously, smashing the nine ball decisively into the corner pocket. The kid stood up quickly, his eyes toting up the remaining balls. He strode like a young lion to a new position and ran the eleven ball cleanly into a side pocket.

Jack Fontaine, a middle-aged hustler, stood to one side, his green hat tipped back on his blond hair. A cigarette stuck in one corner of his mouth lazily trickled smoke as his eyes squinted impassively at the table.

Finally the kid sank his last ball and walked over to Fontaine, a sneer on his face. He stuck out one palm and said, "Pay up, sucker."

Fontaine brought out a wad of bills, dropped them into the waiting hand, and walked away. The kid smiled insolently at the spectators, picked up his coat and hat, and strutted out.

Farrell went over to the bar next to Fontaine. He held up two fingers to the bartender. "Rough day, Jack?"

"Shit," Fontaine said in a flat voice as he picked up the shot of rye and downed it. "Thanks for the drink."

"Have another," Farrell said, pointing out Fontaine's empty glass to the bartender. "Take you for much?"

"Even the butter-and-egg money," Fontaine said. "Stake me to twenty bucks and I'll pay you back double next Tuesday."

"Sure," Farrell said. "Seen that kid before?"

"Yeah, but not to play. I wouldn't have played with him this time, but he was waving around a lot of dough," Fontaine said as he sipped the rye. "I figured him for a punk."

"Wonder where he got it?" Farrell said.

"Beats me," Fontaine said, taking off his hat and scratching his scalp vigorously.

Farrell took out a money clip, peeled off a twenty, and pushed it into Fontaine's breast pocket. "See you next week?"

"Check," the hustler said as he slid from his stool and strode away.

Farrell drew smoke into his lungs and let it trickle back out his nose as he looked at himself in the long mirror behind the bar. He had things to do that day, including trips to another club he owned, three illegal betting parlors, two houses of prostitution in which he had an interest, and a couple of floating crap games that he backed unofficially, but yesterday's visit from the little old woman had started memories, like faded movie film, flickering irritably inside his head. His memories of Willie Mae Gautier were sharp, distinct, and unpleasant. Now here he was, doing her a favor, something he'd never thought he'd even consider. It was just like the scheming old shrew to use his memories of his mother to get something out of him.

His thoughts were interrupted when he felt someone come

up behind him, then slide onto the bar stool recently vacated by Jack Fontaine. "Hey, boss, y'hear the news?" a rasping voice asked.

"That's what I pay you for, Moe, to keep your ear to the ground and then tell me about it," Farrell said without glancing at the man on his right.

"Not this," Moe said. He was a heavy-shouldered ex-boxer with cauliflower ears and ridges of scar tissue over each eye. He wore a cloth cap on the back of his head, and a lock of jet-black hair hung down over one scarred eyebrow. He was only half as punchy as he looked, which meant people said all kinds of things in front of him. "Chance Tartaglia got rubbed out last night."

Farrell's eyes darted from the mirror and fixed on those of the heavyset man beside him. "Who by?"

"Shit," Moe said. "Chance had more enemies than Carter's got liver pills. Gambling, protection, women—Chance had a pinkie in those and more. He died happy, though."

"How do you mean?" Farrell lit a new cigarette with the butt of the old one.

"He was with Holly Ballou last night," Moe said, with a wink and a grin. "Boy, if I had the cash, I'd take a crack at that li'l honey, myself."

"You and ninety-seven percent of the other guys in this town," Farrell said.

"You sound like the three percent that's already been there," the ex-fighter said, leering at Farrell in the mirror.

"I'm part of the one percent that don't give a damn," Farrell said impatiently. "This town's full of women: white, black, and everything in between. You don't have to take out a second mortgage just to scratch an itch. Tell me about Tartaglia."

Moe licked his lips and folded his scarred, big-knuckled hands on the bar. Farrell knew he wanted to keep talking about Holly Ballou because he was the kind of man who enjoyed fantasizing about a woman more than having her, but Farrell was in no mood to humor him.

"Happened after midnight, so I hear," Moe said. "Somebody gunned him but good outside a building he owns down on Magazine Street. Two pills in the chest, like that.'' Moe snapped his thick fingers loudly, twice. The bartender looked up from polishing some glasses, then went back to what he was doing when he realized Moe wasn't signaling for a drink.

''Sounds like a professional hit,'' Farrell said. ''Who'd you get the news from?''

''Li'l Lenny Schwartz,'' Moe said.

''Who?''

''You know, that fat little guy works in the morgue downtown. Hey, Mike, gimme a beer, willya?'' Moe asked, waving at the bartender.

''What else you know?'' Farrell asked after the bartender had been and gone.

''Not much,'' Moe said, wiping beer foam from his lips with the back of his hairy hand. '' 'Cept the cops'll play hell findin' out who did it. Thinka all the people Tartaglia squeezed for protection money over the past ten years, or the legs he broke collectin' on welshed gamblin' debts and such.''

He'd had a lot of juice, too, Farrell thought silently. A cop couldn't get away with all that without friends in high places. Farrell wondered fleetingly whether it was an enemy or a soured friend who'd pulled Tartaglia's plug.

Farrell got up and slid a folded five-dollar bill into the breast pocket of Moe's black alpaca jacket, then dropped two half-dollars on the bar.

''Hey,'' Moe said, ''where ya goin'?''

''I got business, Moe. Take care of yourself.''

''Right, Mr. Farrell. Be seein' ya.'' Moe put his nose back into his beer glass and sucked noisily at the foam as Farrell walked through the gloomy interior of the pool hall and out the door.

Marcel Aristide was in high spirits, the way he always was when he beat a white pool shark at his own game. At such times he forgot who he was and what color he was, and felt like a giant.

He glanced at the face of the cheap strap watch on his left wrist and saw it was going on noon. The realization cut into his euphoria, and a chill ran the length of his spine. The big white man with the Irish accent he'd met three weeks before at Guido's had told him he was looking for some men who liked easy money and weren't too particular how they got it. The Irishman's smile had reminded him of the alligators in the Audubon Park Zoo, but he'd felt an undeniable pleasure from the white man's attention. The man had treated him like an equal, and not a little boy, as Aunt Willie did.

"I like money too much to care about its past," Marcel had answered with a swagger.

"Have a drink on me, then, and we'll talk some business," the Irishman had replied, placing his huge, hairy hand on Marcel's shoulders.

The first several jobs had been a snap; a handful of hold-ups and several grocery store and gas station robberies. Although the money hadn't amounted to much, the ease in getting it had impressed both Marcel and Lester Medley, another young Negro who frequented Guido's. But the big man clearly wasn't satisfied, and he'd told Marcel he needed to build a stake before he left the city, and was after bigger game. He'd made plain the youth was to call him for instructions at noon today.

A block from the pool hall, Marcel walked into a phone booth, dropped in a nickel, and dialed. His eyes darted up and down the street as he waited. Finally a deep, accented voice answered.

"This is Marcel," the youngster said. "Anything shakin'?"

"Right," the voice said. "Meet me and Lester at the corner of Galvez and Perdido tomorrow morning, seven-forty-five."

"What we doin' that early on a Saturday, Griff?" Marcel asked. "Ain't nobody open then."

"Nuts," Griff growled. "This is something I had Lester look into. An old guy with a hardware store. He's doing pretty good, Lester says. He always waits 'til Saturday afternoon to bank the week's receipts. It'll be like shooting fish in a barrel, so bring your artillery.'' The deep voice laughed at the ridiculous image the words had conjured up.

"Okay," Marcel said, feeling his blood start to race. "Seven-forty-five. I'll be there."

Chapter 4

Farrell drove through the Quarter to Basin Street, where his largest and most lucrative club was located. It was still before noon, and the famous street was quiet, with only a few pedestrians idling their way down the sidewalks. He pulled up in front of a large brick building with a neon sign over the door reading CAFE TRISTESSE. A Negro was sweeping the walk under the canopy, and he stopped long enough to speak, and open the the door for his boss. Farrell touched two fingers to the brim of his hat, winked, and passed through the open door.

Inside, several men and women were engaged in cleaning and waxing, and a mixed trio of one white and two black musicians was jiving its way through a Mills Brothers song, "Glow Worm." The white guy gave the piano a lot of English, rippling the keys like Eddy Duchin.

The bartender, a lanky, horse-faced man with a lock of honey-colored hair falling over one eye, caught Farrell's attention and indicated with a toss of his head that he should come over.

"Hi, Harry," Farrell said.

"Hi, boss," Harry answered. "You got company in your office. And I don't mean the Duke of Windsor."

"Cops?"

"Just one, but he's one of the big ones this time," Harry said.

Farrell said nothing, nodded his thanks to Harry, and headed to the back and up the stairs to his private office and apartment. He unconsciously squared his shoulders at the top of the stairs, and walked through his office door with a slow, unconcerned saunter.

"Nice you could make it, big shot." It was the big, florid-faced police captain. He had his wide-brimmed Borsalino down low over his eyes, and his feet propped on Farrell's big cherry-wood desk.

"Make yourself at home, Moroni," Farrell said, "just like you were invited." He hung his Stetson on a hat rack made of buffalo horns, unbuttoned his jacket, and sat down behind the desk. "Why the visit? Somebody stealing from the church poor box again?"

"You heard about the Tartaglia kill already," Captain Moroni said with a smug look, "so you can guess why I'm here."

"So Tartaglia got gunned. I'm surprised it didn't happen sooner," Farrell said, taking a cigarette from a handsome little mahogany box on top of his desk. "So why come to me about it?"

"There was bad blood between you and Tartaglia," Moroni said, helping himself to a cigarette. "Everybody in town knows you knocked him silly and threw him down the stairs. He said he'd get you for it one day. Could be you decided to beat him to the punch." He grinned, and smoke leaked gently from his nose and from between his large, yellow teeth.

"Bullshit," Farrell said, blowing a stream of smoke into the air between them. "That was months ago. Besides, I can prove where I was last night. And I was there all night, copper."

"A woman, I'm guessing," Moroni said musingly. "Probably one who couldn't make it into the Church Ladies' Temperance Union." Moroni took his feet off the desk and leaned toward Farrell. "I figured you to have an alibi, but I just thought I'd come in and . . ."

"You just thought you'd come in and my guilty conscience

would make me tell you I'd done it because I wanted to cleanse my soul," Farrell said, crushing out his cigarette in a crystal ashtray. "Either you're dumber than I think, or you take me for a patsy. Even if I wanted Tartaglia dead, which I didn't, I sure as hell wouldn't have done it in a way that you'd luck on to."

"Chance was taken out by somebody who knew what he was doing," Moroni said, changing the subject. "Two slugs in the pump. Chance never even got his gun out of the holster. I hear you're a pretty good shot, Farrell. I also hear you've taken a few guys down in your time. What kind of gun you got?"

"A .38 automatic," Farrell said.

"Let's see it," Moroni said, holding out one huge hand. His eyes were as blank and cold as two old pennies.

Farrell thought about telling him to go to hell, but he knew Moroni was itching for a reason to take him downtown. He decided to humor the big, florid-faced detective just to get rid of him. He swallowed the rage sticking at the back of his throat, opened a drawer in his desk, and removed a pistol.

Moroni reached out and took it from Farrell's hand. It was an almost perfect right angle of blue steel with a little rounded nub of a hammer. He hefted it, looking it over appreciatively. "A model 1902 Colt automatic. I ain't seen one like this in a lot of years." He ejected the clip, and saw that it held a full magazine of eight. He jerked back the slide, peered down the sight, and snapped the hammer down on the empty chamber.

"You've taken good care of it," Moroni said with a smile. "That's a nice quality to have. Maybe the only one you've got." He laughed at his joke. "What's this?" he asked, pointing to a piece of spring steel welded at one end to the right-hand side of the pistol's slide.

"I had a gunsmith put that on there," Farrell explained. "It hooks into the waistband of my pants, keeps it from sliding down."

"Cute trick," the captain said, a corner of his brutal mouth turning up in a hideous half smile. "This the only gun you got?"

"Yeah, why?"

"Just wondering," the captain said. He pushed the magazine back into the handle and placed the gun in the center of Farrell's desk.

"What kind of gun was Tartaglia killed with?" Farrell asked. "You seem to be satisfied that it wasn't with mine."

"Somebody's being cute," Moroni said. "Lab boys say he was hit twice in the chest with a .455 Webley navy automatic. Ever seen one of those?"

"I wouldn't know a Webley automatic from the *Hindenburg,*" Farrell said. "And I don't know anybody who does."

"You know," Moroni said, standing up and pulling down on the points of his vest, "you interest me, Farrell."

"Why's that?" Farrell asked, keeping his face blank.

"I got a strong hunch you ain't everything you're cracked up to be."

"If you think I know what you're talking about, you've got another thing coming," Farrell replied.

"Yeah, you do," Moroni said, his voice thick with insinuation. "I've lived in this town almost all my life, and I been a cop for twenty years. Something about you stinks like rotten cheese." He walked to the center of the room, then turned back to Farrell. "You might not have killed Tartaglia, but you're sure as hell guilty of *something*. If I can't send you to Angola, I'd be just as satisfied to ruin you in this town; ruin you so's you couldn't even walk down the street no more."

Farrell stood up, his eyes hot and the skin around his mouth white and strained. "If you've got anything on me, take me downtown. Otherwise, get your miserable ass out of my club."

Moroni smiled that grotesque smile again. "I'll be seeing you some more, kid," he said. Then he lumbered out of the room, slamming the door behind him.

Farrell stood there for a long moment, immobilized by an icy clutch of fear to which he could put no name. He reached out, picked up the old pistol, and held it loosely in his hand. After a time the unyielding weight of the blue steel calmed him, and he put it back in the drawer.

Chapter 5

Friday was one of the Cafe Tristesse's best nights. The trio was a good one, popular with the local crowd, and the floor was filled with well-dressed white couples dancing while a long, cool brunette warbled the lyrics to "These Foolish Things Remind Me of You." Farrell, dressed in a white dinner jacket that emphasized the width of his shoulders, made several circuits of the club, chatting with regulars and greeting new arrivals.

A little before eleven that night, three men walked into the club and stood on the edge of the large room. Two of the men were professional muscle, dressed in dark, expensive suits, their biceps straining the sleeves of the fabric. Their eyes held nothing but intense watchfulness.

The man between them was smaller in stature but clearly the leader. He stood there, holding a freshly blocked Homburg hat against the satin lapels of his black dinner jacket. He, too, was watchful, but he was looking for someone in particular. When he spotted Farrell, leaning against the bar sipping from an iced glass of straight vodka, he stared at him until Farrell finally glanced over and saw him. When he had Farrell's attention he smiled thinly and gently inclined his head. Farrell nodded, put down his glass, and wandered through the tables to a door that led up to his office.

He beat the trio upstairs and was standing at the window behind his desk when the knock came. "It's open," he called.

One of the bodyguards opened the door and entered the office first, followed by the small man in the dinner jacket. The second bodyguard came in last, closing the door. Then he and his partner stationed themselves on either side of the entrance and stood there silently with their hands clasped in front of them.

"They'd make a nice set of bookends, Ganns," Farrell said. "Drink?"

Ganns chuckled merrily. "They would, indeed, Wesley. Brandy if you have it." He seated himself in a red leather chair in front of Farrell's desk.

Farrell poured a small dose of Hennessy's cognac into a heavy, cut-crystal tumbler and handed it to Ganns. "You're a little out of your neighborhood, aren't you?" he asked. "I didn't think you went in for nightclub life."

"Quite true, Wesley," the dapper Jew replied. "And I credit you with enough imagination that you can probably guess why I am here this evening."

"You can't mean anything but Chance Tartaglia," Farrell said. "Nobody seems to want to talk about anything else."

"Again true," Ganns said. "I must confess to feeling distressed at his demise. He and I had a nice little . . . association between us. He made it possible for me to run my collection of interests without too much interference. He had become— how shall I put it—indispensable to my operations."

"So why come to me?" Farrell asked. "Tartaglia was the square root of nothing as far as I'm concerned. He was too crooked for me to like, and not dangerous enough to bother me. But there must be more than a hundred people in New Orleans he did bother—plenty." Farrell leaned back in his swivel chair and let smoke feather out of his nostrils.

"I believe you, Wesley," Ganns said, his round face lit with a warm smile. "Shooting someone in the middle of the street, even in the small hours of the morning, is far too crude for you." He laughed in a soft, indulgent way. "No, you'd have been waiting for him in his bedroom, with a knife, most likely."

"It's real nice that you dropped by, Ganns," Farrell said, impatience evident in his voice, "but if all you came to do is blow pipe dreams . . ."

"Not quite," the older man said. "Tartaglia's death is a sizable inconvenience to me. I'd like to know who did it."

"You must have gotten wrong directions someplace," Farrell said. "This is a nightclub, not the studio for 'Information Please.' "

The little man leaned forward in his chair, his small fists bunched on his impeccably tailored knees. His soft, cultured voice became harsh, guttural. "It would be worth your while to assist me in this, Wesley. I can afford to be very generous to those who bother to cater to my whims."

Farrell's eyes narrowed. "I'm in the business of minding my own business, Ganns. You've got a lot of money, but not that much."

"There are things other than money, my boy," Ganns replied, taking a thin gold watch from his vest and massaging it. "One of my hobbies is collecting people that interest me. Unusual people—like you, for example." Ganns pursed his lips into a sly smile as he played with the watch. "It's a rather harmless diversion, but I take great pleasure in, shall we say, investigating the backgrounds of the people who interest me the most."

Farrell said nothing, but he felt a familiar tingling deep in his gut.

Ganns replaced the watch and buffed his nails on the lapel of his dinner jacket. As he admired their gloss, he said, "For example, you have a rather fascinating background, Wesley, one that took me a great deal of time, and a substantial amount of money to probe. But I am persistent in the pursuit of my fancies, and what do you think I found?"

Farrell's chest felt as though it was gripped in a vise, but he kept his gray eyes locked fiercely on Ganns's.

"It is a strange facet of this fair city of ours that there are a large number of people who walk about with Negro blood in their veins. Oh, some hide it very well," Ganns said, waving a deprecatory hand, "but even one-sixteenth Negro blood still makes them Negro according to state statute. Imagine how devastating it could be to such a person, to his friends, his family—his livelihood—if it should become common knowledge that he was a Negro passing for white." He looked back up at Farrell and gave him a winning smile. "Weigh that possibility against the certainty of the ten thousand dollars I will pay you for your help."

Farrell had played poker with the best and knew he was beaten. He fought the clot of sick fear in his throat, keeping his facial muscles under rigid control. Looking Ganns straight in the eye, he said, "Hell, if you've got that much money, why not just buy yourself a new pet cop?" He pushed back his chair, walked over to the table where he kept his liquor, and poured himself a shot of cognac.

"You know as well as I that Tartaglia was hated by any number of police officers, all of the straight ones and a number of the ones no more honest than he," Ganns said. "It could well have been one or more of them responsible."

"I wouldn't bet on it," Farrell said, turning back from the bar. "Tartaglia was killed with a heavy-caliber British automatic. A cop wouldn't have that much imagination. No, this was a professional hit. Something you might have thought up yourself."

Ganns's eyes lit up, though he kept his composure. "That is interesting, indeed. Just how did you come by that piece of information?"

"Captain Gus Moroni was in here earlier today, hoping to get me to confess that I did it," Farrell answered.

"Moroni can be an irritant, but no more than that," Ganns said, waving a hand dismissively. "There are ways of . . . shall we say, short-circuiting him when necessary." Ganns got up from his chair and brushed an imaginary speck of dust from one of his satin lapels. "May I count on you, then?"

Farrell regarded Ganns through narrowed eyes, weighing the prospect of killing him and his men here and now, before things got more complicated than they already were. But, in a silence that lasted no longer than five seconds, he realized he'd have to play along for the time being. "I guess so," he said in a light voice.

"Good," Ganns said, shooting his cuffs. "I'll look forward to hearing from you."

Farrell nodded silently as the man and his two bruisers left in the same order in which they'd arrived. When they were gone he sat down heavily behind his desk and leaned his forehead into his right hand as he tried to still the nerves jumping in the tensed muscles of his arms and legs.

Chapter 6

After midnight Farrell changed into a gray shantung suit, a yellow oxford-cloth shirt, and a dark blue tie with brilliant red starbursts. After checking with Harry the barman, he put on his pearl gray Stetson and went out into the street.

New Orleans just begins to come to life after midnight, and the streets were crowded with men and women of varying shades of black, brown, and white. The mellow sounds of trumpets, saxophones, and clarinets floated from the open doors of cabarets, soft as wine-scented caresses.

Farrell passed a newsstand and bought a copy of the late edition of *The New Orleans States*. The paper was still full of the murder of Detective Chance Tartaglia. He stood under a streetlamp and read through all the columns related to the crime. Not one mentioned the use of the British automatic in the murder, nor did any of them suggest a possible motive for the slaying.

He dropped the paper into a trash barrel and crossed Rampart Street to the entrance of the Moulin Rouge. A steady stream of customers was entering the club, and through the open entrance, Farrell could hear Doc Pardee, the famous jazz clarinetist, and his girl singer, Bonnie Celestine, improvising their own arrangement of "La Paloma."

Farrell joined the crowd, making his way to the bar. "Savanna in?" he asked the barman.

The bartender jerked his head toward the back as he poured a drink with either hand. Farrell touched two fingers to the brim of his hat and made his way through the rapt crowd as it swayed to Pardee's music. In the back, and up a long flight of stairs, Farrell found a doorway marked PRIVATE and rapped on it twice.

"It's unlocked," a throaty female voice called.

"Hi, baby," Farrell said when he was inside. The woman behind the desk got up and walked over to him. She was a tall, full-figured, brown-skinned woman dressed in a red sheath, slit up one side to the thigh. Her lightly squared face held large, liquid black eyes and a pouty, voluptuous mouth. Her thick hair was parted on the left and hung loose to strong, square shoulders. Without a word she wrapped herself around Farrell, enveloping his mouth with hers. He hadn't come for that, but he couldn't help responding. He pulled her hips into his own and kneaded her flesh. When she broke the kiss both of them were breathing heavily and their eyes were hot.

"Where the hell you been?" she demanded. "You think I got nothing else to do but wait on you?"

"Business, Savanna," he answered. "Business won't wait on anything, or anybody, and you know it."

"Bull," she said in a hard voice. "What do you want this time?"

"Nothing much," he said, lifting a placating palm into the air. "I just wondered if any of your girls mentioned a punk, waving around a lot of cash, talking big. A good-looking quadroon, about twenty, light brown hair. Five-nine, one-forty, slick dresser."

"What's in it for me?" Savanna asked, folding her arms under her bosom.

"What do you want?" Farrell asked, dropping his eyes.

Savanna reached under her left arm and undid a catch on

the sheath. It fell to the floor, leaving her standing in nothing but her red high-heeled pumps. "Turn the key in that lock."

Farrell threw his hat into an armchair and locked the door. When he turned she took him by the hand and pulled him into the adjoining room, where she lived, and closed the door behind them. She turned on him then and started pulling at his clothes. Her dark eyes were filled with sparks, and her mouth smiled in a way that was almost predatory.

He had known her for a while, but the rapacious character of her sexuality still had the power to shock him. There was no softness in Savanna, no sentimentality, only a demand for quid pro quo. Almost in self-defense, his caresses became as demanding and brutal as hers, and their desire for each other became a physical contest.

As they bit and kissed each other, Savanna ran her hands up under his arms and over his shoulders. She pulled herself up, locking her legs around his narrow hips, and ground herself against him. The sound of her breath hissing through her teeth almost drowned out the roar of his own breath in his ears. His legs were nearly trembling with strain when she began to shout and pound his muscular back with her fists. His own release was almost lost in the relief of collapsing on the bed behind them.

As he lay on the bed, his heart nearly exploding within him, he heard Savanna begin to laugh in that throaty way of hers. "Don't you go and die, boy," she said. "I ain't through with you yet."

He laughed weakly and closed his eyes. He had once boxed an opponent for twenty-five rounds, but that had been no more arduous or taxing than being Savanna's lover. As she rolled on top of him, he lay passive, letting her tease him back to life again. It was quick this time, and as tender as Savanna was capable of being. When she groaned and sighed for the last time she collapsed on top of him, and sleep overtook both of them almost at once.

The sun shone through the trees in the park, and a cool breeze washed over him. He liked the park, and the shade they found from the sun there. He could hear the soothing sound of a fountain behind him and turned to see a slim, bronze statue of a girl there, with water cascading over her naked, supple limbs.

He looked up and saw his mother's face leaning over him. Her mouth smiled, and her gray eyes danced as she touched his face with her soft fingers. Her loose, honey-colored hair fell over his face as she cooed and talked nonsense to him, and he laughed happily. He tried to talk back to her but couldn't make his mouth say what he wanted.

He smelled his father, and felt his father's mustache nuzzle his face, and he gurgled with pleasure. He raised his hand, looking for his father's face, but it wasn't there anymore. Another face was there now. It was an older face, with dark, shoe-button eyes. The thin lips were bent into something that was a smile, but at the same time wasn't. He felt a consuming terror, and waved his small hands frantically in the air as he tried to fend it off. The face began to laugh mockingly as he tried desperately to pull himself away. Her face got bigger, and the laugh more horrible, and he could feel something lash and sting his skin unmercifully. He felt himself screaming.

"Uhhng!" Farrell's body jumped as if it had been touched with a live wire. Savanna fell off him and grumbled sleepily.

"Jesus," she said. "What the hell's wrong with you?"

Farrell sat up, rubbing his face. His body was damp with sweat, as were the sheets beneath him. "A dream. I had a bad dream," he mumbled.

"Goddamn, I'll say you did," she said. "You liked to scared me to death, jumping like that." She got up and went into the bathroom. He heard water running, and soon she came back. He started again as the damp washcloth touched his body; then he relaxed as she wiped the sweat from his chest, neck, and back.

"Was it bad?" she asked.

"Yeah," he said, embarrassed.

"I wish I could've seen what it was," she said with a sardonic smile. "I didn't know you were afraid of anything that walks, crawls, or flies."

"Forget it," he said shortly. "I gotta get out of here." He got up and began to search for his underclothes in the debris on the floor.

"Ain't you got time for breakfast?" she asked.

"No. Thanks. I . . . I'm not hungry right now."

She shrugged her shoulders. "Suit yourself. I'll ask around about that kid you told me about last night."

"Thanks," he said. "I appreciate it." He pulled on his slacks and roughly pushed the tail of his yellow shirt into the waistband. He shoved his feet into his brogues and quickly knotted the tie around his neck. He started to say something to Savanna, but her head was turned, and she seemed to be looking at something through the bathroom door.

"You don't like me, do you, Farrell?" she asked, still looking away.

Farrell jerked and stiffened. "You're crazy," he said. "I . . . I'll see you later."

Savanna said nothing, and a second later she heard the outer door open and close. She turned toward the sound, staring after it. Her large, dark eyes were wet, and she bit her bottom lip.

Chapter 7

The gray-haired old Negro parked his Chevrolet panel truck in front of his hardware store on North Dorgenois Street and got out into the cool, clear Saturday morning air. He stood there for a moment, admiring the lettering that read LOUIS'S HARDWARE across the side of the truck. He'd just had it done the day before and was really proud of it.

This was going to be a good day for a lot of reasons, not least of which was the fishing trip he'd be taking after he closed up at noon. He could already taste the cold Jax beer that would be iced down in his bait box. He smacked his lips as he unlocked the door.

Once inside, he walked through, snapping on the lights and ceiling fans. The store had a fresh, clean smell, and he looked over the shelves contentedly, thinking that he had it made. Having so much while the Depression caused other folks so much grief gave him a strange feeling of pleasure. It was wrong, he knew, but he couldn't help it. Maybe he'd talk to the preacher after church tomorrow, ask him to pray with him about it.

At precisely 8:00 A.M. the little bell on the door tinkled, and he turned around to greet his first customer. His smile of welcome froze when he saw the three men standing in front of the counter. All wore bandanas across their faces and hats pulled down low over their eyes. One of them was a young Negro. Maybe the second one was, too, but his skin was that peculiar shade of tan that made it hard to tell for sure. But the larger man, who seemed to be the leader, was white.

"Keep it quiet," the white man said in a thick, strangely accented voice. He shoved a heavy automatic in the hardware store owner's face.

"Give us the money and you won't get hurt, old man" one of the younger men said. He was dressed in an expensive brown gabardine suit and a beige hat with the brim snapped down in front. He brandished a gun, too. It looked to the old man like a cheap, nickel-plated Owl's Head .38 revolver.

"Wha . . . what do you want?" the old man stuttered.

"Open your ears, you old bastard," the white man said. "We know you take your week's receipts to the bank when you close today. Now, move!"

The store owner's raised hands were shaking, and his eyes rolled wildly in his head. "Don't hurt me," he begged.

The white man shoved him roughly into the office at the back of the store, pushing him down in front of the big iron safe. Struck dumb with terror, the old man began fiddling clumsily with the dial.

"Tell him to hurry up," the young man who was obviously a Negro said. He was of medium height, with dark skin, and was dressed in a cheap cloth coat and cap.

There was something familiar about his voice, but the old man's mind was racing and he couldn't think straight. Finally he heard the tumblers click, and he pulled the heavy door open. The white man grabbed him by the shoulder and threw him up against the wall. "Hurry up and get this dough bagged," he said.

"Got the bags right here," the dark-skinned youth said.

This time the voice tripped a switch in the old man's memory. "Wait a minute," he began. "I know you. You're . . ."

The white man turned with shocking speed and fired once. The heavy roar of the automatic was deafening in the small room. Blood and blobs of gray brain matter spattered against the wall where the old man's body sagged.

"Jesus," the well-dressed youth said. "You didn't have to kill him."

"Shut up and take one of those bloody bags, damn you," the white man shouted.

The dark-skinned boy moved swiftly, shoveling bundles of rubber band-wrapped bills into the two bags. When the safe was empty, he got up, grabbed one bag, and moved quickly toward the store entrance. The well-dressed youth stood there, gaping at the body until the white man pushed him violently out of the office.

"Move, stupid," he said. "He recognized Lester. I had to kill him."

The youngster moved on leaden feet, still glancing back over his shoulder as the white man propelled him out into the quiet autumn morning.

Chapter 8

Inspector Francis X. F. Casey sat in his office in the detective bureau in the dim light of early Saturday morning, reading the coroner's report on Detective Sergeant Chance Tartaglia. He sighed as he finished reading it for the third time and leaned back in his oak swivel chair, rubbing sticky eyes with long, graceful fingers that didn't seem to belong at the end of his thick forearms. He didn't see the appearance in his open doorway of a short, dark man with the sleeves of his white dress shirt rolled up over hairy, sinewy arms.

"Why don't you go home, Inspector?" the man asked.

Casey sat up and grinned blearily at the younger detective. "You know how it is, Parker. Once you get your teeth into something, you can't let it go. Besides," he added, rubbing the back of his neck, "Chance was a friend of mine once. I've got kind of a personal stake in this."

"I thought you'd say something like that," Parker said as he laid a brown paper bag on the desk.

"What's this?"

"A carton of coffee and a fried egg sandwich," Parker answered. "Maybe you can get a little inspiration with some chow in your belly."

"You're a good kid, you know that?" Parker grinned and waved a brief farewell.

Casey opened the bag and the aromas of hot coffee and hot grease assailed his nostrils. He realized instantly that he was ravenous.

When he had a few bites of the sandwich in his stomach and had chased them with some of the coffee, he reached across the desk and pulled a large manila clasp envelope toward him. One-handed, he pried open the clasp and tilted the envelope so the contents spilled out onto the desk.

Taking another bite of the sandwich, Casey sorted through the remains of Tartaglia's life. A rectangular gold Hamilton wristwatch on an alligator band, a two-blade pocketknife with jigged green bone scales, a silver ring with four keys on it, a Sheaffer fountain pen, and a handful of coins Casey pushed to one side of his cluttered desk. He stacked an alligator-hide wallet, a matching notebook, and a diary, and laid them beside the paper wrapping of his sandwich.

The wallet didn't tell him much more than he knew already. It held $177, mostly in large bills—far too much for a detective sergeant to have on him, particularly when a sergeant's salary was only $44 a week. The celluloid windows contained a membership card in the Knights of Columbus, a police benevolent association card, and an old photograph of a pretty blond woman and a cute little girl.

He paid a little more attention to the photograph because he remembered standing up with Chance at their wedding over thirty years ago. Her name was Helen, and he'd never seen anyone as happy as she'd been at the church that day. Chance had been happy, too. Casey wondered how two people so pleased with each other could have gone so wrong. Within a year of the wedding the marriage had begun to unravel. They'd had a blue-eyed, button-nosed little girl whom Chance was seldom at home to play with. Arguing about Chance's job, and how it kept him from home, escalated into physical brawling. Twice police had been dispatched to their house to break it up. Only the fact that Chance was himself a police officer had prevented them from taking him to the tank.

He'd gotten a chewing out from his district commander, but it hadn't helped. Within three years, the blond woman, no longer happy, had disappeared, taking the little girl with her. No amount of looking had turned them up, and after a while Chance had quit searching. He was never really the same after that, and Casey marked that time as the beginning of his friend's long slide.

His gaze slid over a sepia-toned portrait photo of a beautiful woman that also sat under the lamp on his desk, lingered there for a moment, and then went back to the picture of the woman and little girl.

He closed the wallet, put it to one side, and consulted the leather-bound diary. Most of the daily entries were unintelligible, sets of initials and times. A number of them were merely women's first names, with a little corkscrew pattern drawn next to them. Casey thumbed through the pages quickly until he found the date of the killing. That date, too, had a set of initials, "H. B.," with the little corkscrew. Casey frowned and pursed his lips. He had seen that combination enough times to guess the corkscrew pattern meant a date for a sexual encounter.

The notepad also had a small address book attached to it. Casey thumbed through that until he found the *B*'s; "H. B." was there, too. There was no address, but a telephone number was penciled beside the initials. He reached into the bottom left drawer of his desk and pulled out a special telephone directory that listed alphabetically by exchange, then chronologically by number. The number in Chance's book was assigned to an H. Ballou, a name Casey recognized. He wrote the woman's address on a scrap of notepaper, then took his long-barreled Colt Police Positive from the kneehole drawer of his desk and holstered it under his arm. He grabbed his suit coat and hat from the coat tree on his way out of the office.

Chapter 9

Farrell stood under the shower in his apartment, his hands braced against the wall as he watched the soap disappear through the metal drain at his feet. He felt rotten, and the hot shower wasn't much help. Suddenly he reached out, shut off the hot water, and stood there in the shock of the stinging cold, gritting his teeth until he could stand it no longer. He got out of the stall, still trembling, and rubbed himself dry with a rough white towel. A bottle of Old Overholt rye sat on a table just outside the bathroom door, and he picked it up and drank from the neck until the shaking ceased.

As he put down the bottle, he glanced up to see himself in the mirror. The bleak, sick look in his eyes made him turn away abruptly, and he began pulling clean underclothes and a shirt from the bureau. Five minutes later, he was tying a Windsor knot in a maroon silk tie. He turned slowly to the mirror and saw that the knot was perfectly centered beneath his chin. The look of misery in his eyes was gone now, and the tension ran out of his body like the water down the drain.

Before he put on the jacket of the summer-weight brown tweed suit he'd chosen, he went into his small living room, and opened the drawer of a dropleaf plantation desk. He removed an

Italian spring-blade stiletto and a bone-handled Solingen steel
straight razor. The stiletto he placed in a leather sheath that he
strapped to his forearm with a pair of elastic bands. The razor
he slid into a narrow pocket in the lining of his coat, just below
the right-hand inside pocket.

Farrell's public face was that of a respectable businessman,
but money came to him through a number of enterprises that,
while catering to relatively acceptable public vices, were still
illegal. Other men managed these enterprises for him now, and
as tough as they were, none dared cross Farrell. His reputation
for violence had not diminished in the face of his apparent
respectability.

Even before he'd made a place for himself in the New Orleans
underworld, Farrell had learned the lore of the blade from
men who knew it with loving intimacy, men who owed their
livelihoods—and sometimes their lives—to a piece of sharp-
ened steel. As a boy on the streets, Farrell had watched such
men at work, and had learned quickly the moves that made the
difference between life and death. Before he left the shadows
of the Negro back streets for the white world a rumor sprang
up that he was descended from Basile Croquere, the nineteenth-
century mulatto swordmaster. He laughed when he heard it,
but he did not deny it.

There were few men living who could attest to firsthand
experience with Farrell's skill in this arena, and when they did
speak of it, it was always in hushed, nervous tones.

As he put on his hat, Farrell cast one backward glance into
the mirror, but the face he saw there now told him nothing.

Holly Ballou lived in a stylish brick apartment building with
a little wrought-iron balcony that was located near the corner
of St. Charles and Louisiana avenues. If the neighbors had
known what she did for a living, there would have been loud
cries of complaint, but so far no one was the wiser.

Holly, whose real name was Rose Gregorio, had been born
in Newark, New Jersey, but upon re-locating herself in New
Orleans she soon found that men did not warm to her nasal

northern tones, no matter how well she flaunted her body. She'd hired a girl to drill her in the ways of southern speech, and now her honeyed Delta drawl was more perfect than that of any Louisiana-born belle.

She had also learned to perfection the art of insinuation by simply altering the tone of her voice and placing certain emphasis on selected syllables. Well-born gentlemen, and members of the nouveau-riche flocked to her door bearing flowers and jewelry, almost as if they were vying for her hand in marriage. A few thought they were the only men in her life, a joke that she particularly relished in her private moments.

She was lazing in bed that morning after a strenuous evening with the second son of a shipyard president. The boy wasn't particularly skillful, but he was athletic. Holly was just old enough to feel a lingering fatigue after he made his departure at four that morning. She was still half asleep when the door buzzer sounded. She rolled over and tried to ignore it, hoping the caller would go away. He didn't. The buzzer droned on in short, irritating spurts.

She opened her eyes wide and threw back the covers violently and pulled on the sheer silk wrapper that lay draped across the foot of the bed. Her nipples puckered as the cold, smooth material whisked across her naked limbs. When she got to the door she tore it open, her teeth bared in a snarl.

"Who the hell are you, and what do you mean by ringing my doorbell at this hour?" she demanded in her almost-forgotten northern voice.

No other words were spoken. The caller pushed through the door and kicked it shut behind him and, before Holly could speak or cry out again, silenced her with one big hand. She kicked and tore at him, but her fury was as nothing in the grip of his strength. He grabbed her throat with his free hand and bore down with a single callused thumb. Her pale face flushed with trapped blood and her tongue began to protrude from between her tiny white teeth. Within seconds she was unconscious, and in less than a minute she was hanging dead in her killer's hands.

He dropped her like a piece of used tissue paper and she

crumpled to the floor, the silk wrapper draped open to reveal the body so many men had coveted. The killer wasted no time moving more deeply into Holly's apartment.

Farrell left his Packard parked at the corner and entered the apartment building. He checked the mailboxes and saw that Holly Ballou's apartment was located on the fourth floor. He was nearly to the top when he heard rapid footsteps coming his way. He paused at the next-to-last landing and saw a big, heavyset blond man heading down the interior stairs at a fast clip. The big man vaulted the last five steps down to the landing, swinging a heavy blackjack in his right hand. Farrell ducked and feinted to the left, knowing the right-handed swing would go in the opposite direction of his movement. He came up with the cold steel of the Solingen razor open, the flat edge of the blade bent back over his knuckles. His downward-slashing hand missed the big man's neck but ripped a large gap in the front of his coat and shirt, and blood spurted from a cut.

The big man roared in pain and swung the blackjack again. This time he moved to the other side, catching Farrell momentarily off guard. Farrell got his left arm up in time to catch the blow on his forearm, but it was a hard hit that numbed the arm to the elbow. Fighting the shock and pain, Farrell shot out a foot and kicked the big man's legs out from under him. He fell forward, nearly catching Farrell's body in his grasp, but Farrell threw himself aside and the man tumbled down the stairs like a rubber ball. The man was resilient, though, and found his feet on the lower landing. Before Farrell could right himself, the big man was pounding down the porch stairs for all he was worth. Farrell knew he would never catch him with his injured arm hindering his movements.

He sat for a moment on the steps, gritting his teeth against the pain in his arm. His breath was coming in short pants, like those of a winded dog. Eventually he found the presence of mind to wipe the razor on the stair runner and place it back inside his coat. There was a considerable amount of blood, and he guessed he'd given the man a deep wound. A smaller, weaker man might have gone down from it.

After about five minutes he mastered the pain enough to stand, and dragged himself up the stairs. At the top he saw the door to Holly's apartment half open, and felt a dread grow inside him. He pushed the door wide and sagged against the doorframe when he saw the woman's crumpled body. He forced himself to walk over, kneel, and dig his fingers into the side of Holly's neck. As he expected, there was no pulse. He was squatting there, feeling sick to his stomach, when a voice sounded.

"Don't move a muscle," the voice rapped out. Farrell froze. "Now, very slowly, with your hands away from your sides, stand up, and turn to face me."

Farrell could barely move his left arm, but he raised his right to shoulder level, uncoiled his long frame into a standing position, and turned to face the owner of the voice. He saw a red-haired, stocky, middle-aged man of medium height who held a gold badge in his left hand and a cocked .38 in his right. The long, six-inch barrel was pointed at the middle of Farrell's chest.

"Start talking," the man said.

"I was coming to see Holly," Farrell said. "A man jumped me as I came up the stairs. After he got away I came up here and found her like this. Who're you?"

"Inspector Frank Casey," the man replied. "Anybody else see this guy you're talking about?"

"Nobody I know of," Farrell replied.

"What's the matter with your arm?" Casey demanded.

"I caught a blackjack on it when the guy jumped me," Farrell answered. "It's still kind of numb."

"I saw some blood on the carpet," Casey said. "Yours?"

"No, his," Farrell said. "He hit the first lick, though, so I kind of felt like he had it coming."

"What are you doing here?" the detective asked.

"I wanted to talk to Holly."

Casey smiled nastily. "Holly charged too much to just talk to, fella, and it's too early to be calling for what she sold. If you don't want to come down to headquarters with me, you'd better start giving me some kind of answer I can make sense of."

Farrell stood there for a moment, working to keep the indecision from his face. He decided to see what a little truth might buy. "Holly was the last person known to see Chance Tartaglia alive. I wanted to find out if he said anything to her, and if so, what."

Casey frowned. He wasn't sure what he'd expected the tall, bronze-skinned man to say, but it wasn't that. He uncocked his long-barreled revolver and lowered it to his side. "What makes that any of your business, podnuh? A police murder investigation isn't open to private citizens."

"Tartaglia was a bagman, and a crook," Farrell said. "Even the Dominican nuns down on Broadway knew that. But there're people who want to know why he was bumped."

"Like who?" Casey asked.

"It wouldn't do you any good to know that," Farrell said. "But Tartaglia was worth too much alive for them to have wasted him. That much you can believe."

"Yeah," Casey said, holstering his gun. "It makes sense to me that Chance's extracurricular bosses might be a little sore at whoever spoiled their party. We'll say for the sake of argument that I believe you. Who might you be, kiddo?"

"My name's Farrell; Wesley Farrell," he answered, rubbing the muscles of his sore arm.

There was a strange look in Casey's eyes, and he looked Farrell sharply up and down for a full minute before he spoke again. "I've heard of you," he said. "You own a couple of small nightclubs. I also hear you're a fair hand with a knife. A knife wouldn't be connected to that blood on the stairs, would it?"

"It's against the law to carry a knife," Farrell said.

Casey smiled sardonically but let it pass. "Get that arm into a basin of crushed ice; it'll take some of the stiffness out of it. You might need it again soon. Got a description of the guy who hit you?"

"Big. Big and blond," Farrell said. "About six-four, two-ten. Moves real fast for his size."

"Anything else?" Casey asked as he kneeled over the body.

"Not much. He was dressed in a dark coat and pants and a crew-neck sweater. Square jaw; hair cut close, military style. I didn't get the color of his eyes."

Casey nodded and looked at the bruises on Holly's throat. "Big hands, too. Don't get lost or anything, Farrell. I might want to talk to you again." The inspector looked up, but he was talking to air; Farrell was nowhere in sight. Casey's eyes were thoughtful as he looked out the open door; then he rose and found the telephone.

"Inspector Casey," he said in reply to the voice at the other end. "I need a meat wagon and some crime lab boys at 5763 St. Charles Avenue. Tell the ambulance guys that it's on the fourth floor, and the elevator's too small for a stretcher. Yeah, yeah, I know. They'll just love that part."

Chapter 10

Sunlight filtering through stained glass cast multicolored patterns on the floor and pews of St. Louis Cathedral. Farrell sat near the back of the church, listening to the deep, haunting sound of Gregorian chants spoken by an invisible choir. Down in front of the ornate altar a mahogany casket with silver handles and fittings rested, draped with a white pall.

Not many people were here to mourn the passing of Chance Tartaglia, and there were no policemen at all, except Inspector Frank Casey, who came in, knelt to the cross, and then stood with his hand on the edge of the rearmost pew. When he spotted Farrell he acknowledged his presence with a two-finger salute and a thin smile.

Farrell had not been to Mass in many years, yet the Latin chants unlocked doors in his mind and he began to remember the many times he had come here with his mother. She always dressed in an elegant black suit that fit her like a glove and a black hat with a veil that offered only a tantalizing glimpse of her beauty. When he walked down the aisle in his velveteen jacket and short pants, and the little bowtie she so lovingly tied for him each Sunday, he always felt an intense pride in being with her.

He was stirred from his reverie by a movement at the front of the church. He saw two women enter from the sacristy, kneel to the cross, then rise and move to a front pew. The younger of the pair was dressed in a well-cut black dress and wore a black, sombrero-shaped hat on her platinum-blond hair. Farrell guessed her age at somewhere in the early thirties.

She held the left arm of the other woman, who was dressed in a dark suit. She, too, wore a black hat, a large pillbox fitted with a heavy veil that completely obscured her face. The pair walked slowly, as befitted the solemnity of the occasion. Farrell watched as they took a seat in the front pew.

"I haven't seen them in years, but I expect that's Chance's widow and daughter," Casey's low voice said from behind him.

"Tartaglia didn't leave many mourners behind, did he, Inspector?"

Casey moved around, entered the pew box, and sat down beside Farrell. "Chance was a good guy once, a good friend," he answered. "He just got to liking money too much. So much he never cared whose shoes he pissed on."

"He ever piss on yours?" Farrell asked.

"No," Casey replied, "but then, I never judged him. I haven't lived a blameless life, either."

"Let he who is without sin cast the first stone," Farrell found himself saying.

"Yeah," Casey said. "Something like that. Why're you here?"

"Curiosity more than anything else," Farrell said. "Thought maybe I'd learn something useful."

"Have you?"

"Not so far," Farrell answered, "but the day's still young."

"How's the arm?" Casey asked.

"Feels like a wrecking crew took it off at the elbow," Farrell replied. "You going to pay your respects to the widow?"

"I thought I might follow them out to the cemetery and say something to them there," Casey said. He paused for a moment, then asked, "You wanna tag along?"

Farrell cut his eyes over at the policeman's face, looking for something there that might justify the mistrust he felt for all cops. When his intense scrutiny failed to uncover the guile he sought he said, "Why not?"

The two men sat in silence as a young priest came out and blessed the casket with incense. His homily was brief but reflected on the mystery of life and death and related that to the mystery of Chance Tartaglia's murder, and to the irony of a police detective becoming the victim of a faceless killer. The two women in front took it all in with silent equanimity.

After a short eulogy the priest invited the few in attendance to follow the hearse to the cemetery, and the pallbearers removed the expensive casket. Within ten minutes Farrell and Casey were inside Casey's old Marmon roadster, following the small caravan to the cemetery.

"You're a Catholic?" Casey said when they were rolling.

Farrell cast a glance over at Casey. The detective was slumped comfortably behind the wheel, his eyes watching the progress of the funeral home limousine ahead of them. "I was raised one," he replied. "My mother was devout, but I couldn't see it ever did her any good."

"What do you mean?" Casey asked in a puzzled voice.

"My father ran out on her when I was small," he replied in a flat voice. "She never got over it. It killed her in the end."

Casey shifted in his seat. "How old were you? When she died, that is?" he asked, concern evident in his voice.

"About thirteen," Farrell replied. The questions were making him irritable, and vaguely uncomfortable. "I lived with a great-aunt until I was sixteen; then I went out on my own."

Casey moved in his seat again, and he cleared his throat several times. Finally he said, "I'm sorry. I know how you feel, in a way. My dad was a uniformed sergeant in the old Sixth District. He got killed when I was twelve, trying to subdue a Civil War vet who went crazy with the heat one day and was running around with a bayonet. I . . . I never got over that." He cleared his throat again.

Farrell said nothing, and they were silent for the rest of the trip.

At the dogleg where Canal Street becomes Canal Boulevard,

the caravan turned off onto City Park Avenue and entered the grounds of Greenwood Cemetery. It was one of the larger, better-kept cemeteries in New Orleans, filled with elaborate monuments and mausoleums almost large enough to live in. As they drove down the well-tended avenues of tombs, Casey mused, "Even dead Chance manages to put on the ritz."

He pulled up behind the limousine and got out. Farrell followed suit. The two of them walked up to an open mausoleum and watched as pallbearers removed the casket from the hearse and bore it up to the vault.

A hot, dry wind had picked up, and only snatches of the young priest's prayers reached Farrell's ears. At the committal to the earth Tartaglia's daughter came forward and dropped a handful of crumpled rose petals on top of the casket. The hot wind snatched them aloft, like a hawk grabbing fish from a stream. After the priest blessed the casket with holy water and incense and gave a brief closing prayer, he took each woman by the hand and whispered some words of encouragement. Farrell noticed that neither of the pair had shown any sign of grief thus far.

As the priest took his leave, Casey led Farrell up to the women.

"Hello, Helen," Casey said. "It's Frank Casey. I'm sorry about Chance."

The older woman lifted back her veil to reveal a handsome, yet time-ravaged face. Through the lines of worry and resignation that marked her, Farrell could see the remnants of beautiful girlhood yet there.

"Hello, Frank," she said in a dry voice. "I recognized you in the church. You were a good friend to us once. It was nice of you to come." She gave Casey a small, brave smile and squeezed his outstretched hand. "You remember Sandra, don't you?"

"The last time I saw Sandy," Casey said, smiling, "she was small enough to ride on my shoulders. You've really turned into a beauty, Sandy."

Up close, Farrell could see that the younger woman's eyes were such a pale blue as to be almost translucent. Her face was a nearly perfect oval framed by silvery-blond hair. Dark eyebrows stood out in sharp relief against her pale skin. Her firm, shapely mouth, lightly outlined with pink lip rouge, smiled thinly, but the pale eyes held no warmth or humor.

"Hello, Uncle Frank," she said in a low, resonant voice. "I guess those days are gone forever. You're looking well."

"Not bad for a geezer my age," Casey replied. "This is Mr. Farrell. He knew your father slightly."

Sandra turned to Farrell, and something in her face changed. Her smile became more genuine, and something unreadable flickered across her pale eyes. "Your name is familiar for some reason, Mr. Farrell. Why is that?"

Farrell returned her penetrating look, trying to read what he saw there. He felt the sudden stirrings of physical attraction. "I don't know, Miss Tartaglia. I'm just one businessman out of a thousand in this town." As he spoke, he noticed Helen Tartaglia give her daughter a sharp, thoughtful look.

"Would you like to come back to the house for a drink or some coffee, Frank?" Helen asked quickly.

"I can't," Casey said. "Got too many things piled up on my desk. I'll call you in a couple of days, though, and maybe we can talk over old times."

"I'll look forward to that, Frank," Helen said with a brief smile.

Farrell, still looking into Sandra's eyes, rubbed his chin reflectively and said, "I need to go uptown, Mrs. Tartaglia. Would you mind if I catch a lift with you? At least as far as you're going?"

She turned and looked at him for a second, then said, "Certainly."

"I'll see you around, Inspector," Farrell said, glancing at Casey's retreating form.

Casey turned and stared at Farrell. "Yeah, I'm sure of that," he said. When Farrell said nothing in reply he turned again and walked back to his car.

Chapter 11

The funeral home's Negro limousine driver carefully negotiated the narrow streets of Greenwood Cemetery, and soon had them back on Canal. He took a right at Carrollton Avenue, then headed uptown.

"I *have* heard of you, you know," Sandra confessed. "You don't look quite as I pictured you, Mr. Farrell."

"Maybe you thought I'd have no neck, and red side-whiskers," Farrell said.

Sandra laughed a deep, rich laugh, sounding like an older woman than she seemed, and jaded. "No, I just thought you'd be older. Farrell's an Irish name, isn't it?"

"Is it?" Farrell asked, glancing over at her. "It never occurred to me."

"Your father never talked about it?" she asked.

"I never knew him," he said. "He left my mother and me when I was very small." He felt again the vague irritation he'd experienced when he and Casey had been on this same subject.

"I sympathize with you," Sandra said. "I never really knew mine, either."

"Sandra, there's no need to talk about him now," Helen said with a weary tone in her voice. "We never really had him in our lives, so we can't miss him, or think much ill of him at this late date, can we?''

"You're a forgiving woman, Mama," she replied, glancing at her mother.

"Not really," Helen said. "It just seems pointless to talk about it, somehow."

Silence fell over the trio as the limousine crossed Claiborne Avenue and passed a small, elegant park. The driver turned right at the next street and drove down two blocks before stopping in front of a large, raised house situated on a corner. The yard was surrounded by a wrought-iron fence, and sky-rocket juniper trees flanked the front yard on both sides.

As the car rolled to a stop, Helen said, "Since you've come this far, Mr. Farrell, why not come in and call a taxi."

"Yes," said Sandra, "you can have a drink while you wait."

"Sure," Farrell said. "Sounds like a good idea."

Helen thanked the driver and handed him a dollar bill. Then she led them up a gently spiraling brick stairway and into a large living room with salmon-colored walls and ivory carpets, with a marble fireplace at one end. Once inside, Helen excused herself and walked down a long hall to another room at the back of the house.

"Pretty nice," Farrell said as he put down his hat on an antique chest of drawers that sat against one wall.

"Paid for by me, not my father," Sandra said with an edge to her voice. "He never sent Mama anything after the first year. She worked to keep us alive and saved enough to send me away to school."

"And what is it that you do?" Farrell asked. He heard the anger lying just beneath the surface of her voice and couched his question in tones of casual curiosity.

"I'm in the import-export business," she said as she removed her own hat. "Make yourself at home. The bar's in the corner. I'll just go check on Mama and be right back."

Farrell built himself a drink of Peter Dawson scotch and some soda from a siphon. From the back of the house he heard a radio begin to play, and he could make out the voice of Ella Fitzgerald singing "Goodnight My Love." He was staring at a pair of ancient, hand-colored pictures of some Hindu warriors torturing a few unhappy-looking captives when Sandra came back.

"Interesting, aren't they?" she asked. "I've always wondered what they did to be so unspeakably punished."

"Maybe they were just in the wrong place at the wrong time," he said. "Like your father."

"Why do you say that?" she asked, walking to the bar and picking up a glass. She kept her back to him as she poured a drink for herself.

"Just thinking out loud," he replied.

"You have any ideas about why he was killed?" she asked as she turned back to face him. She bowed her head slightly as she put the glass to her lips.

"Nothing you could pin any hopes on," he said. "Your father had plenty of enemies."

"Like you?"

"I didn't care about him one way or the other," Farrell said, his eyes fixed on hers. That tingling of excitement he'd felt earlier was back, and he pushed it away quickly. "I'd never met him until he tried to interest me in what he had to sell one time, and I had to let him know I wasn't having any of it. That was the first and only time I ever saw or talked to him."

"What was it he was trying to sell?" Her unblinking pale eyes surveyed him from over the rim of her glass.

Farrell stared back, chewing on the corner of his lip. "Protection," he said finally. "Seems he had some idea I needed it, and that he could supply it."

"And what did you do?" she asked, smiling a little.

"He was hard to persuade; I had to throw him down the stairs to get his attention." He found himself returning her smile with one of his own.

She laughed her deep, jaded laugh again, and took a seat on a white leather sofa. "Sit down, Mr. Farrell. You don't have to be anywhere soon, do you?"

He sat in a leather wing chair across a coffee table from the sofa. "Nothing that can't keep. I notice that you and your mother don't seem all that broken up."

"We aren't," she said. "There wasn't anybody else to bury my father, so we tried to do the Christian thing. No more than that."

"What do you know about your father?" Farrell asked.

"Not much," she answered. "When Mama left him she took me to Jackson because she could find work there. We stayed there until a few years ago, then went to the Orient, where I got involved in import and export. Six months ago we decided to relocate the business here." She kicked off her shoes and shifted her body to curl her legs beneath her on the sofa. "Naturally, I had some curiosity as to whether my father was still here after all these years. I made some discreet inquiries and discovered very quickly that he was living far too well for a mere policeman. I'm surprised nobody at headquarters noticed that."

"This is New Orleans, Miss Tartaglia," he said. "There aren't enough honest people here to fill the Blue Room at the Roosevelt Hotel. The few who cared what he was up to probably didn't have the clout to do anything about it. Your father had more than one friend in high places."

"Which brings us to why you care about it," she said.

"Just money," he replied. "Nothing more. Your father kind of belonged to a heavy hitter named Ganns." Farrell drained the last of the scotch and carefully placed the empty glass on the pale oak coffee table. "Ganns doesn't like other people interfering in his business."

"So you're some kind of hired gun," she said.

"Wrong. Ganns wants to know who killed your father, and I agreed to try to find out." He stood up, buttoning his jacket over his flat stomach. "After I do that I'm out of it. I've got no personal stake in a couple of gangsters trying to eat each other up."

Her eyes were full of cool appraisal. "I haven't been completely candid with you," she said. "In the process of finding out about my father, I heard how you threw him down the stairs. Since my father seems to have been the kind of person who'd do almost anything for money, I couldn't help but be a bit intrigued by someone tough enough to slap him down."

Farrell's eyes were trapped by hers again, and her words rooted him to the spot.

"I was intrigued enough to ask around about you and discovered that nobody knows much about you at all. How did you get to be such a mystery man, Wesley Farrell?"

Farrell felt the hairs on the back of his neck rise and knew he had to beat a strategic retreat. She was really something, but no woman was as important as maintaining his anonymity. No flirtation, no matter how alluring, could make up for all he would lose if his secrets became known. "I'm just a guy trying to mind his own business and make a buck, Miss Tartaglia," he said, letting his face and eyes go flat. "I can't be bothered by what other people think or don't think." He glanced down at his watch. "Guess I'd better be going now. Thanks for the hospitality."

"Don't you want to call a cab?" she asked, shifting her body forward on the sofa.

"It's a nice day," he replied. "Think I'll walk to Carrollton Avenue and catch the streetcar downtown."

"Well, if you must," she said, still smiling. "I hope you'll come again when you can stay a bit longer."

"Thanks," he said as he opened the door. "I'll remember the offer."

Chapter 12

After leaving Farrell with the Tartaglia women Casey drove back uptown and over to Magazine Street. As yet, there had been no systematic search of Tartaglia's apartment; it was a job he'd been saving for himself. Police work was largely a series of repetitive, mundane activities, performed by rote as the investigators searched for the one thing that didn't fit or didn't make sense in the scheme of known facts. Every policeman, no matter how smart or stupid, began an investigation in this same routine way. Casey was smarter than most, but he still went through the motions because he enjoyed doing it, because he had a tidy, orderly mind.

Tartaglia's apartment was above a shop in a block of art, book, antique, and other stores catering to those with recreational money to spend. Even in the midst of the Depression there were those in New Orleans who had money for the finer things, and the merchants in the block often stood smiling in their open doorways because of it.

Casey entered through an alley between two shops and walked back into an elaborate brick patio garden. Although it was landscaped with banana, palmetto, and banyan trees, it was well kept, with only a few scattered leaves littering the floor of the patio. A small pool was stocked with fat, active Japanese goldfish. Casey mounted an iron staircase to the door, where he was met by the uniformed officer stationed there at his order. After exchanging a short greeting with the cop he took out a key and unlocked the door.

Once inside, Casey put his hands into his pockets and gazed admiringly about the room. "Chance, m'boy, you really knew how to live," he said to the air.

The outside of the building gave no clue to the opulence within. The living room was elegantly furnished in French Provincial furniture, much of it made from oak or maple and upholstered in royal blue. The walls held paintings of landscapes Casey didn't recognize, and the windows were curtained in fabric to match the upholstery. One wall supported a large glass-doored bookcase filled with sumptuous leather bindings. Casey figured they were just for show.

He strolled casually through the other three rooms and found a breakfast nook off a small but modern kitchen, a bathroom furnished with elegant art-deco style Kohler fixtures, and a bedroom. Casey laughed gently as he stood in the doorway to this last. In contrast to the subtle taste of the other rooms, this one looked like a Hollywood producer's notion of a high-grade brothel. A tall four-poster bed sat under a ceiling set with mirrors. Small pieces of statuary sat around the room on marble pedestals. All were representations of classical figures engaged in sexual intercourse, the bodies contorted into positions Casey doubted he could have duplicated even in the flower of his youth.

Shaking his head, Casey took off his hat, coat, and pistol harness and began to search the room. He didn't know what he was looking for, but that hadn't stopped him in the past. He was counting on his instincts to alert him to anything that might stand out from everything else.

Tartaglia must have had a cleaning woman, because the room was remarkably neat for a bachelor. Even the floor under the bed was clear of dust balls. Casey stripped the bed and turned over the mattress. All he found there was a long, graceful Model 1922 Browning automatic pistol, fully loaded, and a condom, still in the foil wrapper. He registered the unintentional humor of this pairing by turning up one corner of his mouth in a wry grin.

None of the drawers in the bureau or the nightstands yielded anything of note, nor did the closet, which held no less than ten finely tailored suits and as many pairs of hand-lasted shoes. Imported silk ties, and several alligator or lizard-skin belts hung from brass hooks on the inside of the closet door. None of the ties, belts, or the five hats on a high shelf appeared to have anything hidden inside them. There was a pair of matching pigskin suitcases at the back of the closet, both unlocked and empty.

Casey tackled the bathroom next, sifting through all the talcum powder, toothpaste, shaving soap, and everything else in there. The inside of the toilet tank was empty save for water and some rust scales. Casey ran his hand up around the bottom of the tank and the sink; then he unfolded the towels, sheets, and blankets in the linen closet, all to no avail.

The kitchen took less time than he thought. Tartaglia apparently hadn't done much eating in. There were a few unopened cans in the pantry, along with a substantial stock of whiskey, gin, and brandy, all the best brands that money could buy. The electric icebox contained even less. A few cans of Snow-Crop frozen orange juice in the freezer, a pair of shriveled lemons in the fruit bin, a loaf of bread, and a partially used stick of butter rounded out the inventory.

All that was left now was the living room. By this time Casey was beginning to feel a little frustrated, but he was too old a pro to get sloppy now. Something called to him from the bookcase, and he turned to consider it. He couldn't figure Chance giving a happy damn about a book, much less an entire case of rare volumes. He walked closer and opened the glass doors to get a better look.

He checked each shelf systematically, removing every book in turn, riffling the pages, and squinting down into the openings between the spine and the gathered signatures. Midway through the second shelf he got a surprise. A set of four books in a red-cloth slipcase turned out to be a little wooden box with leather spines from a set of Rousseau's commentaries glued on one end. He heard things rattling around inside and began trying to open it.

He was on the verge of getting out a pocketknife to force it open when a little section of wood slid open to reveal a spring-loaded button. He pressed it, and the side with the spines popped loose. There was a stack of twenty-dollar bills inside, still wrapped in the bank band, a tiny Colt .25 automatic with pearl grips, and a key. He took the key over to the window to get a better look. It was too small to be a door key, and the head was a queer triangular shape he'd never seen before. He took it back into the bedroom and tried it on the suitcases, but it didn't fit either lock.

He tossed the key up and down in his hand, musing over it for a few minutes. Then he pocketed it, went back to the bookcase, and checked the rest of the shelves. Within fifteen minutes he had put all the books back and left the apartment.

The big blond-haired man sat holding a telephone receiver to his ear in a dingy room at the back of a shabby rooming house on South Cortez Street. He was shirtless, and a big bandage ran around his torso and over his left shoulder.

"I couldn't help it," he growled into the telephone. "She was kicking up a row, and I was afraid somebody would come looking before I had a chance to look. I didn't mean to kill her, but there you are. Things happen sometimes. Yes, I looked everywhere I could think, but I couldn't find it."

He stopped talking for a moment and listened to the voice at the other end of the wire. "I can't go back there now. I bloody near got my throat cut as it is. No, I never saw the bloke before, but he weren't no cop, I can tell you that. He was dressed in a fancy suit and carried a razor. No cop ever went about like that. What about that money you promised me?"

He stopped talking again, and his face darkened as he listened. "Don't try to sweet-talk me. I used up the money you gave me last week. All right then, but don't blame me for getting money the only way I know how. I'm bloody well not going to starve to death while you work out your scheme. Just call when you've doped this thing out. I'll help you if I'm able.''

He hung up the telephone and poured himself a shot from a bottle of Johnny Walker. He stared broodingly into the corner of the room as he sipped the whiskey and gently rubbed the bandage on his chest.

Chapter 13

Farrell walked the three blocks from Sandra Tartaglia's house to the streetcar stop at Carrollton and Claiborne avenues, his mind buzzing. He felt the powerful pull of mixed emotions, and an indecision that was rare for him. He'd never met a poised, sophisticated woman like Sandra before, and he felt an attraction to her that was impossible to ignore. Still, something about her set off warning bells in his head, and he'd stayed alive all these years by paying heed to those bells. His interactions with Savanna, Casey, and now Sandra had made him edgy and irritable.

It was no accident that Sandra Tartaglia had found out so little about him. When he'd made the decision to put his past life behind him at the age of sixteen and emerge as a white man named Wesley Farrell, he'd divested himself of everything that might tie him to the Creole community. While his mother was alive he'd been known as Wesley Farrell Delvaille, and he'd spoken French more often than English. On the day he disappeared from Willie Mae Gautier's neighborhood, he'd dropped his mother's name and moved into the Quarter.

He'd learned quickly in those early days that there were few people he could trust. On his second day out two other boys had jumped him in an alley, beaten him unconscious, and stolen what little money he had. He'd come to with a mild concussion, an empty belly, and a newly discovered capacity for rage. He'd realized that in order to survive he must view everyone he met as a possible threat, and be ready to defend himself.

In the years that followed he'd moved frequently, used different names, and generally done whatever was necessary to stay alive.

Not long after the beating, he'd taken a job in a gymnasium and after a time traded his labor as a janitor and all-around handyman for boxing lessons. His size, lightness of foot, and capacity for controlling and focusing his anger at an opponent made him a natural, and more than once he was offered the chance to turn professional.

But he was already too smart for that. He was surrounded by ample evidence that there were no rich or old fighters. Most ended up as addled booze hounds, their brains turned to mush from the years of killing blows received in the ring. He'd taken his newfound experience and moved on, changing his name and his address as he went.

Along with his talent for fighting, he'd discovered another skill—cards. As with many discoveries, it was made by accident when he found himself invited to sit in on a penny-ante game with some fellows at the gym. The rules for poker, blackjack, five-card stud, and the other games of chance came to him as easily as reading them off a page. By the end of that first evening, he was eight dollars and seventy-six cents richer, and it dawned on him that this might be a way of making a living.

But gambling had its own pitfalls. There were the cardsharps who dealt from the bottom of the deck with invisible ease, the soreheads who brought guns to the game, fully intending to use them if the cards went against them, and the welshers who played with money they didn't have and lost with depressing frequency. The ever-wary youngster quickly learned to spot them all, though not without earning scars along the way.

In a game in the Bywater section one night, a man who'd lost too many pots accused Farrell of cheating. Farrell had already learned that to back down from such an affront would mean the end of his gambling career. Slowly he stood up and invited the man to step away from the table. The other players remained frozen, waiting to see what would happen.

The bad loser met Farrell in the middle of the room, bringing a straight razor from inside his sleeve with shocking speed, the glittering blade springing open in his hand like a striking snake. Before Farrell could react, the man had cut him badly on the arm and across the chest. The sight of Farrell's blood made the man grin with anticipation. Confident of his kill, he moved in to deliver the final stroke. Farrell, no stranger to pain, had taken the punishment in silence as he watched his adversary's moves, and when the man stepped in a bit too close Farrell's right hand shot out and captured the wrist with the razor. He dislocated the wrist with a quick flip; then, with deliberate calculation, broke most of the bones in the man's face and several of his ribs.

As the man lay on the floor with blood oozing from his shattered face, Farrell's eyes had caught the glint of light reflecting from the open razor blade. Ignoring his cuts, he reached down and picked up the weapon, finding it strongly built but uncommonly light. As he worked the blade in and out of the bone handle, he heard the distinctive chatter it made, not unlike the sound of a cockroach flying. He'd seen men use razors before, and he realized for the first time that his fists would not always be enough. Sometimes a man needed an edge, in more ways than one.

Prohibition was in full swing as Farrell came into young manhood, and New Orleans was a hotbed of the manufacturing and transportation of illegal liquor. For a man living on the edge, always alert to new ways of making money, it was perhaps inevitable that Farrell would try his hand at this form of enterprise. He was a good driver, and made good money driving trucks full of smuggled scotch and Canadian rye from the coastal shallows outside the city.

It was clear from the beginning that a bootlegger was in as much danger from rival gangs as he was from the poorly equipped and manned Coast Guard and state and federal Prohibition authorities. The narrow two-lane roads through marshy

bayou country and along the Mississippi River were ripe locales
for ambushes by both law and law breaker alike. Farrell sur-
vived three such attacks, one only narrowly when his two guards
were killed in a running battle with redneck competitors outside
of Morgan City.

Farrell lost the truck, but he left his mark on his attackers.
Two who followed him failed to return, learning too late what
a potent weapon a straight razor can be on an unsuspecting
prey. From the body of one Farrell picked up the Colt .38
automatic he'd carried ever since, mastering its use as he had
mastered so many other things.

As Farrell moved from enterprise to enterprise, and from
one part of New Orleans to another, there were women in his
life, as there would be in any man's who possessed Farrell's
size and looks. He learned to dress well, enjoying the attention
women paid to him, but he never let his feelings for any of
them get out of control. His mother had died and Willie Mae
had abused him, a pair of lessons that had worked on his
subconscious in ways he could not fully appreciate. Often he
left women as he felt his attraction or theirs growing into
something he did not want.

Savanna had been different than the others, perhaps because
she was so self-sufficient herself. There was never anything in
her behavior that smacked of sentimentality, and often Farrell
felt himself being tested by her in ways that intrigued and sometimes irritated him. Her remark that he didn't like her had been
somehow out of character, and it had troubled him in a way
his mind could neither define nor explain. The tantalizing intru-
sion of Sandra Tartaglia into his world was an added complica-
tion.

Only two other people waited at the stand with him: a large,
heavyset white man in a brown work uniform and a tiny, wiz-
ened old Negro woman in a print dress who propped herself
upright with a hickory cane. He paid scant attention to them
until the sound of the streetcar bell roused him from his reverie.
He turned as he heard the mechanical door open and saw the
large man elbow the little black woman roughly out of the way.
All hell flew through Farrell then. As he caught the little old

woman and set her upright again, he grabbed the big man by the shoulder in a grip so tight that the man cried out.

"What the hell . . . ?"

"Help the lady up the stairs," Farrell said in a voice so guttural he almost didn't recognize it as his own.

The man sneered and turned to face Farrell head on. "What's it to you if I get on before the nigger?"

"I said help her up the stairs," Farrell said. "Do it quick, and don't talk anymore."

"You mouthy son of a . . ." Before the man could finish his sentence Farrell grabbed him by the shirtfront with one hand and around the throat with the other. The big man felt fingers like steel bite into the flesh of his neck, and all the starch ran out of him. For a moment he thought his bowels would break loose. The flatness of Farrell's gaze, and the white, taut skin around his mouth were the most terrible thing the man could ever remember seeing. He turned pale under his tan and croaked out, "Y-yeah, okay, mister. N-no need to get upset. Here . . ." He pulled himself desperately from Farrell's grip and quickly turned to take the old lady's elbow.

The little woman looked at Farrell strangely and said, "Thank you, suh. Thank you ver'a much."

Farrell nodded but did not speak. What he had done was stupid, and he did not like to do stupid things. He followed the pair onto the streetcar and saw the man sit down in the first seat he could find. Then he tucked his head down and began to read a newspaper in a way that was comically frantic.

A few seats from the back was a sign that read COLORED, and Farrell saw all of the few seats allocated for Negroes were taken, and most of the standing room was jammed with Negro day workers. Farrell saw the weariness in the old woman's posture and knew she'd be exhausted from standing up on the bouncing, jostling car by the time she got to her stop. His gesture outside the car had not only been a stupid risk, it had been meaningless as well. No matter what he did for her today, there would be a tomorrow, and a day after that, when she would have to experience the same bone-wrenching weariness and face the same humiliations. He grabbed a strap from the rail overhead and turned his face away from her as the streetcar began its uncomfortable journey downtown.

Twenty minutes later, as the car reached Lee Circle, Farrell had a thought that snapped his head up. He pulled the bell cord, exited the car, and headed for a telephone booth across the street in front of the old Carnegie public library building. Inside, he dropped a nickel and dialed Guido's pool hall.

"Guido," he said when the man answered the ring.

"Yeah, who is that? Mr. Farrell?"

"Right. Listen, is Moe Gilhooley in there?"

"Yeah, I t'ink so. Wait a minute."

"Yeah, Mr. Farrell, this is Moe," the ex-fighter said after a few minutes.

"Listen, Moe, I've got a question for you. The other day you told me that Chance Tartaglia had been with Holly Ballou the night he was shot."

"Yeah, that's right."

"Who told you?" Farrell asked.

"Oh, yeah," Moe said. "I shoulda said. It's the li'l guy who's the building super. I talked to him right after the word come down about Chance. Said he saw him go up the night before."

"What's the guy's name, Moe?" Farrell felt a strange excitement.

"Leo Terranova," Moe said. "Him and me used to fight on some of the same cards, only he was a flyweight on account of he's small. What you want with him?"

"Tell Guido I said to give you a drink and put it on my tab," Farrell said before he hung up.

Frank Casey pulled his Marmon to the curb a half block up from Holly Ballou's apartment house in time to see Farrell get off the uptown-bound streetcar. He got out of the car and met Farrell with a scowl on his face.

"What're you doing here?" Casey demanded.

Casey's flinty gaze made it plain there was nothing friendly in the question.

"I had a hunch I wanted to play out," Farrell replied in a neutral tone. This had to be played just right.

"Maybe you didn't catch my drift the last time you were here," Casey said. "Private citizens aren't allowed to meddle in murder investigations. Particularly when they have the kind of reputation you've got."

Farrell knew he was on dangerous ground, but his fear of Ganns outweighed the potential danger of the policeman's anger. "Listen," he said quickly, "did any of your guys talk to the building super after Holly was killed?"

"Sure, they took a statement," Casey said. "So what?"

"A guy I know tipped me to Tartaglia's visit to Holly the night he was killed," Farrell explained. "Today I thought to ask him how he knew, and he said the building super told him he'd talked to Tartaglia that night. I got a feeling there's something in that."

There was something Casey liked about the big bronze-skinned man, but forty years of police work had built a distrust in him that wasn't easily ignored. He rubbed his chin for a moment, considering Farrell's information, then made up his mind. "Let's play it out, then," Casey said.

They found Leo Terranova in the basement, cleaning out the building furnace, singing "Diga Diga Doo" along with a recording of Duke Ellington and the Harlem Footwarmers that emanated from a little radio sitting on the floor nearby. He was small, with a fringe of curly brown hair sticking out from under a cloth cap. He looked to be in his forties but moved with the graceful economy of a young athlete.

"You the super?" Casey asked, holding up his badge.

"Yeah, Leo Terranova," the small man said. He pulled out a rag and wiped his hands as he turned to face them. "I already told the officer yesterday, I didn't see nothing that could help 'em find poor Miss Ballou's killer." His face took on a sad look, and he shook his head.

"I want to ask you about something else," Casey said. "Two nights ago she had a visitor. You remember?"

He reached up and slapped his forehead. "Yeah, it was Sergeant Tartaglia," Terranova said. "Jeeze, you'd'a thought

I'd'a remembered to say something, him gettin' killed and all. What's this world comin' to, I ask ya?''

"You talked to Tartaglia that night, didn't you?" Farrell asked.

"Yeah," Terranova said. "He was feelin' pretty good." The small man smiled at the memory. " 'Course, anybody goin' to see Miss Ballou would be happy. She was real nice."

"Did he say anything in particular to you?" Farrell pressed gently.

"Well, you know," Terranova said, scratching his head, "he come here pretty often. Him and Miss Ballou was real good friends. I didn't see him every time he come, you understand; just when he had somethin' to drop off."

"Drop off?" Casey asked. "What kinds of things did he drop off? Old clothes?"

"Aw, no," Terranova said, waving a hand in the air. "He just sometimes left a li'l suitcase here, and another guy would come and pick it up from me, usually the next day." Terranova got a peculiar look on his face, and fingered his chin. "Ya know, now I think about it, the guy didn't come the next day like usual. I guess I forgot about it, on account of all the excitement here, ya know?"

Farrell and Casey turned to look at each other. Casey noticed that Farrell, normally imperturbable, had a hot, interested look in his eyes.

"You still got the case?" Farrell asked.

"Sure," Terranova said, thumping his forehead with his hand again. "Lemme go get it."

As the little man went to get the case, Casey turned to Farrell and said, "You've got some instincts for this business, Farrell, or you're bringing me luck."

Farrell said nothing, though he felt a strange, secret pleasure.

Terranova soon reappeared with a small, expensive-looking suitcase made of russet leather. "Here it is, Officer. I'm sorry I didn't remember it the other day, but Miss Ballou's death— it hit me kinda hard. She was always nice to me, ya know?"

"Yeah, I know," Casey said. "Thanks for keeping this. We'll see it gets to the right people. By the way, I'd like to go up and look at Miss Ballou's apartment. Have you got a key you could let me borrow?''

Terranova pulled on a cheap brass chain fastened to his belt and brought out a ring of keys from his pocket. He fiddled with them until he found the one he wanted, took it off the ring, and handed it to Casey. Casey thanked him, and the small man went back to his work.

"What are you going to do now?" Farrell asked when the building superintendent had gone about his business.

"Well," Casey said in a musing voice, "I came here hoping to find something like this. Now that I have, I figure on moseying upstairs and taking a gander at whatever's in this case."

"I'd like to take a look, too," Farrell said.

Casey shook his head. "I don't have any reason to trust you, Farrell, and besides, I've told you twice to keep out of this. If I find you sticking your nose in again, I'm liable to toss you into the can for obstruction of justice."

"You wouldn't have found that suitcase without me," Farrell pressed. "Terranova's so punch-drunk, he'd probably never have thought to contact you, himself. You owe it to me to let me see what's in there."

Casey started to snort, but grudgingly admitted to himself that Farrell was right; he might not have found the suitcase by himself. It was just possible that Farrell could provide another useful revelation if he saw the contents. He nodded, motioning to Farrell to come with him.

Casey led him back out to the front entrance and showed him a small elevator, tucked out of the way behind the stairs. When it stopped at the fourth landing they got out and walked to Holly's door, which Casey unlocked.

Once inside, Casey put down the case on the coffee table and sat down on the crushed velvet sofa behind it. Casey removed the small key he'd found at Tartaglia's apartment from his pocket and unlocked the case.

"How is it you didn't know about the case but you had the key all the time?" Farrell asked, a little mystified.

"It's a secret of the trade," Casey said, grinning. "I'll pass it along to you when I think you're old enough."

When he threw open the lid he could do nothing but stare. Farrell gave a long, high-pitched whistle.

"Holy Mother of Jesus," Casey said, his voice awestruck. "There must be a million bucks here." He took out one of a number of cellophane pouches and poured its contents out into his hand. A pile of diamonds caught glints of sunlight from the living room window, and Casey's mind began spinning like a bobbin on a loom.

Farrell picked up one of the stones and held it up to the light. "This is real high quality. They'd fetch a good price. Where would Tartaglia get anything like this?"

"That's a good question," Casey responded. "He usually ran to protection and loan-sharking. This is a hell of a lot bigger than anything I knew he was into. Holly must have put him in touch with a fence who helped him unload stuff like this. If Terranova is telling us the truth, he must have been bringing it through on a regular basis. I'll bet Chance has a safe-deposit box full of cash somewhere," Casey said thoughtfully.

"The guy who jumped me on the stairs must have been looking for them," Farrell said. "He either killed her to keep her quiet when he busted in here, or by accident, trying to force her to talk. A big guy like that, it could have gone either way."

"What I'm wondering now," Casey said, stroking his chin, "is whether the big man killed Chance to get the diamonds, or if Chance was welshing on somebody bigger than he was, and they killed him for it."

"Holly might have known," Farrell said. "It's too bad she can't tell us."

Further conversation was halted by sounds coming from the door. To Farrell's surprise, Casey quickly put the diamonds back into the case, closed it, and shoved it under the coffee table. Both men were on their feet when the tumblers fell in the lock. As the door opened, Casey unbuttoned his jacket and reached for the butt of his revolver.

"What th ... Frank!" spluttered Captain Gus Moroni.

"What's this guy doin' here?" The big policeman glared at Farrell.

"He and I've been tossing around a few ideas, skipper," Casey said. "We met outside on the walk, and I invited him up while I cased the joint."

"Let me clue you in on your little playmate, Frank," Moroni said in a hard, nasty voice. "He's been hauled in three times that I know of for violation of state gambling statutes. The only reason he's out enjoyin' the fresh air is because there was insufficient evidence to hold him. Which is to say, the evidence disappeared before he made it to trial." Moroni walked the rest of the way into the apartment and kicked the door shut behind him.

"And then there's the little matter of a gambler shot dead over in Jefferson Parish six months ago," Moroni continued. "This bird was at the scene when the sheriff's deputies arrived, holding the gun that did the shooting. And guess what? He has three close friends, all ex-cons, right there to say it was self-defense. Howdaya like that, huh?" Moroni's face was beet red, and flecks of spittle had collected at the corners of his lipless mouth.

"That's all true." Casey nodded. "Checked up on him myself. By the way, skipper, what're you doing here?" He kept his voice casual but watched the captain closely.

"Investigating this broad's murder, what else?" Moroni answered.

Farrell had listened to Moroni's tirade with his muscles tensed and his mouth set in a hard line. He knew the chief of detectives hated his guts, but Casey's offhand comment that he was aware of the gambling and murder charges surprised him, as did Casey's seamless change of the subject. He found himself watching the red-haired detective closely.

When Moroni was slow to answer Casey's question Farrell said, "The chief of detectives investigating the death of a whore? Holly must have had more clout in this town than I realized." He removed his pack of Camels as he spoke, shook out a cigarette, and placed it between his lips.

"Chance Tartaglia was here getting his ashes hauled the

night he was killed," Moroni said, glaring in Farrell's direction. "The next day his chippy turns up dead. I call that a hell of a coincidence. A coincidence I thought I'd look into."

"How did you know Chance was here, skipper?" Casey asked, moving around the coffee table.

Moroni fixed a baleful eye on his subordinate. "I ain't so chained to that desk downtown that I don't still have some snitches on the street. I started out a street man, and I'm still a street man. What the hell kind of question is that, anyway?"

Casey laughed, low down in his chest, and waved a deprecating hand. "Hey, take it easy. It's taken me all this time to come up with the dope, and it just startled me for you to know it already, that's all."

Somewhat mollified, the captain settled down, and the heated color began to leave his beefy face. "Forget it, Frank. Two murders in two days puts a lot of pressure on me, particularly when they're sensational cases like these. What've you found so far?"

"Not much; but then, we just got here," he answered. "Farrell was just about to leave. I'll stick around and help you search the joint. How about it?"

Farrell shot a quick glance in Casey's direction but remained silent.

"Sure," Moroni said. "I'll start in the back; you start in the front. We'll meet in the middle and compare notes."

"Right, skipper," Casey said agreeably. "Go ahead; I'll get to work after I see Farrell out."

When Moroni had lumbered to the back of the apartment Casey moved with lightning speed to pull the case from under the coffee table.

"What the hell are you doing?" Farrell asked in a low voice.

"Put this in a safe place," Casey breathed. "I'll contact you later. And Farrell . . ." Casey said, catching the other man's wrist in a tight grip, "don't think I'll forget where this is. If I say give and you don't, I'll haul you in and take you apart. Don't think I won't."

Farrell was flooded with misgivings, his mind racing as he tried to figure out all the angles. He still wasn't out of the

SKIN DEEP, BLOOD RED   79

woods with Ganns by a long shot. Casey was a cop, and not to be trusted under ordinary circumstances, but these circumstances weren't ordinary. He was trapped in both directions, with nowhere to go but up. He grabbed the case and left the apartment without a backward glance.

Chapter 14

"This place is a real mess, Frank," Moroni said from the rear of the apartment.

Casey walked to the bedroom and found the captain standing in the midst of piles of scattered clothing. The mattress and springs were shoved askew on the tester bed, and the drawers of the bureau, makeup table, and nightstands lay on the floor, emptied of their contents. "Yeah," he said. "The guy who did Holly was after something here besides strangling her. Wonder what it was?"

Moroni gave no answer. He seemed particularly engrossed in his search, going about it with systematic doggedness. He sifted through each pile of clothing, then went into the closet, where Casey heard him shifting things on shelves and thumping on the walls.

"Looking for a secret passageway, Cap?" Casey asked.

"Holly wouldn't have nothing valuable just laying around," Moroni's muffled voice said. "Whatever the killer was looking for would be pretty well hidden." Finally the noises stopped, and the big man emerged from the closet, his beefy face red with exertion.

"You don't figure this for just a simple burglary, Cap?"

Casey asked, scratching the side of his neck. "Maybe the guy thought Holly was gone, then panicked when she came out."

Moroni looked at Casey, his eyes hooded, unreadable. "It could be that way," he said, "but I'm betting it was something bigger."

"How come?" Casey asked carefully.

Moroni was silent for a few seconds. "I've got my reasons, Frank. Reasons I can't talk about just now." He paused, pointing a finger at Casey. "But I'll tell you one thing: If I had any doubts about this being mob connected, your friend just rubbed them out."

"You mean Farrell?" Casey asked. "He's too much of a lone wolf to be connected to the mob."

"You goddamn betcha I mean Farrell," Moroni said, a hard edge in his voice. "That guy's guilty of about six crimes I can almost prove, and probably a hundred I can't."

"I've heard some off-color things about the guy myself, skipper," Casey said, "but I got a feeling about him. He seems like a straight shooter."

"You're a good guy, Frank, and a good cop, but you get soft-headed sometimes," Moroni said, shaking his head. "If you wake up one day with a razor against your throat, or looking down the barrel of that bastard's gun, remember that you heard it from me, okay?"

"Sure, Captain," Casey said. "I'll be careful."

Farrell caught the streetcar on the fly after leaving Casey and Moroni. He rode it for six blocks, then got off near Lee Circle and flagged a taxicab. He sent the cab on a roundabout route to a bordello he had an interest in on Soraparu Street, two blocks down from the Tchopitoulas Street riverfront warehouse district.

The house was typical of the rest of the neighborhood. Its look was neither too poor nor too prosperous, residing amid blue-collar dwellings rented mostly by longshoremen, warehouse workers, and other people in the bottom ranks of the shipping industry.

Farrell made certain that nothing too loud, too bawdy, or too violent happened in the house. People in the neighborhood had come to know him by sight. A few had approached him when they had problems, and had received relief, protection, money, or whatever else they'd required. The neighborhood paid Farrell back by respecting his privacy.

A handsome middle-aged black woman was at work cleaning the front parlor when Farrell walked in. He saw her quick eyes take in the leather case in his hand, but she said only, "Evenin', boss."

"Anything shakin', Marie?" Farrell asked.

"Naw," she replied, " 'cept Harry called from the club, said you should call back if you showed up here."

Farrell touched two fingers to the brim of his hat and strode to a small room at the back of the house. He put down the case on a desk, then rubbed the cleft in his chin reflectively for a second. He was still puzzled as to why Frank Casey had hidden the case from Captain Moroni. Moroni was a bad enemy, and Farrell knew it wouldn't do him a bit of good if the captain discovered he had the diamonds. Farrell had no choice but to trust Casey, to play along with him for the time being.

He kicked a small, oval braided rug away from the center of the floor, revealing a section of worn hardwood flooring joined with large wooden pins. Farrell pressed two of the round pins at once, then a third pin separately. A section of planking popped up, which he lifted away from the rest of the floor. The hole was lined with cedar and gave off a pleasant aroma. Inside there were two pistols wrapped inside oily wool socks, two yellow cardboard cartons of Peters .38 pistol ammunition, several bundles of currency with the bank bands still on them, and a cloth sack of gold and silver coins, all of it a hedge against hard times. Farrell dropped the leather case inside the hole, replaced the section of flooring, and smoothed the rug back into place.

He sat down and dialed the number of the Cafe Tristesse. Harry answered on the second ring.

"This is Farrell."

"Yeah, boss," Harry answered. "There's a woman over

here asking for you. Name of Sandra Tartaglia. What should I tell her?''

Farrell was silent for a moment, then said, "Take her upstairs to my apartment. Tell her to make herself comfortable. I'll be there in about an hour."

"Right," Harry said, then rang off.

"Marcel, where are you going, son?" Willie Mae Gautier asked, trying to keep a pleading note out of her voice.

"Out, Grandma, just out," Marcel answered. He was looking at himself in the mirror, arranging the Windsor knot in his bright red necktie. The pleats and creases of his gabardine suit were as neat and sharp as new razor blades.

"Son, you never stay home anymore," Willie Mae said. Her face was drawn and old with worry. It was a far different face from the hard, confident one she showed Wesley Farrell. "I— I get worried about you sometimes. I'm afraid you're going to get into trouble. Your mother begged me on her deathbed to watch out for you."

Marcel turned his smooth, good-looking face toward his grandmother. His eyes were diamond hard. "I'm a grown man now, Grandma," he said. "I'm gonna do what I want for a change."

Willie Mae's face hardened as anger crept into it against her will. "You're not a grown man. You're a boy of eighteen. You'll do what I say or . . ."

"Or what? Throw me out?" Marcel laughed. "I'm makin' my own money now, and I'm gonna move out soon anyway." He ran a hand across his wavy brown hair, smoothing it down before putting on his fedora.

Willie Mae clenched her fists impotently, her jaw tight as her anger got the better of her. "I'll call the police," she cried in a shrill voice. "I'll have you put into reform school."

But Marcel was already gone. The door slammed behind him, and Willie Mae's shoulders sagged with defeat. She was too used to dominating the men in her life, too used to getting her own way, to know how to deal with Marcel's rebellion.

Outside, Marcel looked up at the darkening sky, tipped his hat rakishly over one eye, and laughed quietly to himself. He reached back to his hip and brought up the Owl's Head .38 in a swift, practiced movement. He twirled the old revolver on his finger, then smoothly moved it back to his hip, out of sight. He laughed again, this time a little louder, then strode down the street, rolling his shoulders cockily as he went.

Chapter 15

Farrell parked his car at the back of the Cafe Tristesse and walked up an iron staircase to a private entrance. When he opened the door he could hear Benny Goodman's clarinet, and the voice of Helen Ward coming from the Victrola in his living room. Helen was singing "Goody, Goody," in that deep, go-to-hell-voice of hers, and Sandra Tartaglia's voice was helping her. He took off his hat and walked quietly to the front.

He found Sandra lounging on the leather sofa with a highball glass in her hand that she swung in time to the music. She had a dreamy smile on her face, and her pale blue eyes had lights in them. She was wearing a summery yellow dress with a plunging neckline. A matching bolero jacket was draped over the back of the sofa, and a wide-brimmed straw hat rested on top of the jacket. One high-heeled yellow sling pump lay on the rug, and the other dangled from her toes. She turned her head and smiled at him as she joined Helen Ward in singing, "And I hope you're satisfied, you rascal you."

"This is the damnedest excuse for a wake I've ever seen," he said as the song ended and the Victrola switched itself off.

"Well, since the funeral is over, I decided I was tired of being in mourning," she said gaily. "I'd rather celebrate the end of a beautiful fall day, and the beginning of new acquaintences. Have a drink?'' She raised her glass to him.

''Why not?'' he asked as he moved over to the bar. He threw some ice into a tall glass and poured rye and ginger ale over them. ''What brings you to see me?''

''I had just decided that I liked you when you left so abruptly this morning,'' she said. ''I thought it would be nice to get to know more about you.'' She lowered her feet to the floor and made room for him on the sofa.

''There isn't that much to tell,'' Farrell said as he sat down. He liked this woman in a way he'd never liked anyone before, but the liking was fighting hard against the alarm bells inside his head. ''I'm thirty-seven years old, I've never married, and I pay my taxes when they tell me to. I voted for Roosevelt the past two elections, and I spend most of my time minding my own business. It's not very exciting, but too much excitement isn't good for you, I hear.''

She laughed. ''You don't do much of a selling job on yourself, I'll say that for you.''

He sipped his drink and looked at her over the rim of the glass. ''The only things I sell are the dinners, cocktails, and music downstairs in the club. The prices are pretty reasonable, if I can go by the number of people who come in.''

''That explanation doesn't go with the rest of the things I've heard about you,'' she said. The light, bantering tone that had been in her voice disappeared, to be replaced by something low and solemn. ''I've been told you can be a pretty dangerous man when you have to be.''

''They say a lot of things in New Orleans,'' he countered. ''It's a pretty small town, and sometimes there isn't much else to do but talk.'' He shifted his body on the sofa to face her. ''Maybe you should quit beating around the bush and tell me what you want.''

''A man who cuts to the heart of things. I like that,'' she said, some of the banter back in her voice. ''I told you I'm in the import-export business,'' she said, flicking her eyes down to her glass. ''It can be . . . difficult sometimes.''

''Like now?'' he asked.

"Like now," she replied. "I could use a friend who doesn't scare easy. Somebody who could do my fighting for me when it got dirty. I asked around about you, and I heard you might be that kind of man."

"I've got all the work I can handle right now, Miss Tartaglia," he said.

"Sandy," she said.

"I'm a businessman, not a bodyguard," he said. "What you want is a couple of five-dollar-a-day loogans."

She smiled and swirled the ice in her glass. "What's a loogan?" she asked.

"A guy with fists bigger than his brains," he replied, putting down his glass on the coffee table. As he turned to face her again her arms went around his neck and her body slid into his.

"No, that wouldn't do," she said softly, her face very close to his. "Brawn is nice, but I prefer my men to have a few brains."

He started to say something but knew that more talk wouldn't do any good. She was offering him something he wanted, and the alarm bells weren't loud enough to make him stop wanting it. After a moment he responded, but his eyes remained open, and there was a thoughtful look in them.

Frank Casey sat in the darkness of his Marmon eating a muffaletta sandwich as he watched the office building on Howard Avenue. He was thinking to himself that the secret to a good muffaletta was the olive salad you used. Without that, all you had was a lot of cold cuts and cheese on bread.

Between bites he was considering the many reasons Captain Gus Moroni might have for being in the building. He'd been following the captain around all afternoon and into the evening. Moroni had been a busy boy. He'd stopped at five different places that Casey knew were bookie joints, and he knew that each betting parlor was high volume. He also knew that Moroni didn't bet on horses, or on anything else. Since the parlors were illegal, and Moroni had made no arrests, there was only one thing he could be doing at each place.

Casey wasn't so much surprised as disappointed. A chief of detectives ought to be involved in a more dignified kind of graft than taking protection money. Of course, with Chance Tartaglia so suddenly dead, Moroni probably hadn't had the opportunity to break in a new apprentice. It was a shame, Casey thought, that it was so difficult to get good help.

As he was putting the last bite of his sandwich into his mouth, Moroni came out of the building, paused, looked down both sides of the street, and then got into his blue Mercury. Casey liked the Mercury, admired Moroni for getting it. It wasn't so flashy a car that anybody on the force would be suspicious about him having it. After all, a captain made a respectable salary, and Moroni had no wife or family to support. The Mercury made good sense.

Moroni started up and drove down Howard toward the Union Railroad Depot, then turned right on Loyola Avenue. Casey started the Marmon and followed at a discreet distance, with only his parking lights on. At Canal Street Moroni turned left and headed toward the lakefront. Casey had no trouble tracking him; Moroni had one taillight out, and there was little traffic.

They drove the length of Canal Boulevard until they reached Robert E. Lee Drive, where Moroni took another right. About a mile down he turned off into an enclave populated entirely by wealthy people who could afford big yards and very few neighbors. Casey cut the parking lights and continued until he saw Moroni brake to a stop in front of a large brick house blazing with light. Casey saw the front door open, and Moroni lumbered into the house.

When the door closed Casey got out and crept across the yard, listening intently for the bark of a dog. When he heard none, he continued around to the back of the house, keeping to the shadows cast by large trees. The house had a large, glassed-in sun porch at the rear, and Casey saw two men sitting in armchairs talking. He crept closer, hugging the trunk of a large elm tree. He could see Moroni clearly now, but the other man had his back to the window. They were talking animatedly,

and Casey became increasingly frustrated because he couldn't
see the other man's face, or hear what they were talking about.

Suddenly the second man got up and walked to a table where
several bottles, decanters, and a soda siphon sat. As he turned
to face the window, Casey saw that it was Emile Ganns.

Marcel stood in the shadow of the building on Perdido Street,
watching the door to a bar across the street. The bar was the
only place open in that part of town, and there wasn't much
foot or automobile traffic. He'd known that in advance, had
been counting on it. He had already run through most of his
pool hall winnings and his share of the money from the hardware
store heist, and was hard up for cash. He figured a simple little
mugging wouldn't be much of a risk, and with luck he'd get
enough to tide him over until Griff called the next time.

He heard the clock in the belfry of St. Joseph's Cathedral
on Tulane Avenue chime for 11 P.M., and shifted his weight
to ease a cramp in his left leg. Several people had entered the
bar, but so far nobody had come out. He was beginning to get
discouraged, and a little frightened, when he heard the door
open, bar sounds spilling out into the dark street.

A short, stocky man in a canvas work jacket and a sailor's
knit watch cap staggered onto the sidewalk, pulling a skinny
blonde into the circle of light from a fixture mounted over the
barroom door. The stocky man roared with laughter, and the
skinny blonde responded, her laugh reminding Marcel of the
time his grandmother dropped a handful of silverware on the
dining room floor. He pulled his handkerchief up over his nose
and mouth and drew the revolver from his hip.

As the drunken couple giggled and weaved their way across
the street, Marcel faded back into the shadows and waited.
Within seconds, the couple worked their way up to the mouth
of the alley. As they drew abreast, Marcel sprang out behind
them, dug the snout of his gun into the stocky man's back, and
hissed, "Get 'em up, sucker. Don't make a sound."

The drunk said, "Wha . . . ?" and Marcel brought the butt
of his gun down on the base of his neck, once, twice, and three

times. The seaman groaned and sagged, but Marcel caught him
under the arms and held him upright. The blonde, a shifty-eyed,
careworn woman of about thirty-five, froze on the sidewalk, her
fists pressed to her mouth, her eyes round with fear. Incipient
screams hissed from behind the fists.

"Shut up or I'll kill you," Marcel growled. He motioned
with his gun for her to follow him into the alley. He walked
backward, dragging the unconscious man with him. Once in
the alley Marcel dropped the man, then grabbed the woman,
and threw her up against the brick wall. Fixing her with his
eyes, he deftly patted the seaman's body until he felt the bulge
of his wallet. Marcel's probing fingers found a twenty, two
fives, and three ones inside the shabby, sweat-stained leather
billfold.

"So," he crowed, "you didn't get him to spend all of it yet,
did you?" He folded the limp bills with one hand and shoved
them into his inside breast pocket.

"Please . . . please d-don't hurt me," the woman whined.
Her arms were clasped across her skinny bosom and her knees
were buckling with terror. "I'll do anything . . . anything at
all; just don't hurt me."

Marcel stared at her, blood surging through his body. He
felt a buzzing below his belt buckle, and a feeling of power
such as he had never known. He got up and walked toward
her, the cheap, nickel-plated revolver tight in his right fist. He
reached out with his left hand, rubbing it roughly over her
breasts. "You're damn right you'll do anything," he said in a
thick, cottony voice. "Anything at all."

Chapter 16

He was walking through the grass on a hot day. The heat caused the grass to exude a heavy, pleasant odor. He felt a hand on his shoulder and looked up to see the long, thin fingers of a hand attached to an arm that ran up into a blue sleeve. It was his father, he knew, and he felt safe, even though he couldn't crane his neck far enough to see his father's face. He reached out and grasped two of the fingers in his own small hand, and his father lifted him up, swinging him to and fro. He felt safe, though, and began to laugh with glee. He could hear his father laugh, too, and it made him laugh all the harder.

He awoke slowly, smiling at the laughter in his dream. He started to stretch until he felt her body next to his and checked himself. He looked down and saw her white-blond hair spread out on the pillow, her lips bent into a small, childish smile. She was almost completely bare, and he gently drew up the sheet, spreading it over her.

As quietly as he could, he withdrew from the bed and walked softly to the bathroom, where he relieved himself. Then he stepped into the shower stall, lathered, and began to shave. He was scraping the last of the whiskers from his chin when he felt her step into the shower behind him.

"You're an early riser," she said, rubbing her hands over his soapy body.

"A dream woke me," he said.

"Was it about me?" she asked.

"No, it was about my father. A good dream," he added.

"Do you always dream about your father when you're in bed with a woman?" she asked, laughing.

"Not usually. I never knew him, so I don't know why I've been dreaming about him lately."

"Well, I guess I should be grateful you weren't dreaming about your mother instead," she said, still lathering his chest.

"You're a pretty fast worker, you know that?" he asked.

She laughed and drew his hand low down on her belly. "Life's short, Wesley. I don't want to miss out on anything." She moved her hands slowly down his chest to his belly, then down to his groin, and for a while there was no more talking, only moans and little cries.

"Sure you don't want any breakfast?" he asked later.

She turned from brushing her hair and said, "Don't think so, boy. Breakfasts aren't good for a girl's figure."

Her refusal cut through the pleasure he'd been feeling, and for some reason Savanna's face leapt into his memory. Fighting a strange panic, he said, "Your figure doesn't need any work, baby. You could cheat just this once." He'd meant the words to sound casually humorous, but instead they seemed oddly like an entreaty. His chest felt tight, and his throat burned.

She ran her hand over his freshly shaven cheek and said, "Cheating leads to lying, and lying leads to mayhem, boy. I can't afford to start having bad habits now." She chuckled deep down in her chest as she put the brush into her purse and reached for the bolero jacket. "I'll see you soon," she said as she picked up her hat. It was a statement of fact, not a question.

"I wouldn't be surprised," he answered.

She smiled lazily and walked through the door leading down to the club.

Farrell stood there for a moment, feeling waves of pleasure, loneliness, and worry wash over him. Sandra Tartaglia was something very special, but now she was gone, and the alarm bells were back, loud and insistent. He'd never ignored the bells to this extent before, and it frightened him to break his own rules so cavalierly.

He was standing in the kitchenette, making coffee and trying not to think, when a noise made him whirl around. Savanna was there, leaning against the doorframe. Her long body was dressed in a deep purple suit, and the lacy ruffles of her silk blouse showed at the cuffs and at her lean throat. Her black eyes were opaque, her mouth a brittle line.

"Who's the blond chippy?" she asked in a toneless voice.

"She's Chance Tartaglia's daughter," he replied, feeling a strange, unpleasant pain in his chest.

"Right," she said, disbelief hanging heavy in her voice.

"I met her at his funeral yesterday," he said, a bit defensively.

"What the hell were you doing at Tartaglia's funeral?" Savanna asked. Her frank scrutiny was almost more than he could bear, and an unfamiliar feeling of shame knotted his guts.

"A man I know wants to find out who had Tartaglia killed, and he offered me some money to look into it," he said.

"He offer you money to fuck the daughter, too?" Savanna asked.

"What's it to you?" he demanded, his voice uncharacteristically shrill. "There's no brass plate on me with your name on it."

Without another word she strode to him, her left fist moving in a swift arc toward his jaw. At the last possible moment Farrell's right hand shot up, caught the fist, and stopped it cold. Savanna's black eyes snapped with rage. "You're a sonofabitch, Farrell," she shouted, snatching her hand from his. When he said nothing she turned and walked out the way she'd come in, slamming the door behind her.

Farrell looked down at his hand and saw it was shaking.

* * *

Farrell put down the pencil he was using to make entries in his ledger and rubbed his eyes with a thumb and a forefinger. It was getting dark outside, and the room had become dim with the advance of night. It was time to get up and go to work. He switched on a desk lamp, drew the telephone toward him, and got out his address book. After looking up a name, he dialed. He finally got an answer after dialing three different numbers in succession.

"Let me talk to Nate Stiles," he said when a voice answered.

"Stiles," another voice said.

"This is Farrell," he said. "I need to call in a marker."

"If I got it," said Stiles, "it's yours."

"I'm trying to get a line on Chance Tartaglia's movements on the day he was shot. Who'd know?"

The voice was silent for the space of five seconds. "You're foolin' around in Ganns's territory. Why don't you ask him?"

"If Ganns knew what I wanted, I'd go to him, sap. Tartaglia was playing some angles Ganns didn't know about. Get my drift?"

At first Farrell thought he wouldn't respond. Then Stiles said, "Go see Paul Markowitz. He ran errands for Tartaglia. If anybody'd know, he would."

"Paul Markowitz," Farrell said. "Thanks, Stiles. I appreciate the help."

"Nuts," Stiles said. "I owed you. Consider the debt paid off." He hung up.

Farrell put away the address book and locked the ledger in the bottom drawer of his desk. He strapped the switchblade to his left forearm and made certain he had the razor. As an afterthought he reached into the top right-hand drawer and took out the old Colt .38. He jacked a cartridge into the breech, set the rounded nub of a hammer on half-cock, then tucked the pistol into the waistband of his trousers, over his right hipbone. After calling Harry down at the bar he got his hat and left the club through the rear entrance.

Chapter 17

As Farrell drove his Packard into the Mid-City area, the sky darkened with something more than night. A low rumble of thunder escaped the darkening billows along with a sound like electricity straining at its leash. Dim flashes of light haunted the edges of the muddy clouds.

He turned off Canal Street onto North Murat and drove past several blocks of wood-frame houses that sat atop false basements made of rotting red brick. It was a largely middle-class neighborhood, and everyone was inside at dinner. Three blocks in from Canal, Farrell pulled up in front of a well-kept duplex. A red Chevrolet coupé was parked in the driveway.

Farrell got out of the Packard, raised the canvas roof, and rolled up the windows. At the stairs leading to the porch he checked the mailboxes and saw that the left-hand apartment was where Markowitz lived.

Five seconds after Farrell pressed the doorbell the front door opened. A fat little man, barely five and a half feet tall, stood behind the screen door. His body was so compact and thick that it seemed his head rested directly on his barrel-shaped torso. His hair was tightly curled, and steel-rimmed spectacles rested on a bulbous nose.

"You Markowitz?" he asked.

"Who's askin'?" the fat man asked warily.

"My name's Farrell. I want to talk to you for a few minutes."

"What about?" Markowitz asked, his eyes uncertain.

Farrell opened the screen door with a quick movement of his wrist and body and got his foot into the doorjamb before Markowitz could slam it shut. He could hear the fat man's deep, rapid breathing as he strained to push the door closed. Farrell set his left leg and heaved once. The fat man flew into the room, rolling until an armchair halted his advance.

Markowitz threw himself into a sitting position, his eyes wide and desperate. He fumbled behind him for a large-frame .38-44 Smith & Wesson revolver that lay on the arm of his chair, but just as his questing fingers met the blue steel, something bright and hard flew through the air. The Italian stiletto punched into his hand and on through to the arm of the chair. Markowitz's eyes rolled and his mouth opened to scream, but Farrell's open hand slapped over his face. The fat man was pale with pain and terror, and muffled exclamations came from behind Farrell's hand.

"Listen," Farrell said, shaking Markowitz with his free hand, "I'm gonna pull out the knife, and you're gonna sit there and not say a word, get me?"

The muffled sounds died in Markowitz's throat, and he nodded his head frantically up and down. As Farrell grasped the switchblade, pulling it from the wound, Markowitz squinted with pain. A sigh escaped his mouth as he passed out.

Farrell wiped the knife on Markowitz's necktie, closed it, and replaced it up his sleeve. Then he picked up the big revolver, thumbed the latch, and emptied the six brass cartridges onto the rug. He bent down and inspected the wound in the fat man's hand, saw that it wasn't bleeding too badly, then bound it up with his own handkerchief.

Satisfied that Markowitz wouldn't bleed to death, he went to the kitchen for a glass of water and brought it back to the living room. He kicked Markowitz's leg twice, and when the man didn't move, threw the water into his face as hard as he could. The fat man came up gasping and gagging.

"Feel like talking now?" Farrell asked when the choking stopped.

"I don't know nothin'," the fat man whined, clutching his injured hand to his chest.

"You know plenty," Farrell said, tipping up the brim of his Stetson, "and you're gonna tell all of it. Where'd Tartaglia get the diamonds?"

"W-what diamonds?"

Farrell took the razor from inside his jacket and began to make the handle and blade dance in his hand. The razor made a dry, whisking noise reminiscent of the sound cockroaches make when they fly through the summer air. Markowitz's breath began to sound labored and shallow.

"You can make this as easy or as hard as you like, fat boy," Farrell said. "Tartaglia can't help you now, but you can help yourself. Where'd he get the diamonds?"

"I dunno," he said. "He didn't tell me. All's he said was a new shipment of stuff was due in—something hot. Something that would set him up for life, so's he could quit the cops and Ganns, too."

"How long had Tartaglia been holding out on Ganns?" Farrell asked.

"Maybe a year," Markowitz answered. "I told him it was stupid, that if Ganns found out he'd kill him for sure, maybe me, too." Markowitz shook his head mournfully, like a father with an errant son he couldn't control. "Now Ganns knows, and I'm a walkin' dead man."

"Never mind that. What happened the day of the murder?" Farrell demanded. "Did he do anything different than usual?"

"He called me up Wednesday night," Markowitz answered. "Told me to make the rounds of the payoff spots. Said he was meeting somebody on Thursday morning at the Celeste Street Wharf. Somebody was comin' in on a ship, and he hadda meet 'em." Markowitz's face was bathed in sweat, his body trembling visibly.

"You see or talk to him after that?"

"No, no, I swear it," Markowitz said, a little calmer now. "He told me to visit the payoff drops that day; said he'd see

me that night, or the next day. Only I never saw him again. I
don't even know what happened to the ice.''

Farrell looked at him closely and saw no guile at the back
of his round, frightened eyes. He put the razor back inside his
coat. ''Who was fencing the stuff Tartaglia was stealing from
Ganns?''

''Different ones,'' Markowitz answered. ''I think he was
going to use Luc Bergeron for the ice. He normally left stuff
like that in a suitcase with that punch-drunk fighter who's the
building super in Holly Ballou's apartment house, and one of
Bergeron's guys would pick it up from him the next day. Holly
was friends with Bergeron, and I think she got the two of them
together.''

''How was Tartaglia keeping all this from Ganns?'' Farrell
asked.

Markowitz shook his head again. ''Ganns got so big he didn't
know nothin' about the day-to-day activities no more. Bein'
as Chance was a cop, he was a natural to handle all the gold,
silver, gemstones, and dope that got smuggled in by ship.''
Markowitz paused and brought his wounded hand up to his
chest, where he stroked it gently with the other hand. ''See,
he was able to arrange drops in safe places, where there'd be
no chance of gettin' surprised by Treasury or Customs people.
It was no big trick for Chance to shortchange him, since Ganns
never knew the full value of nothin' that came in. Chance
brought him whatever he felt like and pocketed the rest. I knew
Ganns would find out sooner or later; I just knew it.'' The fat
man sagged in his chair like a wilted flower.

''You better get out of town as soon as you can if you want
to stay healthy,'' Farrell said. ''Whoever had Tartaglia killed
might come to you next, and soon.''

''You mean . . . you mean you're lettin' me go?'' Markowitz
asked.

''You're no use to me,'' Farrell said. ''Ganns wants to know
who killed Tartaglia, but he didn't say anything about cleaning
house for him. Just get the hell out of here—tonight—and get
on the first train headed north. He won't have anybody follow
you.''

The little man was bobbing his head up and down, looking pitifully grateful, as Farrell turned and walked through the door to the porch, closing it behind him. As he continued to the stairs, he heard all the latches snapping closed behind him. He smiled grimly and headed down to the street.

He paused on the steps as thunder rolled above him, and he searched the sky for rain. Then, as the thunder receded, he heard an engine idling somewhere and paused to scan the street. His eyes raked the block from one end to the other before he noticed movement inside an old black Plymouth touring car. An arm came out of the window, and Farrell leaped over the side of the steps as the first shot sounded. A slug ricocheted off concrete where he'd been standing and whined off into the night.

Farrell got his Colt loose and threw two quick shots in the Plymouth's direction. His gunfire was answered by a reckless string of shots that sent him ducking for cover. As he reached his gun over the edge of the stairs for another shot, the car roared to life, streaking past him up the street. He ran out after it, firing low to hit a tire, but none of his three shots appeared to have any effect. The big black automobile careened around the corner and out of the neighborhood.

Farrell stood in the middle of the street, a murderous fury rippling through the length of his body. His teeth were bared in a snarl and his eyes flicked around him, searching for other targets. As he turned toward his own car, a broad flash of lightning split the darkness, and his eyes caught something gleaming in the street ahead of him. He walked to it quickly, bent down, and saw it was a spent cartridge case. As he held it up to catch the pale rays of the streetlamp, he saw stamped in the base the words ELY BROS .455 WEBLEY. He tossed it up and down in his hand for a moment, then got back into his car and left the neighborhood.

Chapter 18

Casey had been watching Ganns and Moroni for nearly an hour when he saw the two men get up and walk back into the house. Moving quickly, he was back inside the Marmon as Moroni stood on the front porch, shaking hands with the smaller man. Soon Moroni was negotiating the winding, landscaped street, past several more elegant homes, until he picked up Robert E. Lee Drive again. There was enough traffic on the drive to allow Casey to switch his lights back on again without fear of discovery. The broken taillight on the Mercury made it possible for the red-haired detective to follow his quarry from the lakefront all the way uptown without effort. Casey amused himself by listening to Bob Hope's "Pepsodent Hour" on the radio as he drove.

Casey had been watching Moroni for months, certain that he was in league with Chance Tartaglia but still unsure who had been pulling their strings. Casey had begun the investigation hoping that Moroni was playing at being a crooked cop in order to discover the identity of Tartaglia's boss. He still wanted to believe that. When a policeman turns crooked he tars all of his fellow officers with the same brush.

As he followed Moroni through the streets of the city, Casey decided to give Moroni a chance to come clean with him. Although they weren't friends, Casey had worked for Moroni for more than ten years. He decided to go up to Moroni's apartment and give him an opportunity to explain himself. If he took it, Casey could offer to begin working with him. If he didn't—Casey would know what that meant.

At about 9:00 P.M. Moroni pulled off Jefferson Avenue into the parking area behind a stylish, four-story apartment building at the corner of St. Charles Avenue. Casey pulled to the curb at a discreet distance and admired the building's art-deco corners, concrete decorations, and glass-and-metal Frank Lloyd Wright windows. When he thought Moroni had had sufficient time to get inside he got out of the ancient roadster and entered the building's main entrance.

A check of the mailboxes in the lobby told Casey that Moroni lived on the top floor, so he took the elevator all the way up. As he walked softly down the thickly carpeted hall, Casey tipped his hat back on his head, rubbed his face with both hands, and pulled his necktie down from his collar. After he rang Moroni's buzzer he leaned against the doorframe and assumed a weary, bedraggled look.

Moroni opened the door with his vest unbuttoned and his own tie undone. He had a highball glass in his hand, but it contained nothing but ice.

"Frank," he said with some surprise. "What're you doin' here this time of the night?"

"Been tracking leads on Tartaglia's death, and the Ballou woman's," he said. "It's been a hell of a long day, but a pretty profitable one."

Moroni regarded Casey with blank, impenetrable eyes and a tight-lipped mouth. "Well, as long as you're here, c'mon in and have a snort," he said finally.

"Thanks, don't mind if I do," Casey said affably. He straightened up and walked past the captain into a comfortably furnished living room.

Moroni had an expensive Kroeller sofa with two matching armchairs and a heavy mahogany coffee table grouped around a fireplace equipped with a gas log. A small oak-paneled bar sat in one corner of the room with a lot of crystal decanters on top. A big Philco cabinet radio sat in another corner, and Casey heard the theme music to "The Adventures of Bulldog Drummond" emanating quietly from the speaker.

The walls were filled with framed photographs of a younger Moroni posed in front of cannon and machine guns with other men dressed as soldiers. There were also a few latter-day photos of Moroni shaking hands with the mayor and other civic and police officials. Over the mantel Moroni had mounted a cavalry sabre and an old British Martin-Henry service rifle.

"Nice place you got here, Cap," Casey said as he dropped his hat on the coffee table.

"It'll do until something better comes along," Moroni replied tonelessly. "It's kind of late for a social call, ain't it, Frank?"

"Well, skipper," Casey said as he sipped his drink, "this has been kind of a crazy case so far. I guess I wanted to talk some of it out with you; see if maybe you could help clear up some things."

"I don't know, Frank," Moroni said as he tinkled the ice in his glass. "So far it's all Greek to me. I doubt I've gotten much further than you have."

"Don't be so modest, skipper," Casey said heartily. "You know the criminal element in this city better than anyone I know. You're bound to know some things I don't."

Moroni said nothing, but his face grew flushed as his knuckles whitened with strain. The fire in his face seemed to make his eyes glow.

"I got a funny feeling about this business, though," Casey went on. "For instance, I'd bet my next week's pay that whoever killed Holly thinks Chance left something with her. Something valuable."

"These feelin's you got, they tell you what it was that Tartaglia's supposed to've left with her?" Moroni asked, the tension in his voice growing.

Casey got up from his chair. "I already know what he left, and it's hotter than a two-dollar pistol." He smacked his right fist into his open left palm for emphasis.

Moroni was silent for a minute, his eyes fixed unblinkingly on Casey's. The fire in them was out now; they looked cold and distant. "You gonna tell me what it is or not?" he asked finally.

"Not just yet, skipper," Casey said as he picked up his hat, "but I've only got a few more loose ends to tie up before I can give you the whole package." He walked to the door, then turned and looked back over his shoulder.

"By the way, I found out something interesting about you today," he said. "Something I didn't know. After you raised all that hell down in Central America with Lee Christmas you went to England with the A.E.F. They had you over there teaching doughboys all you knew about machine-gun tactics."

"So?" Moroni said. "A hell of a lot of guys went to England during the War. What of it?"

"I was just thinking that England must be lousy with Webley automatics," Casey said, smiling. "You've got quite a collection of war memorabilia here; I was just thinking how funny it is you didn't think to bring one back as a souvenir." Casey yawned elaborately. "Jesus, it's gettin' past my bedtime, Cap. I guess I better be getting on home. Thanks for letting me talk some of this over with you." Casey waved and let himself out of the apartment.

Moroni stared at the door after Casey left, the skin around his eyes and mouth hard and white. Unconsciously, his hand began flexing around the highball glass, and suddenly it broke with a loud pop. He didn't seem to notice the sound, or the blood that dripped from his hand to the hardwood floor.

Marcel leaned back in a wooden chair across from the bar of the Negro tavern at the river end of Jeanette Street. It was dim and quiet, since most of the mechanics, domestics, and day laborers who normally frequented the tavern had gone home to sleep, resting up for the coming workday. Marcel had nothing to get ready for; he still had at least thirty of the thirty-three dollars he'd taken from the seaman he'd slugged the night before.

His groin itched from the brief, semi-satisfying rape of the dishwater blonde in the alley, and he scratched himself absently. He wanted another woman tonight, somebody he could really pile into. He had a full head of steam up, and the whiskey he was drinking seemed to inflame him all the more.

As he sat there considering whether to stay or go, a trim little brown-skinned girl entered the tavern. He took in her carefully cut and straightened pageboy haircut, the ripe round-ness of her breasts, and the way her fanny wiggled as she sauntered up to the bar. He got up, walked over, and casually stood beside her. As he dropped his hat on the top of the bar, he turned his head and said, ''Buy you a drink, baby sister?''

The girl turned her head and leveled a pair of eyes that were a hundred years older than the rest of her on him. They were eyes that knew every cheap pitch and hard pass that had ever been thrown. She was about to tell him to go to hell when his light-colored, handsome face and expensive clothes began to register in her calculating little mind. Her eyes got interested, and she turned her body on the bar stool until she faced fully in his direction.

''A drink?'' she said. ''That would be real fine, honey. That all you want?'' Her smile was full of promises now that she knew he could pay for a little fun first.

Marcel grinned back at her and motioned to the bartender to set up a round. He took the girl's small, fine hand and knew he had it made. ''A drink is good for starts, baby sister. We can play it by ear from there, can't we?''

She grinned knowingly and slowly nodded her sleek little head up and down.

Chapter 19

The big red-brick building that housed police headquarters had the same pitiless and grimly efficient look as a medieval keep. Farrell had never visited police headquarters in his life and found some irony in the fact that he was now entering it on police business.

He used the irony to cover over an unpleasant tickle of fear. For years, he had thought of this only as an enemy stronghold. He was a gambler, with a gambler's instincts, and he knew that it was only luck that had kept him from being dragged through the wide double doors in chains on a one-way trip to prison or the electric chair.

Unlike a lot of gamblers, Farrell had learned from the experience of others that every lucky streak has an end, and that you had to be good enough to know when to fold. Until now he'd kept a lot of distance between himself and the police, and violating that habit was a supreme testing of the limits of his luck.

Farrell asked the desk sergeant how to find Inspector Casey's office and was directed to stairs that would take him to the third floor.

Farrell walked down the hall and up the stairs on cat feet,

willing himself to be as inconspicuous as possible in this hostile
environment. But his tall, muscular frame, and the expensive
Harris tweed suit he wore, made him as out of place as a crab
salad at a bar mitzvah, and attracted as many curious glances.
At the third-floor landing he consulted a floor directory and
found Casey's name and office number without difficulty.
Within another minute he had located the office and knocked
gently on the pebbled-glass door.

"It's open," Casey's voice called.

Farrell opened the door and stepped in. Casey was seated at
his desk, his shirt sleeves rolled up, leafing through a bunch
of papers. The light coming from the window behind him made
his face indistinct, his expression unreadable.

"What brings you here so early in the day?" Casey asked,
looking up from his reports. "I didn't think you nightclub
proprietors got up before noon."

"I'm on a health kick. I get up by ten A.M. and take a thirty-
yard walk," Farrell said. "Besides, I want to fill you in on
some things." He sat down in a heavy oak side chair with a
red leather seat.

Casey rested his chin on the backs of his clasped hands.
"This must be something in particular to bring you over here,"
Casey said, his eyes gleaming with interest.

Farrell said nothing, but reached into the breast pocket of
his jacket, fished around for a second, then brought out an
object and placed it in the middle of the desk.

Casey's right hand left his chin and moved toward the dull
brass object, picked it up, and brought it up close to his face.

"A .455," he said. "How'd you come by this?"

"A guy threw about five of them at me last night. He wasn't
a very good shot," Farrell said.

"You do any better?" Casey asked.

"No, but there's going to be another time."

"Where'd this happen?" Casey asked as he placed the cartridge case down in the center of his desk blotter.

"I found out that Tartaglia had a man who did some of his
scut work," Farrell replied. "His name's Markowitz. Lives
over in Mid-City."

"Yeah, and what else?" Casey asked.

"I asked him about the diamonds," Farrell said, taking out a pack of Camels and placing a cigarette in the corner of his mouth. "Know anything about a fence named Luc Bergeron?"

"Sure," Casey said, nodding his head. "Tartaglia connected to him?"

"At the hip, from what Markowitz told me. He said Tartaglia had been taking possession of gold, silver, jewelry, and drugs for his boss, and fencing them with Bergeron and several others."

"Well, well," Casey said, lacing his hands behind his head. "I'll bet the next thing you're gonna tell me is that Chance was holding out, skimming the cream before he delivered the milk to his boss." He smiled and cocked a knowing eyebrow at Farrell.

"On the nose," Farrell said. "Which gives me reason to think that his boss might have been the one to rub him out, after all."

"What makes you so certain Markowitz was telling the truth about all this?" Casey asked.

"I made it worth his while to play straight," Farrell said as he lit the Camel. "He was willing to be reasonable."

"I'll just bet he was," Casey said, his fingers moving back to the dull brass shell on his desk. "He tell you anything else?"

"Not much. Tartaglia just told him to collect the payoffs that day. Said he'd see him later, only he didn't." Farrell blew smoke into the air.

"So who fired the shots at you?"

"I'm not sure. It was getting dark as I was leaving Markowitz's place. I saw a '30 or '31 Plymouth touring car with the motor running. I smelled a rat and took cover just as he started shooting. I shot back, but he got away." Farrell paused a moment to draw smoke into his lungs. "I couldn't be certain, but it was a big guy. It could have been the same one I saw at Holly's a few days ago."

Casey mulled over Farrell's story in silence as he rolled the cartridge case around on his blotter.

"Got any other ideas?" Farrell asked.

"A few," Casey responded, "but I'm not quite certain how they hook up. For example, I've got a strong hunch that Emile Ganns is mixed up in this somehow."

Casey watched Farrell's face; although his expression didn't change, Casey was certain that something in his eyes did. Farrell wasn't making it any easier to trust him. "You know Ganns fairly well, don't you?" he asked.

"Who doesn't?" Farrell asked, shrugging. "He draws a lot of water in this town."

"I'm not much for giving advice," Casey said, "but if Ganns brought you into this, I'd watch out. All those old-world manners and that polite English he talks won't mean damn-all when the chips are down. There's at least five guys lining the bottom of the river on account of him. Some of them were pretty good boys."

Farrell smiled at the red-haired cop and stood up. "I'm not used to having anybody concerned about my welfare, Inspector, particularly a cop. But you don't need to worry; I don't trust Ganns and I never have. I haven't lived this long by turning my back on anybody."

"One more thing," Casey said. "You're in this pretty deep. How deep I don't know. You've been some help to me, but if you've got any dirt on your hands when the dust settles, I'll take you down just like any other crook." He leaned back in his chair. "If there's anything else you'd like to tell me, this would be a good time to do it."

Farrell saw his seriousness and wiped the smile from his face. He nodded and said, "I hear you," then touched two fingers to the brim of his hat and left Casey's office. After he closed the door behind him he stood there for a minute in indecision. He knew he could save himself a lot of grief by telling what he knew about Emile Ganns, but in doing that, he'd end up having his bloodline exposed. He reached for the knob, checked himself, then turned quickly and walked back down the hall.

Inside the office, Casey rocked back in his swivel chair and scowled at the closed door. He found himself in the uncomfortable position of wanting to trust Farrell and not really knowing if he should. He was certain that Farrell was working for Emile Ganns, and he'd given him a chance to say so. Farrell's failure to come through on that issue had caused Casey to hold back on something, too.

He looked again at seven recent robbery reports, dating back as far as three weeks. In two of the robberies, the most recent at a hardware store on Saturday morning, a .455 Webley automatic had been used by one of the holdup men.

Although the last shooting had been a fatality, the other had left a witness behind. That witness had given descriptions of a large, blond-haired white man, a young Negro, and another young man of indeterminate race. Those descriptions fit five other robberies in which no shots had been fired. The bullets and cartridge cases matched the ones from the Tartaglia kill. Casey couldn't see the connection between an itinerant heister, Tartaglia, and Emile Ganns, but he was certain there had to be one.

He leaned back in his chair and regarded the photograph on his desk. He stared at it for a minute, then combed his fingers through his hair, got up, and left the office, taking the .455 cartridge case with him.

Chapter 20

Casey left the cartridge case with the crime lab and went outside, got in his car, and drove over to the offices of *The New Orleans Times-Picayune*. After speaking to the uniformed guard at the front desk he walked up several flights of stairs to the newspaper morgue. A pretty young woman, who tried to hide her looks behind a set of steel-rimmed spectacles, smiled brightly at him as he strode up to the desk.

"Hello," she said. "It's Inspector Casey, isn't it?"

"Darlin'," he said, "you'd make a good cop with a memory like that."

"What can we do for you today?" she asked.

"I need to see the shipping news for the last three weeks, up until last Thursday."

"Right," she said. "Have a seat and I'll bring them over."

Casey sat at a study table, taking off his hat. Then he took out a notepad and his fountain pen and set them down next to the hat. He was leaning back in his chair, cracking his knuckles, when the young woman came back with a formidable stack of papers on a wooden book truck.

"Can I get you anything else?" the young woman asked.

"Not right now," Casey replied. "I'll look through these and let you know later."

The young woman had returned to her desk, and Casey opened the oldest issue, turned to the shipping news, and located the "Arrivals" column. Five ships had arrived that day, and he made notations on his pad for the S. S. *Southern Cross* out of Adelaid, Australia, the S. S. *Maxwell* out of Belfast, Ireland, and the S. S. *Broor Mickkelson* out of Capetown, South Africa. He also wrote down the names and addresses of the shipping agents for each vessel.

Slowly and methodically, he went through each paper, writing down the names and agents for each ship fitting the same criteria as the first three. Finally, an hour and a half later, he capped his fountain pen, replaced it and the pad back inside his jacket, and then gathered the newspapers neatly and carried them back to the desk.

"That didn't take long," the young woman said.

"It may not have looked like a long time to you, but I think I left about five years of my life back in that chair," Casey said, grinning. "Still, if any of this information pans out, it will have been worth it."

"Cracking a big case, huh?" the young woman said, grinning back at him.

"Could be," he said, "just could be. If it pans out, I'm coming back here to take you out to dinner."

"Promises, promises," she said, but Casey could see she was pleased by his attention. He reached out, squeezed her hand, then left the building.

After Farrell left Casey's office, he gave into an impulse to visit Emile Ganns. Ganns had a suite of offices in the Pere Marquette Building on Common Street. It was a modest building, in keeping with the fiction that Ganns was a legitimate businessman. Farrell found an empty space on the street around the corner from the building, and parked his Packard there. Inside the building, he found the elevator, and told the Negro porter to take him to the fifth floor.

Ganns's suite took up most of the fifth floor, so Farrell had little trouble locating it. Instead of a plain, pebbled-glass door, Ganns had a large set of oaken doors, stained dark, and set into a gothic arch, also made of oak. A brightly polished brass plate was set into the door, elaborately engraved with the legend, EMILE GANNS, INCORPORATED.

Farrell heard the tumblers in the latch fall, and heard faint voices filtering through the crack. Although he couldn't hear the words, the timbre of one of the voices was familiar. Playing a hunch, he drew into the recessed doorway of a lawyer's office and peered cautiously around the edge.

The voices grew somewhat louder as the door opened, and then Sandra Tartaglia backed through the doors and out into the hallway. She was smiling until the door closed; then her face took on a look of calculating shrewdness. Farrell drew back into the recess and waited. When she didn't come past him he quickly checked the hallway and saw her retreating form disappearing around a bend in the hall. Farrell waited for five seconds more, then left his hiding place and walked through the door to Ganns's office.

A smart-looking young Jewish woman with long hair as dark as a raven's wing turned her handsome profile from her typewriter. "Yes?" she said. Her eyes were so black that it was impossible to differentiate the irises from the pupils.

"I'd like to see Mr. Ganns," Farrell said. "Tell him it's Wesley Farrell."

The woman picked up a telephone handset, pressed a button, and spoke softly into the mouthpiece. After a brief pause she replaced the handset, turned back to Farrell, and said, "You may go in now."

Farrell nodded to her and walked to the office door. Before he could open it, it swung open and Ganns, as neat and precise as a Swiss watch, beamed at him from the opening.

"Wesley! What a pleasant surprise. I was just thinking of you," he said heartily.

Farrell said nothing, but let Ganns lead him to an armchair covered in leather the color of old gold.

"You'll have a spot of brandy?" Ganns asked. "I've got a splendid calvados for you to try."

"Thanks, it's a mite early for me," Farrell said.

"You won't mind if I have one, then," Ganns said. "It isn't often that such a rare potion finds its way to this rather provincial place."

Farrell said nothing, and watched the little man measure out an eyedropper's worth of the amber fluid into the bottom of a small snifter.

"I hope you've come with news," Ganns said as he sat down behind his huge antique maple desk.

"I've found some things out," Farrell began, "and I'm beginning to understand why Tartaglia may have been killed."

"Capital," Ganns said. His eyes glowed with enthusiasm. "Who do you think did our friend in, then?"

"That part I'm not so sure of," Farrell said, absently tracing the cleft in his chin with his thumbnail. "In the beginning I figured this for a casual hit, somebody Tartaglia had scared, or threatened, or hurt. Somebody who was tired of being bled every week for a loan they knew they'd never pay off, or somebody who was tired of paying protection money." Farrell paused and stuck a Camel into the corner of his mouth. "Trouble is, I don't think this was some small-time revenge kill."

Ganns lowered his nose and lips to the snifter, took some of the apple brandy into his mouth, and rolled it around on his tongue for a few seconds. He swallowed, and then favored Farrell with an appreciative smile. "This is really quite good calvados. Perhaps the best I've ever had. Are you certain you won't have some?"

Farrell lit his cigarette and let the smoke trail out of his nose as he fixed Ganns with a blank, expressionless face. "You know, there are a lot of things I don't like about this setup. Things that don't seem exactly on the up-and-up."

"Oh?" Ganns said, his nose inside the snifter again.

"Ganns, you know me," Farrell said. "It wouldn't do to try to double-cross me, or leave me holding the bag. It wouldn't do at all."

"Wesley," Ganns said, a mildly aggrieved note in his voice,

"I know I took unfair advantage of you to secure your help in this matter, and I'm justly ashamed of it. But surely you don't suspect me of dishonest dealings with you. No, no, my boy. My honor forbids it."

Farrell smiled, but his eyes held a cruel gleam. He got up, placed his hat on his head, and crushed out his cigarette in a crystal ashtray on Ganns's desk. "Just so we understand each other. Thanks for the conversation, Ganns. I'll be seeing you, okay?" Then he turned and left the room.

Ganns picked up the snifter and drained it quickly. When he placed the empty snifter on his desk his pale cheeks had a warm, unhealthy glow, and his eyes flickered with worry.

Chapter 21

Casey got back into his Marmon and drove from the newspaper office directly to the riverfront district. It was still before noon, and he hoped he could catch a couple of shipping agents in their offices before they broke for lunch. His first stop was the Bienville Street Wharf at the end of Canal Street. There he quickly located the office of the shipping agent for the company owning the S. S. *Southern Cross* and four of the other ships on his list. He spent more than two hours with the man, quizzing him and going over freight manifests and passenger and crew lists. He neither saw nor heard anything that seemed to have any bearing on the case, so he thanked the man and left.

He sat in his car for a moment before going on, trying to think. He'd been on this case without let-up since Chance Tartaglia's body had been found early on the previous Friday morning, and he was bushed. He took off his hat and ran his fingers through his hair while he drew in a couple of deep breaths. Each time he inhaled, he exhaled noisily through his mouth. As he placed his hat back on his head, something that had been dancing around in the dark background of his mind suddenly jumped out into the center spotlight. He remembered seeing a newsreel once about the diamond mines in South

Africa. There were three ships on his list with that registry. He checked the list for an address and started up the car.

Marcel was hung over, as sick as a dog. The sleek-haired little brown-skinned girl had really put him over the jumps. He was back home in his own bed, the sunlight coming through the window stabbing through his closed eyelids into his brain like a flaming Apache war arrow. All that kept him from groaning aloud was a fear that the noise would split open his head. He lay perfectly still, hoping the nausea would subside and he wouldn't have to get up and stagger to the toilet again. The retching from the last attack had almost torn his head from his shoulders.

Twice his grandmother had come to his door and called to him, and both times he had lain perfectly still and made no answer, in the hope she would go away and leave him alone. Oh, Jesus, he thought. There the old bitch is again. Just be still.

"Marcel. Marcel," she cried, banging on the door. "Wake up in there, you hear me? There's a man on the telephone wanting you. Wake up, I say. It might be about work." She banged on the door two more times for added emphasis.

Marcel's eyes opened at once. The only man calling him about work would be Griff. Clumsily, he threw the blanket from him and pushed himself into a sitting position. The smell of his unwashed, love-sour body almost made him throw up again, but he bit back the nausea, pulled an old flannel bathrobe on over his nakedness, and staggered to the door. "I'm comin', Grandma, I'm comin' already."

Somehow he made it down the stairs without falling, but each time one of his feet hit the floor, it felt like a French 75 going off inside his skull. This time he couldn't quite suppress a loud groan, and the dyspeptic belch that followed. Finally he made it to the telephone stand in the hall and brought the receiver to his ear. "Yeah, this is Marcel," he said shakily.

"Jasus, bhoyo, you sound like a man near death." Griff laughed coarsely at the other end of the line.

"I'm okay, Griff," Marcel said. "You got somethin'?"

"I got a little surprise for you tonight, my wee man," Griff said in his customary growl. "That is, if you can walk." Griff exploded into laughter again, and Marcel flinched away from the receiver.

"I'll be all right," Marcel managed to say. "Where and when?" Suddenly his head didn't bother him as much as the cold chill of fear racing down his spine.

Farrell called Sandra Tartaglia's house and was told by her mother that she had her own office, about six blocks from Ganns's, in the D. H. Holmes Building on Canal Street. As he walked there, he saw dark storm clouds gathering in the west and heard a low, distant rumble of thunder. As the sky darkened, Farrell walked faster to beat the rain.

Farrell found Sandra's office on the third floor of the department store building. When no one answered his light knock on a door that read ORIENTAL IMPORTS, LTD., he tried the knob and found that it turned easily. The anteroom was vacant except for a small desk with a telephone on it. He heard talking going on behind a second door marked PRIVATE and rapped lightly on the pebbled glass. The voice said something else, and then he heard the sound of a telephone receiver being hung up. Two seconds later the door swung open.

"Why, hello there, boy," Sandra said, her arms going around his neck. Before he could say anything she molded her mouth to his, and he almost forgot what he was going to say.

"Whew!" she breathed into his ear. "I need to get more rest if you're going to pop in unexpectedly like this." He felt her sharp little teeth grab the lobe of his ear and bite it teasingly.

"I'm kind of unpredictable," he said when he had his breath back. "Sometimes I don't even know where I'm going or when, myself." He ran his hands down her back and around the curves of her bottom.

She laughed her jaded laugh, let go of his neck, and leaned back into his embrace. "You must have known it was time for my lunch."

"Sure," he said. "Let's go downstairs and grab something in the tea room."

She nodded brightly, picked up her handbag, and, taking him by the hand, led him out of the office and down to the elegant tea room on Holmes's second floor.

They found a table by a window where Farrell held out a chair for Sandra, then took a seat with his back to the window. A waitress came, took Sandra's order for chicken salad and iced tea, and Farrell's for coffee, then left them. Knowing that the sunlight coming through the window would mask his expression, Farrell watched Sandra intently.

"That certainly was a nice time we had the other night," she said. "I didn't expect to find such congenial company so soon after returning to town."

"Yes, it was nice, wasn't it?" Farrell agreed with a smile. "You haven't been back that long, eh?"

"About a week this time," she said. "I built up a network of business contacts in another country, but Mother and I got lonesome for the States about a year ago. We bought the house and live here permanently but go out of the country periodically on buying trips." She leaned her chin on the flats of her interlaced fingers and smiled at him. Her pale eyes seemed to give off a warm glow. "What about you? How'd you get into the nightclub business?"

"I won the first one in a card game a few years ago. It made so much money, I was able to buy another one," he said. "It adds up to a living, I guess."

"A pretty nice one, if I can tell by the way you live," she said.

Farrell was quiet for a moment, then said, "When we first met you said you needed some kind of help. Maybe this would be a good time to start telling me about it."

Sandra put her hands in her lap and looked down at them. Farrell had a sinking feeling that she was getting ready to lie to him, and he waited patiently to see how big a lie it would be.

"Suppose," she said, "I told you I was sitting on top of

something big. Something that would make me—make us—rich.''

"I like money," Farrell said laconically. "I haven't made nearly as much as I need. What's it going to take?''

"Last week I brought something into the country on the sly—something extremely valuable.'' She looked up, braced her elbows on the table, and leaned forward, speaking in a low, urgent voice. Her eyes were as wide and guileless as a Swiss milk maid's. "The trouble is, I've lost it. I need your help to get it back.''

Farrell said nothing, but took out his deck of Camels, put one into the corner of his mouth, and lit it. As the smoke began to rise, he squinted through it at Sandra, and said, "What's your connection to Emile Ganns?''

Sandra's body jerked as if she'd been touched with a live electric wire. Farrell caught an upset water carafe as it rocked on edge.

"Is Ganns responsible for losing that valuable something you were talking about?'' Farrell asked.

"How did you . . . no. No, Ganns was the one who was going to fence it for me," she said, somewhat recovering her composure.

"That's damned interesting," Farrell said, half to himself.

"What did you say?'' Sandra asked. Before Farrell could answer the waitress showed up with Sandra's lunch and Farrell's coffee. They sat staring at each other across the table until she had gone.

"I'm going to make a wild guess," Farrell said finally. "Your father was a bagman for Ganns. Ganns sent him to get the item from you. But before he got back to Ganns with it somebody killed him. How close am I?''

Sandra's eyes were shocked. She looked down at the plate of chicken salad and lettuce, then pushed it away from her. "You've been stringing me along the whole time, haven't you?'' she said, a trifle bitterly.

"No more than you've been stringing me, baby," he said, stirring sugar and cream into his coffee. "When your daddy got iced you got scared. I'll bet you figured Ganns did it and was using the confusion to pretend he didn't know where the stuff was. Only I think Ganns doesn't know either. He asked me to find out who killed Tartaglia, probably hoping I'd stumble onto the package in the process.''

"Goddamn," Sandra said. "Goddamn it to hell."

"I'm curious, honey," Farrell said as he sipped his coffee. "When you passed the package over to Tartaglia did he know who you were?"

"No," she said, taking out a green package of Lucky Strikes. "I told Ganns my name was Flynn, but I didn't introduce myself to my father. Ganns instructed me to wait at a certain place and to wear a yellow gardenia on my lapel; that way I'd be easily recognized by his courier, and there'd be no need for any talk. But I knew him immediately. Mother had an old wedding photo she'd saved. I knew his face as soon as he came into the room." She shook out a cigarette, placed it between her lips, and leaned across the table to get the light Farrell held out to her. "I'd never heard anything good about him, so I guess I wasn't surprised to find out he was a crook." She drew smoke into her lungs, then let it out in a long plume. "It's funny, though; I was a little disappointed he didn't recognize me. Ridiculous, isn't it?"

"No," Farrell said. "Not really."

"What happens now?" Sandra asked after they'd been silent for a moment.

"I've got some more looking to do," he answered. "I know a lot of what this was about, and pretty soon I'll know the rest of it."

"And my . . . package?" Sandra said. "What about that?"

"I think I can lay my hands on it," Farrell said as he gazed calmly into her eyes. He'd needed to know who all the players were, and now he knew. She hadn't lied to him, after all, even if she was trying to use him. It didn't matter all that much anymore. Any dreams he'd been building had already blown away like smoke in an autumn breeze.

Chapter 22

Because there was no main street directly approaching it, Casey arrived at the Celeste Street Wharf a little after 4:00 P.M. and had to fight some of the traffic resulting from the shift change. The neighborhood was poor, and Casey, worried he might come back and find his car stripped, or stolen, did something he rarely did; he locked it and left a POLICE placard in the windshield. He wasn't certain it would do any good but decided it was worth a try anyway.

It took some time, but he eventually managed to find the office for the South African Steamship Lines. A heavyset Dutchman wearing a roll-collar sweater was sitting behind a battered desk using a couple of rubber stamps on a stack of papers. A bakelite nameplate on the desk identified him as James Brinkerhoff.

"Inspector Casey, New Orleans Police," he said, holding out his gold badge. "I wonder if I could get some information from you?"

"Sure," Brinkerhoff said. "What about?"

"You had a ship tie up here about a week ago called the *Broor Mickkelson.* Out of Capetown?"

"Yeah, what about it?" the Dutchman asked.

"I'm playing a hunch is all," Casey said. "I need to see a passenger manifest, and a list of the crew. How soon could you get it together for me?"

"Not long, but I usually close up by five. Will this take very long?"

"Maybe not," Casey said. "If what I'm looking for is there, it'll jump right off the paper," Casey said.

Brinkerhoff sighed and looked longingly at the brass ship's clock on the wall. "Okay. Make yourself comfortable."

Marcel was standing outside his grandmother's house on Touro Street when Griff rolled up in an old Plymouth touring car. The car had seen some pretty rough times, if Marcel could tell anything from the rusted-out places under the doors and along the edges of the running boards. Marcel saw that Lester was sitting in the front seat with Griff.

"Get in, lad," Griff said, jerking his chin at the rear door.

Lester reached into the back and worked the lever, and the right rear passenger door opened with a hideous screech of rusted metal. The noise made Marcel's flesh crawl, and he cast a nervous glance behind him before he got into the back seat. Before he had closed the door Griff had the car in gear and rolling. Marcel felt funny, and pressed himself deep into the seat cusion in order to avoid being seen by any of the neighbors.

"What's the matter, kiddo? Sure and you're not embarrassed at the fine company you're keepin'?" Griff guffawed as he clashed the gears shifting into third. "Griffin O'Meara is descended from the lords of Eire, even if he *is* forced to ride in this sorry excuse for a motorcar, right, Lester?"

Lester's eyes showed that he didn't understand anything Griff was talking about, and he laughed nervously.

"Where we going, Griff?" Marcel asked finally. "And where did you get this heap?"

"This fine chariot?" Griff said grandly. "I found it lying unused next to a hovel over on Gravier Street. As to where we're goin' . . . well, let's say we're off on an adventure. A person I've been doin' some favors for has asked for another, one that I'm told will pay handsomely. We're goin' to do a small bit of murder, Marcel. How does that sound to you?''

Lester laughed nervously again and kept his eyes fixed straight ahead. Marcel, stunned by Griff's words, fell back into the seat, his mouth open with shock and his heart beating forty-to-the-mile.

It was growing twilight as Farrell turned down Basin Street and headed for his apartment. After leaving Sandra at her office he'd checked with the people who managed his other club, the two brothels he owned part of, and with the men who ran his bookmaking operations for him. Booze, sex, and gambling were all making him a fat profit. If it weren't for Emile Ganns and the Tartaglia family, Farrell knew he'd be feeling pretty good right now.

He pulled behind the Cafe Tristesse, got out, and was walking up the stairs to his apartment when he heard a voice call his name. He whirled, his right hand streaking toward the Colt before he saw who it was.

''Damn, you're jumpy, Farrell,'' Savanna said.

Feeling vaguely foolish, Farrell let the hem of his coat fall back into place as he walked down the stairs to the alley. ''It's not a very good idea to sneak up on anybody in an alley, baby,'' he said. ''You might even say it's unhealthy.''

Savanna walked out into the light dressed in a dark blue serge suit with ivory pinstripes that emphasized the strong contours of her body. A felt hat with the brim turned up on the left side and a long, maroon feather cast her face in shadow, but her black eyes reached out at him from the gloom.

''Don't waste all that tough talk on me, sweetheart,'' she said. ''I know you from way back, remember?''

''You come over here just to needle me?'' Farrell asked. ''Or have you got something to say that can't wait?''

''I came to do you a favor, though I can't figure out why,'' she replied. "Maybe it's just that I want everything between us to end with something owed on your side of the slate."

Farrell knew she had him on the defensive, but he was damned if he was going to show it. The relationship he'd had with Savanna had always been an equal give-and-take, and it would irk him to owe her anything now.

"That kid you asked me about," she said, "I've got some news that might interest you."

Farrell was about to speak, but a noise stopped him, a sound so faint that only a man used to surviving on the street would notice it. Farrell didn't wait to hear it a second time; he whirled to the left, knocking Savanna back with his left forearm as he turned. His right streaked back to his waist and came up with the ancient Colt cocked and ready.

Bullets were already flying, and Farrell felt a tug at the shoulder of his jacket as he started shooting. He counted flashes from three guns, and dimly made out the shooters crouched behind trash cans and other junk near the mouth of the alley. Farrell ducked behind the fender of the Packard, took careful aim at the nearest head, and fired twice. He heard a scream, saw the man fall over into the alley.

The other two men were still firing, though they were retreating now. Farrell straightened, leveled his right arm across the roof of the Packard, and threw one last well-aimed shot after them. He saw a hat fly into the air, but the men continued to withdraw. As they made for the opening of the alley, Farrell rounded the Packard's fender and pounded after them. Reaching the street, he heard the roar of an engine and checked himself as a battered, rusty old touring car passed him, its engine whining as the car accelerated in second gear. He raised his gun to shoot again, but there were too many people in the street. He cursed aloud with frustration.

Pedestrians were crowding the mouth of the alley, their voices raised in concern and fright. Farrell ignored them and jogged back into the alley. When he reached the fallen man Farrell turned him over with the toe of his shoe. An unfamiliar face stared up at him, eyes wide with shock and mouth opened in an *oh* of surprise. Farrell's shot had entered the man's face just below the right eye and had exited through a ragged, bloody hole at the back that now dripped brains and blood on the dirty pavement.

As he looked up from the dead man, he noticed a stylish, freshly blocked fedora, and had a sudden recollection of the hat flying from the head of one of the other attackers. He picked it up and turned it over. The sweatband had some writing in dark ink, and Farrell quickly got out his lighter and flicked it into flame. In the sudden illumination he saw an address: 2830 TOURO STREET, NEW ORLEANS. His face got a shocked, stiff look as he recognized the address. He killed the lighter, crushed the hat in his hand, and shoved it into the first open trash can he passed as he walked back to the rear of the alley.

He saw Savanna, leaning against the Packard, her head down and her arms crossed tightly at her waist. She was shaking, and he ran over to her. "Hey, baby," he said. "The fireworks are over now. It's okay."

But as he got closer, he saw the shaking was over something worse than fear, something that was darkening the blue serge under her right breast. He got to her just as she crumpled, catching her in his arms.

"Savanna, Savanna," he said, panic rising in his voice. "Jesus, baby, where did they get you?" He tipped back her head and saw that her lips were turning blue. He lay her flat on the ground and tore at the buttons of her suit and blouse until he got to brown skin. He found a hole there under the breast, with blood welling up in it.

Without thinking, he dragged an empty cardboard box over and raised her feet until they rested on top, then ransacked his pockets until he found the pack of Camels. He tore the cellophane from around it, flattened it in his hands, then applied it to the open wound and placed Savanna's hands over it.

"Hold this tight, baby," he said. "Press down on it as hard as you can. I'm gonna get some help."

As he looked up, he saw Harry standing there, his face registering shock. "Boss, what the hell . . . ?"

"Get an ambulance, and hurry," Farrell rapped out.

Harry ran like his pants were on fire, and Farrell kneeled

over Savanna, talking in a low, calm voice. Neither of them were aware of the crowd growing around them, or of the babble of excited questions and useless remarks being made. After what seemed an eternity, Farrell heard the sound of a siren grow louder, then die outside the alley.

"Break it up, break it up. C'mon, let somebody through. Move, you goddamn ghouls," a voice hollered. "Joe, here she is. Move, you friggin' tourists."

Farrell looked up to see a pair of burly middle-aged men wearing white coats and tough Irish faces.

"Quick," Farrell said. "She's got a sucking chest wound."

"Just move, buddy," one of the ambulance attendants said. "We've done this before, so don't worry about nothin'."

The larger of the two men bent down, nodded approvingly at Farrell's first-aid job, and got out a roll of adhesive tape and a pair of surgical scissors. In a blink he'd pulled off and cut four pieces, which he used to tape down the edges of the cellophane.

"She gonna be all right?" Farrell asked, his voice edged with fear.

"Too soon to tell," the attendant said. "But you did all the right things, buddy. Getting her feet up and covering that hole like you did bought her some time. If they can get the bullet out, and there's not too much internal damage, she's got a chance, anyhow."

Gently the two men elbowed Farrell out of the way, got Savanna on a stretcher, and briskly moved her out of the alley and into the interior of the ambulance. Farrell started to follow, but a uniformed cop grabbed him by the arm.

"Not so fast, buster," he said. "I wanna know what's going on here." The cop was big and wide through the shoulders, and had a face like a slab of raw ham. His eyes were deep-set and unfriendly.

Farrell saw two more uniformed officers move to surround him and knew he'd just fallen into a deep hole.

"This is kinda funny, Bill," one of the other cops said. "We got us a dead jigaboo on the ground here, and the ambulance just took a half-dead nigger broad with them. Near's I can find out, this guy was doin' a lot of the shootin'.''

"What's a white man doin' in the middle of this nigger mess, huh?" Bill said with an edge in his voice.

Farrell felt an icy ball forming in the pit of his stomach. "The dead man shot at us, hit the woman," he said quickly. "I shot back in self-defense." Even to Farrell, the words sounded lame and unconvincing.

"Raise your hands, spread your legs, and don't do nothin' funny," the third cop said. He was short and fat, but his face had flat, empty eyes and the smile of somebody who liked setting fire to anthills. Farrell saw that he had a blackjack looped over his right hand that he slapped rhythmically against his thigh.

Farrell was shoved against the car before he could comply with the order, then felt hands running roughly over his body, removing things from him.

"A .38 automatic," the voice said, followed by loud sniffing. "Been fired. Still warm, in fact. Well, well, what we got here? A razor."

The cop named Bill took the razor and held it up in front of Farrell's face. "I've never known a white man to carry one of these, but bet I've taken fifty off'n a bunch of nigger punks."

"Maybe he's a nigger, too, Bill," the second cop said. "They grow 'em down here so white, you'd swear they *was* white." He laughed nastily.

"You're crazy," Farrell blurted in a rising voice. "I'm the owner of this nightclub. The dead man and two others shot at me first." Farrell could see as he spoke that the three harness bulls were ignoring everything he said, and he felt something cold and hard form in the pit of his gut.

Bill produced a flashlight and played it over Farrell's face. "Maybe you're right, George," he said. "It'd explain why he's down in this alley with a bunch of shot-up boogies, wouldn't it? Let's take the sonofabitch in, let somebody else sort it out."

Farrell felt his arms pulled roughly behind him, and the cold steel of handcuffs going around his wrists. His mouth suddenly had a sickening, metallic taste in it, and he fought to keep his knees from trembling. You fucked up, he said to himself. You were such a smart guy, but you forgot that luck can run out. You forgot to know when to quit.

Then the cops dragged him roughly out of the alley, shoved him into the back of a prowl car, and drove him quickly away.

Chapter 23

Brinkerhoff was interrupted twice by telephone calls and once by a merchant marine officer checking on a ship arrival, but finally he was able to get all the information from his files about the passengers and crew of the three South African steamers that had docked in New Orleans over the past month.

The ships had been large ones, and although they were listed as freighters, all had substantial lists of passengers. Casey started with the most recent one to dock, the S. S. *Broor Mickkelson*, because he knew what he was looking for there and expected to find it quickly. Casey was chagrined to learn that they were not arranged alphabetically, which necessitated a lengthy search of the entire list. Eventually, though, he found the name of Sandra Tartaglia, just as he'd expected. He knew he would probably have to ring in some federal badges in order to find who had helped her get the diamonds ashore without going through Customs, but that could wait.

He spent more than another hour going through the passenger and crew lists of the other two steamers and, when he didn't find what he was looking for, went through them again. It was nearly 7:00 P.M. and Brinkerhoff had his face in his hands, leaning on the desk and trying not to look impatient. Casey, totally absorbed in his search, ignored him.

As Casey leaned back, rubbing his eyes, something nagged at his memory. He pulled the passenger list for the ship that had docked three weeks ago, the S. S. *Roark's Drift*, and traced slowly down with his index finger. Finally he came again to the name that had nagged at him, and he stared at it for a long time. All of a sudden his look of intent perplexity was replaced by one of shocked recognition. He sat up straight, replaced the papers in the folder, and stacked them neatly on the shipping agent's desk.

"Anything else I can do for you?" the agent asked hopefully. His eyes went to the clock over Casey's head.

"I'm sorry to have kept you from your dinner so long," Casey said. "I hope your wife isn't going to be sore over this. I was wondering, though, if any of the crew of the *Roark's Drift* might have laid over here, rather than shipping out when she left?"

"I got a feeling I know what you're looking for there," Brinkerhoff said wryly. "I've been waiting for one of you to come 'round asking about that Irish fellow."

"What fellow do you mean?" Casey asked, feeling the hair stand up on the back of his neck.

"The captain reported he had a man jump ship here, although we didn't think too much of it at first," Brinkerhoff said. "After all, New Orleans is a sailor's paradise." Brinkerhoff's wry smile became a thoughtful frown. "But then they found out about the gun, and the captain got a little concerned."

"What gun?" Casey asked.

"Fellow got into the small arms locker before he left the ship," the agent replied. "A heavy-caliber automatic and a box of cartridges were found missing after the ship was halfway down the river to the Gulf. I made a report on it to the police, but nobody ever got back to me about it. Didn't think of it again until just a second ago."

"This guy wouldn't be a tall, heavyset fellow with blond hair, would he?" Casey asked, leaning over the desk at the Dutchman.

"Yep, that's him. Griffin O'Meara," he answered. "Those micks, they can't stay out of trouble, can they?"

Casey was moving before Brinkerhoff stopped talking. He pulled the telephone across the desk and dialed police headquarters. When the desk sergeant answered Casey identified himself and asked for the radio dispatcher.

"Casey here," he said. "I want an all-points bulletin put out on Griffin O'Meara, an Irish seaman. Subject is about six feet, four inches in height, two hundred and ten to two hundred twenty pounds, close-cropped blond hair. Subject is wanted in connection with at least two murders, and is believed to be armed and dangerous. Right, now connect me to the detective squad."

The burly Dutchman looked up, a shocked look on his face. "Murder! You say this guy bumped somebody off?"

"That's right." Casey's head jerked as a voice came over the wire. "Inspector Casey here. I've got an all-points bulletin out for the guy who may have killed Chance Tartaglia and the Ballou woman. What? Say that again. Okay, I'll be right down." He hung up the telephone with a clatter and headed out the door.

"Thanks, pardner," he flung over his shoulder before the door closed.

Farrell sat in the back of the patrol car sweating blood. His natural instinct for self-preservation was locked in a titanic struggle with a mounting panic. He'd spent most of his life perfecting the public persona of a successful white man, and in one unguarded moment he'd been placed in a situation that threw doubt on his identity. He knew that if the headquarters cops decided he was just an octoroon or a high-yellow, they'd bury him in the tank and deny him bail.

"Hey, they're gonna have some fun with you in the back room, boy, y'know that? They got a dick down there likes nothin' better than taking a jigaboo apart. You passin' for white, he'll like it even better.'' The short, fat cop, whose name was Terrill, leered at him from the left-hand side of the back seat. Farrell was in the middle, sandwiched between Terrill and George, the second cop. Farrell decided the best thing to do was to say nothing.

"Aw, the high-yellow's feelings is hurt,'' Terrill said. "Whaddaya think of that, George?''

"I can't believe this guy's a jig, Terrill,'' George said. "He's whiter than you are.'' He laughed uproariously.

"Knock it off, you two clowns,'' Bill said, from the driver's seat. "I got enough worries with this traffic without havin' to listen to your crap.''

"Jeeze, no sense of humor,'' Terrill said under his breath, but he stopped talking.

As the car hove in sight of the large, gothic police head-quarters building, Farrell could feel the sand running out in his hourglass. Casey was the only help he could think of, but he knew, as well, that Casey didn't trust him, and might not believe his story, either.

The three cops were tough, mistrustful old pros. They got him out of the car and led him through the booking room in the middle of a three-man phalanx. The booking sergeant looked up from some paperwork, an expression of complete disinterest on his pale, thin face. "This Farrell?''

"Yep,'' Bill answered. He dropped Farrell's gun and the razor on the desk and said, "He had all this on him, Sarge.''

The desk sergeant looked down at Farrell's arsenal, up at Farrell, and back at the weapons again. "Jesus, you expectin' a foreign invasion or something, pal?'' Farrell said nothing.

"Bill thinks the guy's a high-yellow, on account of the razor, Sarge,'' Terrill said. "Let's get him in the interview room and find out for sure, huh?''

"Nuts to you, Terrill,'' the sergeant said. "Captain Moroni caught the squeal that you were bringing this guy in. Said for you to take him directly to his office.''

"Moroni, huh?" Bill said. "You must be a celebrity, jigaboy. Let's not keep him waiting." He took Farrell under one arm and dragged him roughly down the hall.

Moroni's reception room was empty, and only a desk lamp burned on the secretary's desk. Bill tapped gently on the pebbled-glass door leading to Moroni's personal office and heard the captain's order to come in.

Bill pushed open the door and shoved Farrell across the threshold into the office. It, too, was lit by only a desk lamp. The rest of the room was in deep shadow now that darkness had fallen outside. "Here he is, skipper. You want us to hang around?"

"No," Moroni said. "But leave the cuffs on him. I'll see you get them back."

When the trio of cops had gone Moroni got up from his chair and came, with slow deliberation, around the desk to where Farrell stood. When he reached him Moroni doubled up his huge fist and threw it into Farrell's belly. Farrell made only a hushed, gasping sound, his body folding like an accordian and dropping heavily to the floor.

"Why don't we resume that conversation we had in my office about square dealing a short while back?" a new voice asked.

Farrell lay on his side, struggling to get breath back into his body. He had to exert every ounce of his will to force himself to inhale, and the horrible sound of his labored attempts rattled inside his head. Moroni reached down and grabbed Farrell by the collar, lifting him like a rag doll, and then threw him into a wooden armchair. The abusive gesture knocked some breath back into Farrell's body, and for a few minutes he just slumped there, raggedly breathing in and out.

"Wes," a woman's voice spoke, "I know you know where the diamonds are. Your only chance to stay alive is to tell us. Please, I don't want them to kill you." As Farrell's eyes vainly sought the source of the voices, Moroni walked to the wall and pushed a switch. A bright ceiling fixture leaped into life, flooding the room with a light that revealed Emile Ganns, seated in a comfortable armchair, and Sandra Tartaglia standing behind him.

"Your young lady friend is quite right, you know," Ganns said, flicking an imaginary speck of dust from his impeccably tailored knee. "Captain Moroni is more than capable of beating you very painfully to death. Why not be reasonable and tell us where you've hidden the diamonds?"

"Why . . . why do you think I've got the diamonds, Ganns?" Farrell managed to gasp.

"Because, dear boy, they are nowhere else," Ganns replied. "And because you know too much about what has gone on during the last few days to not know where they are. After all, I recruited you because I knew you to be a resourceful chap."

"Okay, so what if I have the diamonds?" Farrell asked, his brain racing. "What's in it for me if I let you have them?"

"Just your life, dear boy," Ganns said smoothly. "You give me the diamonds and the good Captain Moroni lets you go free. A decent bargain, I think you'll agree."

"Please, Wes," Sandra said, her eyes reminding Farrell of a frightened fawn's, "don't make him kill you. Tell us where the diamonds are."

Farrell thought for a minute. "What's to keep you from killing me after you have the ice?" He shot a glance at Moroni.

Moroni laughed deep in his chest. "Not a damn thing, sucker. I heard you're some kind of hotshot gambler, Farrell. Look at the odds and take your chance." He laughed again.

Farrell looked from Sandra's frightened face to Ganns's blandly smiling one and back to Moroni's hateful leer. "Okay, Ganns. Let's get going. I'll tell you where to drive."

"Jesus, he killed Lester. He killed him," Marcel repeated in a high-pitched voice. "You said it would be an adventure . . . big pay . . ."

"Shut up, you sniveling brat," Griff snapped. "The guy is good; a lot better than I gave him credit for. Lester's luck was bad, that's all."

Lester's luck was bad. Jesus, Marcel thought. It coulda been my luck that was bad. *My* luck. He looked down at his hand, which was shaking like a leaf in a high wind.

"What're we gonna do now?" he asked when he could bear Griff's silence no longer.

"We're gonna ditch this car, that's what," Griff said. "Then I gotta do some thinking."

Chapter 24

Moroni pushed Farrell out into the deserted corridor outside his office, starting him toward the back stairs. Sandra and Ganns brought up the rear. A uniformed officer passed them on the stairs, throwing a salute to Moroni, who acknowledged it with only a grunt and a nod of his head.

Ganns's gleaming black Lincoln sedan waited in the alley behind headquarters, his two bodyguards sitting impassively in the front seat. When they saw the procession approaching the bodyguard in the shotgun seat jumped out and ran around to open the passenger door. At a word from Ganns, he reached inside and unfolded the two jump seats. Sandra got in first and took the folding seat on the far side. Moroni indicated that Farrell should get in next and slide over to the far end of the upholstered rear seat. Moroni got in beside him and Ganns followed, occupying the other folding seat. Once everyone was situated the bodyguard closed the door and got back into the front.

"Well, Wesley, where should we drive?" Ganns asked, his hands folded on top of his gold-headed malacca walking stick.

"Tell the driver to head over to the river, then get on Tchopitoulas Street heading uptown,'' Farrell said. He shifted uncomfortably, his hands still handcuffed behind him.

"What's down that way?" Moroni asked.

"I own some property down there. A whorehouse, if it matters," he said.

"Hah!" Moroni exclaimed. "A nice place to store valuables, eh, Mr. Ganns?"

"History has often noted that money and vice are inextricably bound, Captain," Ganns replied. "Mr. Farrell has made a considerable amount of money through his realization of that fact, haven't you, Wesley?"

Farrell said nothing, but stared bleakly at Sandra. She met his stare for a while but finally lowered her eyes.

"You hooked yourself up with some nice people, sugar," Farrell said softly. "They're going to kill me when they get the ice. If you don't watch out, they might decide they don't need you, either."

"Shut up, Farrell," Moroni said.

"Is diamond smuggling the first thing like this you've done, sugar? No, maybe not. You're a girl used to getting what she wants, any way you can," he said in a musing voice.

"I told you to shut up," Moroni said, reaching over and striking Farrell's face with his fist. Farrell's body jerked and fell into the corner of the limousine.

"Stop it, just stop it!" Sandra cried, balling up her fists. "You didn't say anything about hurting him," she shouted as she turned to face Ganns.

"Dear Miss Flynn," Ganns said mildly, "surely you didn't imagine Mr. Farrell would simply give up the diamonds without a fight. Mr. Farrell is in business to make money, just like me—and like you. This isn't a hobby, you know. It's in deadly earnest."

"I said you were a little wooly lamb, honey," Farrell said, shaking his head. His hat had fallen off and his cheek was cut. Blood dripped from it onto the lapel of his jacket.

"We're on Tchopitoulas Street, Mr. Ganns," said the driver. "Where to from here?"

Farrell kept his eyes, now pale and cold, on Sandra's face.

"Soraparu Street runs into Tchopitoulas about ten blocks down. Turn into it."

They drove in silence past darkened warehouses and rows of shanties that lined either side of the long, dark street. The arresting officers had missed Farrell's stiletto, strapped to his left arm, but with the handcuffs still in place the knife might as well have been in New Jersey. He knew he had to get them to take off the handcuffs if he was to have a fighting chance. Finally the driver spoke again.

"Soraparu Street, Mr. Ganns."

"How far down, Wesley?" Ganns asked.

"Two blocks, on the right-hand corner. You can pull in behind the house." Farrell's body was completely relaxed. The slump of his shoulders and the dull monotone in which he spoke gave the impression of complete docility.

The driver slowed the Lincoln, turned, and bumped gently into the yard behind the two-story clapboard house. He cut the motor; then he and his partner turned to look into the back seat.

"Well, Wesley," Ganns said, "we've reached our destination. Shall we go in and get the diamonds?"

"How about taking off the cuffs?" Farrell asked. "I can't just tell you how to get the diamonds. They're in a secret compartment that I'll have to open. We can go in the back door and nobody'll see us."

Ganns considered for a moment. "You'd better hope no one does see us. And there had better be no tricks. Do we understand each other?" His rich, cultured voice became hard and icy.

"Yeah," Farrell said. "Loud and clear."

"Take off the handcuffs, Moroni," Ganns said, fingering his chin. "You and Baxter should be able to control him. You stay with the car, Pirelli."

"Right, boss," Pirelli said.

"I don't like it," Moroni said, glaring at Ganns.

"Do it anyway," Ganns said roughly. "If anyone sees him in handcuffs, it will cause questions. I want no complications at this stage."

Moroni glowered at Ganns, started to say something, then

changed his mind. He grabbed Farrell roughly by the shoulder, slewing him around on the seat, and unlocked the cuffs. Farrell sat there for a moment, rubbing the circulation back into his hands.

"No more stalling," Moroni said. "Get moving." He showed Farrell a large, nickel-plated Smith & Wesson .44 Special that he'd pulled from under his left arm.

Farrell said nothing, but turned, opened the door, and stepped out. Baxter was already there and waiting, a .45 automatic cocked in his hand. When everyone but the driver was out of the car Moroni waved Farrell on with the barrel of his gun, and Farrell led the procession to the back door to his office.

The night air was crisp, cool, and deadly quiet. Farrell could hear each individual footfall on the dry autumn grass. He fumbled in his pocket for a key, and heard the ominous triple click of a hammer. He stopped dead and looked up to see the dark bore of Moroni's .44 staring at his head.

"Don't do anything stupid," Moroni said.

"I'm taking out a key," Farrell said, and moved his hand with exacting care from his pants pocket. When the key was free of his pants Farrell held it up in the air, where the dim light of distant stars reflected on it. Moroni nodded once, a short, sharp gesture, and Farrell gently turned, placed the key in the lock, and turned it. The sound of the tumblers falling was unnaturally loud in the dark yard.

When Farrell had the door open Baxter pushed him through the opening. Farrell reached out a careful hand and flipped a wall switch, flooding the interior of the office with light. The three men and one woman followed Farrell into the room.

Like fighters in a ring, each member of the group went into a neutral corner, their eyes watchful, their bodies tense. Sandra put her hand into her bag and brought out a little Savage .32 automatic. She pointed it at no one and everyone. Ganns's eyes narrowed, and those of Moroni and Baxter focused intently on Sandra.

"Steady on, dear," Ganns said softly. "We wouldn't want to have any accidents, would we?"

"If anybody does anything stupid, what I'll do won't be an

accident, Ganns,'' Sandra replied. Her mouth was set in a thin line, and her knuckles were white around the black grip of her gun. ''You may think you're going to chisel me out of those diamonds, but think again. We had a deal, and you're going to stick to it.''

For the first time since he'd been taken into police custody Farrell knew he wasn't being closely watched. Whatever chance he was going to take to break free had to happen now. Sandra's presence complicated things for him, but he knew she couldn't do him any good alone. It was now or never.

The air was thick with tension as the three men and one woman traded hard stares at each other over the barrels of their guns. Farrell began edging toward Baxter, the closest gun to his hand. He was within a foot of his quarry when the connecting door to the front opened suddenly.

''Mist' Farrell, can I . . .'' were the last words Marie ever spoke. Baxter swung left, the .45 in his hand exploded twice, and Marie's middle erupted in a geyser of spattered blood. Farrell grabbed Baxter, spun him around, and chopped him in the throat. Behind him, he heard two shots, the sharper crack of Sandra's .32 almost drowned out in the roar of a larger gun. Forcing himself to ignore it, he closed his hand over Baxter's automatic and was swinging to bring it to bear on Moroni when a sickening blow fell across his shoulder, dropping him to his knees. Pain swept over him like a tidal wave, and all his eyes could register were bright flashes.

Chapter 25

After ditching the rusted old Plymouth near the Fairgrounds racetrack Griffin O'Meara led a pale, shivering Marcel on foot to Esplanade Avenue. They walked past large, elaborate Victorian homes toward City Park, until they came to a tavern. The door was open, and the sound of a jukebox came from within. Marcel recognized the Duke Ellington band and Sonny Greer's Memphis Men doing "That Rhythm Man." Griff indicated with a toss of his chin that they should enter. Marcel's legs were rubbery beneath him, and although he didn't want to go in, he lacked the will to disagree.

They took a front corner table where they could see everyone coming in. Griff grinned and held up two fingers to the barman, who nodded his understanding.

A moment later a blowsy, bleached-blond waitress sauntered over with two shots of bourbon on a tray. Griff leered up at her and sought to run his hand over her buttocks, but the woman moved aside with unexpected speed and dexterity.

"Do that again and you'll draw back a nub, buster," she said around a wad of chewing gum.

"Sure, darlin', and I was only tryin' to express my appreciation for your . . . beauty,'' he said, flipping a silver dollar onto her tray. She looked indifferently at him and walked away.

Marcel picked up his glass and bolted the whiskey. He was shaking so badly that the glass rattled against his teeth. "Griff, I'm scared,'' he said. "This ain't workin' out the way you said.''

"You liked the money well enough, lad. Did you think the man wouldn't shoot back, then?'' Griff eyed Marcel with contempt, sipping at his shot of whiskey.

"We weren't no match for Farrell,'' Marcel continued. "I never saw anybody move that fast in my life. I thought all those stories they tell about him were bunk. He heard us before we was even there, and then he snuffed out Lester like a candle before we could draw a bead on him.''

"Any man can be killed, bhoyo,'' Griff said. "I'm not gonna give up so easy as that. You wait here; I got to go make a telephone call.''

Griff pushed back his chair and walked to a telephone booth at the back of the tavern. He dropped his nickel into the slot and gave the operator a number.

"It's me,'' he said when a voice answered. "No . . . no, we muffed it. The blighter's got eyes in the back of his head. He shot one of my boys, nearly got the other, and we had to get the hell out of there.'' He paused to listen to the voice, then said, "No, he's got the wind up so bad, I'm not certain he wouldn't bolt if I asked him to make another try. I'll have to do it by myself.'' Griff's face got a shocked look. "What? You want me to lay off? Maybe it doesn't matter to you anymore, but he's not going to quit snooping around, I can tell you that. No, but you'll care a good deal if he catches up to you. The bloke's a killer, no error. All right, all right, but what about that money you promised?'' He fell silent again, then began to shake his head. "But you promised more than that, a great deal more. If you think you're going to sluff me off like that, you'd better . . . Hello? Hello?''

Griff stared at the dead receiver in his hand for a moment, then hung it up. His face was twisted with rage as he squeezed his bulky body out of the booth. He was halfway to the table before he noticed that Marcel was gone.

As Farrell kneeled on the floor, kneading his wounded shoulder, the smell of cordite assailed his nostrils, bringing him near to vomiting. He gritted his teeth, and gradually the lights stopped going on and off behind his eyes.

The first thing he saw was Marie, lying half in and half out of the room. Her arms were flung wide and her shocked eyes stared fixedly at the ceiling. The two .45 slugs had torn her nearly in half, and blood covered the entire midsection of her body. Ganns stood beside him, his short legs spread wide, the malacca stick raised in his hand like a truncheon.

Sandra lay crumpled on the cheap braided rug. Painfully he crawled over to her and saw that her eyes were half open and her lips slightly parted. There was a large, wet hole in the left breast of her blouse; her hat and purse lay near her on the floor. Farrell reached out with his right hand and gently touched her cheek. He remembered her lying in his bed with a childish half smile on her face. His chest got tight, and for a moment the room seemed too bright for his eyes.

He felt movement to his left and looked up to see Moroni standing there, his eyes blank and stunned.

"Somebody ought to of told her this was a man's game," Moroni said in an odd, strangled voice. "Somebody ought to of told her to stay out of it."

Farrell looked at the hand holding the .44 and saw a tremor in it. Killing a woman had shaken Moroni. Farrell made a silent promise to shake him worse if he could manage to stay alive just a bit longer.

"A great pity," Ganns said. "A beautiful young woman like that. She'd barely had time to know life. But as you say, Captain, this is a man's game." He bent down and picked up Sandra's automatic.

Farrell heard footsteps and saw that Pirelli was in the room now, too, helping Baxter to his feet. The man was breathing hoarsely as he massaged his throat. He looked at Farrell balefully.

"And now, Wesley," Ganns said, pointing Sandra's pistol at him, "we've had far too much foolishness tonight. All I wanted was a collection of diamonds, not all this killing." He, too, was subdued; for once he had lost his insouciant manner. "Bring out the diamonds. Let us waste no more time at this."

Farrell moved cautiously and rolled back the braided rug until he could see the hidden trap. He pressed two wooden pins, then the single one, and the section of flooring popped out on its spring.

"Very clever, my friend," Ganns said. "You're always full of surprises. Now, very carefully, bring out the stones."

Farrell leaned over, grasped the handle of the small suitcase, and pulled it out. He placed it on the floor, opened it, and shook out a handful of stones from one of the cellophane packets.

Ganns bent over, his eyes gleaming with lust. "A fortune. A veritable fortune," he said in a soft, distracted voice. He bent lower and took a few of the diamonds from Farrell's hand, smiling as he watched light from the ceiling dance in the facets of the stones.

"Mr. Ganns," Moroni said after a brief silence, "we'd better make ourselves scarce. Let's get out of here now." His voice was urgent.

"Yes," said Ganns, coming out of his reverie. "Quite right. Baxter, can you walk?"

The man couldn't speak yet, but he nodded his head. His breath was still labored, and his bloodshot eyes blazed at Farrell. He lifted his gun, but Ganns's expression stopped him.

"Not here, you fool. We can do that somewhere else. Pirelli, pick up that case, quickly."

Pirelli took Baxter's arm, grabbed the suitcase, and led his comrade out into the night. Ganns, with one backward glance at Sandra's body, followed suit.

Farrell looked up and saw Moroni, his right arm stretched out at full length, with the barrel of the Smith & Wesson locked on Farrell's breast. "Up, you. And get outside."

Farrell slowly got to his feet, then walked out to the car.

Pirelli had the engine running already, the car's tailpipe exuding a white plume of vapor into the night blackness. Baxter stood at the open door to the back seat, eating Farrell with a look of pure hatred. Farrell got in and took his original seat, and Moroni got in after him. In the space of three heartbeats they were driving out of the yard, down Soraparu Street, and back onto Tchopitoulas.

"Where to, Mr. Ganns?" Pirelli asked.

"Where indeed? Captain?" Ganns deferred to the police captain, who seemed to consider for a moment before making up his mind.

"Head down toward Carrollton," Moroni said. "Stick to the back streets until you can link up with Leake Avenue. I'll tell you when to stop."

The big Lincoln snaked along Tchopitoulas until they reached the Public Health Service Hospital; then Pirelli cut down Henry Clay Avenue to Magazine Street. There was little talking in the car, and Moroni kept his pistol shoved into Farrell's ribs. Farrell sat quietly but was poised on a live-wire edge, alert to the slightest possibility of escape or retaliation.

Where Tchopitoulas Street had been largely deserted Magazine had a brisk traffic that slowed their speed. Farrell cudgeled his brains, looking for an opening, or anything that might give him an edge. As they passed Audubon Park on the way to the Leake Avenue intersection, he was nearly desperate enough to try anything.

As Pirelli negotiated the hairpin turn that signaled the change from Magazine to Leake, he failed to slow down, and didn't see a Ford roadster stopped ahead until it was almost too late. As he jammed on the brakes, all five men were thrown about in the car. Farrell disabled Moroni's revolver by grabbing it around the cylinder, and then hit Moroni with a terrific right cross, knocking him cold. Before anyone else could recover, Farrell wrenched open the door and threw himself out into the street.

He heard yelling behind him but wasted no time looking back. A shot sounded, and he felt the buzzing of the bullet as it passed near his right ear. As he made it across the three sets of railroad tracks running parallel to Leake, he ran flat out for the high, grassy levee that separated the Carrollton District from the Mississippi River.

When he reached the crest of the levee he slowed long enough to turn and throw one backward glance, to see that Pirelli and Baxter were about fifty yards behind him. Three more shots whizzed by as he made a break for a stand of trees that stood between him and the river.

Chapter 26

The two men were still coming as Farrell made the stand of trees. Without breaking stride he merged with the darkness, became one with it. As he stood in the shadows, he felt his body quivering and heard the breath rasping in his throat. He knew he was scared and fought savagely to bring his terror under control. He pulled the knife from his sleeve, flicked it open, and stuck the point into his left forearm. In the flash of pain he forced himself to remember Marie's shocked, dead face and Sandra's body crumpled on the floor, and felt an electric charge of rage rush through him. The trembling stopped. Now he was all right; he was fine. He was in the dark with sharp steel in his hand, and men he hated coming toward him.

While he watched from the underbrush Pirelli and Baxter came panting up to the edge of the grove and stopped, looking first one way, then the other.

"Goddamn that sonofabitch," Pirelli swore, desperation in his voice. "The old man will kill us if he got away. You got a flashlight?" he asked.

"No, but he couldn't have gotten very far," Baxter said hoarsely. "Spread out and beat the bushes. He ain't got a gun, so we can still take him."

Pirelli nodded his assent, and broke north as Baxter moved south. They swept into the thickly grown grove like a couple of bulldozers, each of them making plenty of noise. Farrell moved quietly toward Baxter, allowing the man's noisy movements to mask his own. He could tell that Baxter had never been in the woods before, and so didn't recognize the danger into which his headlong rush had taken him.

Baxter's progress was slow, and his bruised throat made his breathing loud and labored. Occasionally he would stop and listen for a moment, moving the barrel of his automatic like some kind of divining rod.

Farrell followed him until he reached the clearing at the bank of the river. For a second Baxter paused to scan the bank up and down in an effort to see something against the dim moonlight. As he turned to re-enter the stand of trees, Farrell launched himself at the man's legs, toppling him into the water. So swift was the attack that Baxter had no chance to cry out.

Baxter thrashed and churned, but Farrell arched his shoulders and bore the bodyguard's head under the water. Baxter's arms came up and grappled blindly, and Farrell felt the contagion of the man's terror as his hands desperately sought purchase on Farrell's body. Baxter's fingers tore at the material of Farrell's coat and ripped the seam at the shoulder; then air bubbles broke the surface, and the struggles ebbed to nothing.

As Farrell hauled himself out of the water, shivering and sick, he felt a lassitude creep into his mind and body. The cold and the reaction to the killing were strong, and he raged and cursed himself, struggling to bring back the hate that had driven him this far. Finally he shook himself and moved back into the forest, but it was harder this time.

He heard a voice calling and headed toward it. As he reduced the distance, he could make out Pirelli calling Baxter's name, calling for his partner to come out of the forest and give up the chase. As he drew nearer, Farrell could discern uncertainty, and maybe fear, in the man's voice.

By the time he had come to within fifteen yards of him, Farrell could tell that Pirelli had left the stand of trees entirely and was waiting at the edge of the clearing between the grove and the levee.

"Goddamn it, Baxter, c'mon outa there," Pirelli shouted. "He musta gotten to the river and swum away." Pirelli shivered and pulled his coat closer around his body as he stood there, shifting his weight uncertainly from one foot to the other.

A wind had picked up, and the sound of it whistling through the trees cast an eerie pall over the spot of ground that Pirelli unknowingly shared with his quarry. A bird called somewhere in the woods, and when Pirelli jerked his head nervously in that direction Farrell exploded from the woods like a panther. Pirelli shouted something unintelligible and fought to get his gun up, but Farrell was quicker, whipping the blade of his knife in a short arc across the other man's throat. Pirelli's shout became a gurgle, and he dropped the gun as his hands went instinctively to his throat. Still moving, Farrell stepped in, punching the knife into Pirelli's chest just under the breastbone and twisting it viciously as point punctured skin. As Pirelli collapsed to the ground, the air around them was heavy with the smell of his bowels as they were vacated.

As Farrell stood over him, he felt the lassitude hit him again, stronger, accompanied by a nausea he couldn't control. He bent over as the vomit rushed up his throat, gagging until there was nothing in his stomach but air. He looked up, shivering, as he darted glances up and down the river for any sign of Moroni. He knew he had no time for sickness or reflection; his margin of safety was too thin. He wiped his knife on the leg of Pirelli's trousers and replaced it up his sleeve. He saw Pirelli's gun lying on the ground, picked it up, and forced himself to break into a ground-eating northerly trot, toward the place where Carrollton and St. Charles avenues intersected.

Ten minutes later, his lungs nearly bursting from the effort, Farrell saw the bright lights of the Carrollton business district shining over the levee. He stuck Pirelli's automatic into the back of his waistband and climbed the embankment to the crest, from where he could see cars moving slowly through the busy intersection. Farrell worked his way down the slope of the levee and across the street. He heard the bells of an approaching streetcar, and sprinted to the stop in time to catch the downtown-bound car.

The conductor started at the sight of Farrell's dirty face and damp, disheveled clothing, but the press of oncoming passengers pushed Farrell down the aisle to the rear of the car before the man could react further. Farrell sat down on an empty bench and, as the car lurched into motion, allowed himself to breathe easily, and plan his next move.

Casey was beside himself with worry. He'd driven to headquarters the moment he'd heard of Farrell's arrest, but upon his return he'd found Moroni and Farrell gone, and no one he talked to had any idea as to their whereabouts. Telephone calls to Ganns's home and Moroni's apartment had gone unanswered. Harry at the Cafe Tristesse said he hadn't seen Farrell since the shooting of Savanna Beaulieu earlier in the evening. A call to The Roxy, Farrell's other club, was equally fruitless.

It was now after midnight, and Casey was almost desperate enough to go out in his car to conduct a search when the telephone on his desk began to jangle. He grabbed it before the first ring was completed.

"Casey," he said.

"It's Farrell," a voice said. "Are you alone?"

"Yeah," he replied. "Where are you?"

"I'm in a phone booth in front of the public library on Lee Circle. I could use a lift."

"You okay?" Casey asked.

"Just cold and wet. Moroni and Ganns are after me."

"Stay where you are," Casey said. "I'll pick you up in ten minutes."

"Bring some liquor," Farrell said. "I'm damn cold."

Casey checked the loads in his .38 and grabbed his hat and coat on the way out of his office. Taking the back stairs, he was out to the parking lot in two minutes and on the road in three. His eyes were sharp and his jaw set as he left the station. He made a number of turns down side streets until he was certain nobody was tailing him, then headed for Howard Avenue.

Lee Circle was empty except for the impassive statue of General Lee and a couple of nightshift workers waiting for the streetcar. As he rounded the circle toward the old Carnegie-style public library, Casey saw a tall figure emerge from the shadows. Farrell bounded out to the curb, leaped to the running board, and got inside before Casey could brake to a full stop.

"Man, you look bad," Casey said. "What happened?"

"Ganns and Moroni had some idea of taking me for a ride after they got the diamonds," Farrell said.

"Smells like they dunked you in the river," the red-haired detective said.

"You got a drink?" Farrell asked.

"Inside the glove box," Casey said. "You get Moroni?"

Farrell poked his hand into the dark interior of the glove compartment and pulled out an unopened pint of Old Fitzgerald. He uncorked it and sucked a big drink down his throat. The whiskey set his insides on fire, but he drank more anyway.

"Not this time," he said, wiping his lips with the back of his hand. "But Ganns is short two boys. He was paying them too much; they weren't very good."

"What happened?" Casey asked as he turned off St. Charles onto Washington Avenue.

"Bad luck, and lots of it," Farrell answered. "The big man who killed Holly, and two others, tried to take me out in the alley behind my club. They shot a friend of mine, bad, and I don't know if she made it or not. I killed one of them, but the other two got away. The cops came and put the arm on me; then Moroni got me up in his office. Ganns and Sandy Tartaglia were there."

"Yeah, go on," Casey said impatiently.

"Those diamonds we found . . ." Farrell said, taking another pull from the bottle. "Sandy smuggled them into the country. Apparently Ganns was supposed to fence them for her, only he sent Tartaglia to pick them up."

"Jesus," Casey said. "I had Sandy figured for the diamond smuggling, too. Did she know who he was?"

"I think Ganns thought her name was Flynn," Farrell answered. "She told me Tartaglia didn't recognize her. Anyway, when he got gunned neither of them knew where the diamonds were. I'm not certain whether Ganns knew Tartaglia was double-crossing him, but he and Sandy both wanted me to help find them. I'm guessing Ganns was planning to stiff her if he got to them first. She wasn't savvy enough to deal with anybody like him.''

''Yeah, you're probably right,'' Casey said. ''What happened then?''

''Ganns is nobody's chump,'' Farrell said. ''He'd figured out that I probably had the diamonds, and they forced me to take them to where I had them hidden. Things kind of fell apart there, and Sandy got it.'' He stopped talking suddenly and took a couple of deep breaths. It was the first time he'd had a chance to think of Sandra's death, and the memory took the wind out of his sails.

''Sandy?'' Casey exclaimed. His face was numb with shock, and he felt a weakness flood his body. All his memories of Sandra were those of a beautiful, happy little girl. Having lost his own wife and son, Casey had become a kind of unofficial uncle to his best friend's child, and he'd lavished some of the same affection and attention on her that he might have given to his own son. He felt a sick heaviness in his chest and swallowed hard several times.

Casey glanced over at Farrell and saw that his head was bowed on his chest as he rubbed the bridge of his nose with his thumb and forefinger. ''Who did it?'' Casey finally managed to ask.

It took some time for him to answer. ''Moroni did it,'' he finally answered. His voice broke a little at the end.

Casey, too, became quiet in the face of Farrell's unspoken grief. He slumped back in his seat, fighting the nausea that flooded him. ''I need a drink,'' he said finally.

Farrell handed him the bottle. ''I've got to get some clean clothes,'' he said.

''What you've got to do is get off the street,'' Casey said. ''Moroni's going to have people looking for you. The first thing they're gonna do is start busting your operations. If you go back to any of them now, he's gonna haul you in again, and this time he won't make any mistakes.''

"Where are you taking me?" Farrell asked.

"I've got a place over in the Irish Channel," Casey said. "It's not far from here."

Chapter 27

Casey drove down Magazine Street and turned riverward onto Pleasant, a working-class neighborhood composed of shotgun singles and doubles. Three blocks from the river, he pulled to the curb in front of a modest white clapboard house with a lot of gingerbread trim. Casey let them through the white picket gate and led Farrell up the porch stairs and into the house.

When Casey switched on the electric chandelier Farrell saw a small but comfortably furnished room, with a small mantelpiece and gas grate set into one wall. Over the mantel was an oval, hand-colored photograph of a man with handlebar mustachios dressed in an old-fashioned New Orleans police uniform.

The furniture was old but in good condition, and a gaudy Persian rug covered the floor. Farrell, who found that he was near exhaustion, sank down gratefully in one of the upholstered chairs. He was nearly asleep when Casey came back in with a steaming cup in his hand.

"Here," he said. "Coffee and brandy will put you right again."

Farrell gave Casey a look of thanks and took the cup. He'd

never tasted anything quite so good in his life. "You make a pretty good toddy, Inspector," he said when he'd tasted it.

"We Irishmen know about spirits, don't we?" Casey asked in an exaggerated Irish lilt.

"Yeah, I guess we do," Farrell said as he brought the cup back to his lips.

Casey sat down on an upholstered love seat across from Farrell and put his feet up on the coffee table. "It's funny how things happen," he said. "I've been trailing Moroni and Tartaglia for a couple of months now, trying to establish a link between them. I knew all along that Chance had to have somebody up above covering for him. I'd just about gotten enough to go to the district attorney when Chance was shot."

"I thought Tartaglia was a friend of yours," Farrell said. "You were going to put him in jail?"

Casey's face was somber as he stared at Farrell. "When they give you the badge it doesn't say anything about giving your friends a break if they turn bad. I thought as much of Chance as if he'd been my brother, but he was a bad cop, a thief, and other things I don't want to think about."

Casey ran his fingers through his hair. "Nothing else had made him go straight. Maybe in jail he'd have gotten wise to himself and come out a better man. I guess I was hoping so, anyhow." He paused, blew on the steaming mug in his hand, and sipped at the water and whiskey. "But none of that matters now," he continued. "Chance is dead, and Sandy's killing will put Gus in the electric chair before I'm through."

"But who killed Tartaglia?" Farrell asked. "I'm betting it was the big blond guy, but where does he come in? I thought at first he might be working for Ganns, but now I'm not so sure."

"The blond guy is an Irish seaman named Griffin O'Meara," Casey said. "He jumped ship from a South African steamer three weeks ago and stole a gun from the ship's arms locker that I'm betting is a Webley automatic. That seems to make him fit the frame for Tartaglia's death."

"But what does he have to do with Ganns?" Farrell asked.

"That's the sixty-four-dollar question," Casey replied. "If

Ganns knew that Tartaglia was skimming money off the top of his profits, he'd be the most likely candidate to have somebody kill Chance. The trouble is, he has plenty of boys who'd be glad to do it, and do it quiet. He wouldn't pick some heavy-handed lug to do it in a way that would stir up so much trouble.''

"Yeah," Farrell said. "That makes sense." He shook his head confusedly. "Jesus, I thought I knew what this was about. It's a screwed-up mess, isn't it?"

"Maybe. You'd better finish that toddy and get into the shower," Casey said. "You'll be lucky not to come down with pneumonia. C'mon; the bathroom's down the hall on the right. Towels're on a shelf in there."

Farrell smiled in gratitude and groped his way down a narrow, dimly lit hallway lined with photographs and plaques until he found a small bathroom. The footed tub had been converted to a shower with an elaborate array of piping and canvas curtains. The room was already nicely warmed by a small gas space heater that Casey had obviously lit in anticipation of Farrell's need.

He stripped off his ruined suit and shoes, turned on the water, and climbed in. As the water hit him, he found himself overcome with weariness and sat down in the tub, letting the water cascade over his head and shoulders. After a time he got up, soaped himself, rinsed, and then shut off the water.

He pushed back the curtains and saw a wire shelf on the wall at the rear of the tub that contained a half-dozen thick, white terry-cloth towels. He selected one, stepped from the tub, and vigorously rubbed himself dry. He found a heavy flannel bathrobe hanging from a hook on the door and put it on.

He was smiling contentedly as he opened the bathroom door; then something froze the smile, and he was assailed by a dizzy feeling of unreality. A face stared at him from a picture frame on the wall, a face he knew as well as his own. He reached out and took the picture in hands that had suddenly gone numb, bringing it closer to his face.

Casey was sitting in the living room nursing his toddy when Farrell came into the room, his face the color of chalk.

"Where did you get this?" Farrell demanded. "Where did you get my mother's picture?"

"So it's true," Casey said quietly. "I've wondered since I first saw you at Holly Ballou's apartment."

Farrell came across the room with frightening speed, grabbed Casey by his shirtfront, and snatched him to his feet. "What do you mean? Who the hell are you?" His nostrils were flared, and his eyes were filled with angry sparks.

"I'm your father, Francis Xavier Farrell Casey," Frank Casey said. His blue eyes gazed into those of his son, and he waited with infinite patience for Farrell to either speak or smash his face.

As Marcel ran blindly through dark, shadowy streets, he felt fear gripping his bowels like a vise. He remembered seeing the woman in the alley stagger and clutch at herself. Some unknown sense told him it was his bullet that had struck her, and she was probably dead. Now he was something far worse than a holdup man and a mugger. He was a murderer, and the realization staggered him like a blow to the kidneys. In his mind, Marcel could see himself with his head shaved and trouser legs slit; he could see himself strapped into the electric chair. Ole Sparky, they called it. They put it on a truck and took it from town to town, where they plugged it in and fried the life out of whoever they sat in it. Yes sir, come and get it, fricasseed nigger boys a specialty of the house.

Marcel forgot Griff, forgot Farrell, and ran from the image of that hideous wood chair with its leather straps. He ran and ran until his sides cramped, and then he ran some more. Finally he could run no farther and fell to the concrete walk, sobbing with fear and exhaustion. He lost track of time as he lay there.

He heard a noise that brought him to his feet, his eyes darting here and there, his legs poised for flight, until he saw it was only a dog foraging inside an overturned trash barrel. He started walking toward Mid-City, looking over his shoulder from time to time. The panic he'd felt was now honed into a cold, reasoned terror. He felt the wind blow through his hair and realized for the first time that his hat was gone. He tried to remember where he'd lost it, and recalled with a sickening dread that his address was marked on the sweatband. That was a stupid thing to have done, but he'd paid a lot for the hat and was always afraid of losing it. Now either Farrell or the police might find it, and if they did, they'd be coming for him, and soon.

He willed himself into a calmness, knowing he had to find a place to hole up, somewhere neither Griff, Farrell, nor the police would look for him. As he walked, he removed the .38 from his hip, broke it open, and ejected the spent cartridge cases. He put five fresh cartridges in the empty chambers and replaced the gun in his pocket.

He saw lights in the distance and realized that he'd walked through the neighborhood beyond Bayou St. John and had reached the foot of Carrollton Avenue. He heard a streetcar bell in the distance and walked briskly toward it. As he walked, he remembered something. The sleek-haired little whore might hide him. Yeah, that was the ticket. He broke into a trot.

Ganns was in a rare quandry. After Farrell's escape he had jumped behind the wheel of the Lincoln and guided it to the curb at the river end of Broadway. More than an hour had passed with no sign of either Baxter or Pirelli. He was a cautious, reasonable man, a man who prided himself on his logical powers of thought. He knew his men should be back by now with either a report that Farrell was dead or that they had lost him. Since they had not, that could only mean they were dead.

Ganns didn't fear death himself, but he knew that Farrell was a relentless enemy who would, sooner or later, catch up to him. Ganns wasn't about to let everything he'd built be destroyed without a fight. Ganns had many resources, and he began planning in his head how he would use them.

He heard a groan behind him and looked into the back seat of the car.

"God . . . goddamn," Moroni said, shaking his head. "What the hell happened?"

"Farrell got away, you fool," Ganns said sharply. "After

he knocked you out he escaped and ran over the levee. Baxter and Pirelli went after him, but I doubt they'll be coming back.''

Moroni sat up quickly, his eyes showing white in the gloom of the car. "We got to get the hell away from here, and fast. We got to hide, or get out of town, right now." Ganns detected a shivery panic in Moroni's voice and felt a momentary contempt for this tool that was rapidly becoming useless to him.

"Perhaps," Ganns said quietly. "I'll waste no more time hunting Farrell. He's too good. He is a masterful hunter and would eliminate us at his leisure, as he did Baxter and Pirelli." Ganns sat quietly for a moment, fingering his chin. "No, I think we'll repair to my house out by the lake. It's surrounded by open ground, and I can put some other men out to watch. If Farrell gets in, we'll make certain he doesn't get out."

"But Mr. Ganns . . ." Moroni began.

"Enough," Ganns snapped. "Get behind the wheel of this car and drive to my house. Don't waste my time, Moroni, or your own life," he said in a soft, sibilant voice.

Moroni heard the threat, and within seconds they were racing down the darkened street, scattering fallen leaves behind them like frenzied bats.

Chapter 28

Farrell felt he must be dreaming. As he looked the other man in the eye, some dim memories of his father began to mesh with the reality of Casey's long, graceful hands, the mustache, his very smell. Somehow he knew the older man was telling the truth, a truth that nevertheless drove him into an unreasoning fury.

"Every day for years," he said between clenched teeth, "I asked Mama when you were coming back. When you were going to take us home. Her aunt treated her like a dog and me like shit on the parlor rug. All Mama could do was sit there with the tears running down her face. But *I* believed you were coming. *I* still believed," he screamed in the other man's face.

Casey hung there in his son's grip like a rat in the jaws of a terrier. His eyes began to bulge, and his hands instinctively came up to grab Farrell's wrists, but Casey exerted no pressure, seemingly content to let Farrell strangle him to death without resisting. "Don't you want to know why?" he managed to choke out. "Don't you even want to know where I was?"

"Who cares where you were?" Farrell shouted, shaking his father's nearly limp body. "You weren't here when I needed you; that's all I know." Farrell knew tears were streaming down the sides of his face, but he couldn't make them stop. As his vision clouded, he found himself overcome by the same lassitude that had overtaken him when he'd killed the men on the levee. Suddenly he threw Casey into the love seat, knocking it, and him, over into the floor.

Farrell knelt down and retrieved the photograph from where he'd dropped it. The face was as he remembered it—heart-shaped, with a firm, straight nose, large dark eyes, and a delicate mouth that smiled sweetly from the picture. Waves of long, pale hair framed the face, and a few errant locks curled over a high, smooth forehead.

The fall had cracked the glass into a web–like pattern across his mother's face, and the image touched a well of grief so deep inside him, he hadn't even known it was there. The sobs rising in his chest were choking him in their rush to escape his body, and for several agonizing minutes he could not breathe without making sounds more like the moans of an animal than a man's.

Casey lay stunned, but gradually the sounds of Farrell's anguish brought him back to himself. Painfully, he dragged himself upright and limped around the overturned furniture to where his son knelt.

"I know you probably can't believe this," Casey said in a hoarse voice, "but I wasn't the one who left her. I never wanted to leave her, ever. I loved your mother more than my own life."

Farrell pulled himself to his feet and staggered back to the bathroom. He stripped off the bathrobe and began to struggle back into the damp, filthy clothes he'd left on the floor.

Casey appeared in the doorway to the bathroom and leaned heavily on the doorframe. His face looked haggard. "Don't you want to know the truth?" he asked. "After all these years, don't you even want to know what happened to your mother and me?"

"I know enough," Farrell replied as he slipped the straps of his suspenders over his wide shoulders.

"All you probably know is what your mother's aunt told you," Casey said.

Farrell's head snapped up, and his eyes flickered dangerously at his father. "What's Willie Mae got to do with it?"

Casey rubbed his neck where he'd landed after going over the back of the sofa. "I don't know all of it, but your mother's parents were dead. Willie Mae was her guardian, and I've always believed she was responsible for the whole thing."

Farrell stopped moving then. The mention of Willie Mae Gautier had thrown everything in his mind into doubt. His anger at his father cooled to a simmer as his curiosity flared into high heat. "All right, talk," he said, turning to face Casey head on.

Casey walked into the bathroom, his arms still limp at his sides, until he was only inches from his son. "If you'll come into the other room and sit down, I'll tell you all I know. If you don't like it, or don't believe it, you can do anything you want. Even kill me, if it's in you to do it."

As Farrell looked deeply into Casey's eyes, the urge to strike out was almost overwhelming, but he could see no fear there, only a pain and resignation that could not be ignored. Casey had already taken the worst Farrell could dish out, and taken it without fighting back. "All right," he said grudgingly. "I've waited more than thirty years. I can wait a few more minutes."

The two went back to the living room, and Farrell once again took the upholstered armchair. Casey righted the sofa, then got two glasses and a bottle of straight rye, set the glasses on the coffee table, and filled them with ceremonial dignity. When the glasses were full he sat down, picked up a glass, and began to speak in a voice made thick with emotion.

"I guess your mother probably never told you how we met. I was nothing but a kid from the Irish Channel, and under ordinary circumstances I'd never have had the opportunity to meet a Creole belle, much less marry her."

Farrell said nothing, so Casey took a sip of whiskey and resumed. "I met her by accident in 1900," he said. "I was in uniform then, brand-new on the force. I was about nineteen, and pretty full of myself, I guess." He ran his fingers through his hair, a gesture that Farrell realized with a shock was similar to a habit of his own.

"Anyway," Casey went on, "I was walking a beat down in the Gentilly area and heard a woman screaming. I ran as fast as I could, and as I rounded a corner, I saw your mother running from a large dog. I guess he'd gone crazy from the heat or something, because he was foaming at the mouth. I didn't even think about what I was doing, just got out my gun from under my coat and shot him. The girl fainted, and I ran to her, scared out of my mind." He smiled gently and swirled the whiskey in his glass. "I'd never seen a woman faint before."

Casey looked up and saw Farrell's face, rapt with attention. He took that as a hopeful sign, and continued.

"I got her to some shade, and somebody in the neighborhood brought some water. After a while she came back to herself. I've never seen such beautiful gray eyes on a woman, before or since." Casey grinned at the memory. "She told me her name was Marie Elizabeth Delvaille." Casey pronounced the name *Del-vy-yu*, and rolled it around on his tongue like French cognac. "I think I fell for her right then and there. I was stupid, I guess, but first love is like that."

Farrell spoke for the first time in a voice so soft, it was almost as though he were afraid to break the spell of his father's reminiscences. "You didn't belong in her world. You'd never have belonged in a million years."

"Yeah," Casey responded with a smile, "but I didn't know that then. I believed anything was possible. That's another thing love does to you." He paused to scratch his head. "I began trying to see her right away, but your mother said her aunt wouldn't allow me to call on her. I figured it was because I was Irish and poor. I wrote letters to her then. Long, soulful, passionate letters. I even wrote some poems. Eventually she agreed to meet me at the entrance to Audubon Park. It was there that I realized just how impossible things could be."

"That was when you found out she was colored," Farrell ventured. He leaned forward and took the glass of whiskey his father had poured. His voice was still low and soft.

"Yeah," Casey said. "I was shocked, because there was nothing about her to tell me she had Negro blood. Her skin had that same golden tone as yours, but that was all. I guess you only see what you want to see." He shook his head.

"Didn't knowing she was a Negro change anything for you?" Farrell asked. "What kind of life did you think you could have?"

"I didn't care," Casey answered. "It was too late for me to care. Although it was tough for her to get out unchaperoned, we spent a year sneaking around, meeting at the park, the library, at cafés in the French Quarter. We were so young, I think it was the sheer impossibility of it that drew us closer together." Casey paused and looked at Farrell again. "We finally decided that we were too committed to each other to turn away. If we couldn't have a life here, we'd go where we could."

Farrell shook his head in wonder. "But there's no place in the entire country where whites can marry colored people. Nowhere."

Casey nodded. "We thought about it a long time and made the decision to book passage on a boat to Cuba. We were married by a priest in Havana. Intermarriage was pretty common there, so there were no legal problems to overcome."

"How did you live?" Farrell asked.

"Well, I had a good record on the New Orleans force and could speak a fair brand of Spanish. I got a lieutenant I'd worked under to write me a letter of reference, and I joined the police in Havana. It didn't pay much, but then, we didn't want very much, just each other." Casey drained the whiskey in his glass and sat back on the sofa, looking very tired.

"We wrote to Willie Mae, telling her what we'd done, and where we'd gone. She wasn't happy about it, I can tell you." He shook his head slowly. "But by then we had something else to think of. Ten months after we got to Havana you were born. We took you everywhere with us. You especially loved to play in the park. We had a special place, by a fountain with a bronze statue of a girl in the center, and you'd play there for hours. Sometimes I'd let you grab my hand and I'd swing you around in a circle. How you'd laugh." Casey laughed for a moment, himself.

"You still haven't told me where you've been for the past thirty years," Farrell said with quiet intensity. "All the family history is great, but where the hell have you been?"

"One day, about two years after we moved to Cuba, I had a crazy idea," Casey began. "I thought if we came back home, with you, that Marie's family would accept me. Accept us. I was a fool." A single large tear welled up in the corner of each of his eyes, spilled over, and ran down into his mustache. "Marie was afraid, but she finally agreed we should go back and try to make peace with her family. After we got to town she thought it best to take you and go alone to meet her family. I never saw either of you again."

"How could they have hidden us from you?" Farrell asked incredulously. "How can anything or anybody be hidden from the police?"

"I can't answer you on that score," Casey answered. "There's not much as clannish or secretive in this part of the world as the Creole community. There're mysteries about their lives that some of us may never discover or understand. All I know is, your mother's family closed around you like a blanket and would tell me nothing," Casey answered, wringing his hands. "Her Aunt Willie Mae seems to have been the brains of the operation, because she was the only one who would even speak to me. She said your mother did not love me anymore, and told me the two of you had gone far away and would not come back.

"I came to believe that, at least temporarily, you were taken out of the city," Casey continued, "because for months I searched town for you, even asked my friends on the police force to help, but it was all for nothing. Your mother's community stood between us like a brick wall." He reached into his hip pocket, pulled out a handkerchief, and blew his nose into it.

"All these years," Farrell said, his face grainy with fatigue and sorrow, "all this time I thought I was a bastard, with no father at all. They all said Mama had disgraced the family. I thought that was the reason they treated me like I was dirt. If I'd known you were a white man . . ." He looked at his father and balled up his fists. "Why did you do it?" he demanded in a voice thick with outrage. "Didn't you realize you were making something that couldn't belong anywhere?"

"My being white didn't have anything to do with it," Casey replied softly. "The real reason your mother's family did what they did was sheer arrogance. To them, I was nothing but shanty Irish—poor white trash. It was more convenient and expedient for them to pretend you were a bastard than to welcome some-body like me into their family."

"Don't ask me to feel sorry for you," Farrell shouted, pound-ing his chest with one fist. "I haven't had a home or any people to belong to my whole life, and what little of me that's black is just enough to keep me from being anything but a nigger in my own hometown. The only way I've been able to survive is to pretend to be white—and always be scared somebody's gonna find me out." His eyes glowed like two smoldering coals set deep into his haggard face, and his clenched fists seemed caught in the throes of a palsy. "How would you like to live like that, huh? Answer me that."

Casey looked at his son and saw in his anguished features the face of the woman he'd lost. He shook his head. "People in love don't think about things like that, kid. All you know is you can't live without one another. Love is such a miracle, you can't believe anybody in the world would deny you that happiness. If your mother and I made a mistake, we both paid dearly for it." He poured more whiskey into his glass and downed it, allowing the fire in his gullet to give him an excuse for the burning of tears in his eyes.

The pathos in those last words dampened Farrell's anger like water suddenly thrown on a fire. He stared quietly at Casey, then rose and began to walk up and down the room, pounding his right fist into his left palm. He forced himself to rise above his rage, to think rationally again. Although Casey's story sounded fantastic in parts, Farrell knew Willie Mae Gautier was proud and arrogant to a fault. She was more than capable of this particular cruelty. Casey's unaffected sadness was proof enough that the old woman had inflicted a terrible loss on him that the years had done nothing to assuage. Farrell remembered well enough the sadness his mother carried until it finally killed her.

The two men had been quiet for several minutes when Casey finally looked up again and saw Farrell standing at the mantel, staring at him.

"We've got a lot of things to catch up on, when you're ready," Casey said, "but we've got some work to do first."

Farrell looked at Casey and nodded his head. "We've talked enough for now. Let's go," he said.

Chapter 29

It was sometime before dawn when Casey and Farrell drove the Marmon roadster out of the Irish Channel onto Tchopitoulas Street and headed downtown. Fog had rolled in during the night, and the riverfront street was dense with swirling trails of white.

When they turned onto Soraparu Street Farrell and Casey could see there were a few lights on in the house, but no other signs of life. The rest of the neighborhood was tucked in and buttoned up.

"I reckon when the guns started going off your girls and their clientele skedaddled. There's not a joy girl nor a john in America who'd call a cop to a house where they've been doing business," Casey said.

"Yeah, and this isn't the kind of neighborhood where people wake up and start looking out the window when guns are going off," Farrell added.

Casey cut the lights, and coasted to a stop a half block from the front of the house. Farrell made a motion to get out, but Casey stopped him and reached into the pocket of his overcoat. He withdrew a blue-steel Smith & Wesson revolver, which he handed to Farrell.

"Watch out for that thing, kid," Casey said. "It fires a .32-20 rifle cartridge and kicks like a mule."

Remembering that he'd left Pirelli's .45 back in Casey's bathroom, Farrell nodded, then broke the cylinder and counted six brass cartridges in the chambers. He flicked the cylinder shut; then the two men got quietly from the car and approached the house.

The gate to the picket fence hung open, and they could see that the front door of the house was slightly ajar. They split up and cut through the yard so each would come to the opposite end of the porch. Casey went first, quickly checking the window nearest him, then motioned for Farrell to come up. They got to the door at the same time, communicating with silent looks and hand signals. Casey shoved the door wide with one foot, and Farrell darted quickly into the room. Within the space of three seconds he spoke.

"Come on in. It's empty."

Casey entered and found Farrell standing at the foot of the stairs leading to the second floor. At Farrell's gesture, he followed him to the back.

"Jesus Christ," Casey said. "What a mess." He bent down to examine the wounds in Marie's body. From force of habit he dug his fingers into the side of the woman's neck, shivering a little from the chill that had settled over her skin. With his thumb and forefinger he closed Marie's eyes; then he stood up.

Farrell was standing over Sandra. His face was blank, but a nerve began to twitch under his left eye. Casey bent down and saw that, from the location of the hole in Sandra's chest, there was no need to check her pulse either. He unfolded his show handkerchief and draped it across her face, then got up quickly, his eyes sick.

"Moroni was never one to waste lead," he said tonelessly. "At least she didn't suffer any."

Farrell didn't move, but a nerve in his face danced jerkily. "She never knew her father, either," he said to himself.

"What was that?" Casey asked, jerking his head up.

Farrell shook his head irritably, walked across the room to a closet, and began pulling clothes from it.

"I guess I should call the station and get a wagon down here," Casey said to his back. "Or would that cause you some trouble? I forgot for a second that you own this joint."

Farrell looked up from buttoning a fresh shirt and shook his head. "The deed to the house was in Marie's name. I was a silent partner. She did me a lot of favors once, and I gave her most of the interest in this place to pay her back."

"Was it because her name was Marie, too?" Casey asked.

Farrell looked up as he buttoned the vest of the gray pinstripe suit he had chosen and stared quietly at his father. "She'd had a lot of hard times, too, so maybe you're right," he said finally.

Within another few seconds Farrell was completely dressed and tying the laces of a pair of black wingtip shoes. He strapped the stiletto to his left forearm and slid Casey's revolver into his hip pocket as he kicked the ruined suit into the closet and closed the door.

"You got a telephone here?" Casey asked.

"On that table in the corner," Farrell answered

Casey found the phone, an ancient two-piece candlestick, lifted the receiver, and tapped the hook up and down a couple of times. Finally an operator answered. "This is Inspector Casey, New Orleans Police. Get me police headquarters, please. It's urgent."

Within seconds the receiver crackled at Casey's ear, and he turned and began talking into the transmitter in his left hand. "Yeah, this is Casey. Listen, I'm at 202 Soraparu Street, near the First Street Wharf. I've got two gunshot victims here, both female. One Negro, about forty years of age, and a white woman, thirty-two years of age. Both victims are DOA. Yeah."

Casey looked up, and saw that Farrell had vanished like a wisp of smoke. He'd wanted to say something to his son, something useless like "Be careful," and he hadn't gotten to do it. For almost thirty-five years his son had been dead to him, but now he was alive, and Casey wanted to make up for some of that lost time, wanted it even though his son was a killer, and maybe worse. The fear that Farrell would disappear again was all but overwhelming. Then the sergeant at the other end of the telephone line spoke again, and gratefully, automatically, Casey went back to work.

In different parts of the city two women sat and worried. On Touro Street, Willie Mae Gautier walked from the sofa in her parlor to the front window, back and forth, back and forth. Marcel had been gone at night before, but he'd always come in sometime before dawn. Something had happened; she just knew it.

She'd never had any trouble with her daughter, now dead for nearly ten years. She'd had sense. She'd recognized from an early age that as a woman she had to be responsible. Men were congenitally irresponsible, the lot of them. Her son-in-law, Marcus Aristide, had been an attorney, but when Willie Mae's daughter had died suddenly, Marcus had gone off the rails, drinking until he drank himself to death. A woman would have put the boy first, Willie Mae thought. A woman wouldn't have given in to grief like that. In a way, it was just as well that Marcus had died, too, because he'd been a bad influence on the boy, always coming in drunk like that.

Willie Mae had managed to curb her own husband's excesses, and had kept him in his place until she'd buried him. But Marcel, he was too much like Wesley, even though they'd never met. She'd whipped Marcel until her arm ached when he was small, and still he'd grown up bad, running around town drinking, and carrying on with women. She shook her head, thinking that she hadn't scared him enough. If she had, he'd be going to school at Xavier University now, learning to be a schoolteacher, a pharmacist, or maybe a priest. Something dignified, that she could point to with pride.

In her mind she could see Marcel in his fancy suit, drinking whiskey and putting his hands all over some dark-skinned slut he'd found in a bar. The image was so disturbing that she got up quickly and walked briskly into the kitchen to light a fire for coffee.

* * *

On Sycamore Place, Helen Tartaglia was restlessly pacing the floor, too. Sandra was a grown woman, but there was something about having her only child out on the street alone, late at night, that made chills run up and down her spine, no matter how old that child might be.

As she walked about the big, empty house, she thought back to the years in Jackson, after she'd left Chance. Those first few years had been bad ones, when it was hard to find enough money to keep a roof over their heads, much less eat. She'd had to do things she'd never dreamed she would. Illusions disappear fast when you get hungry, she thought with a rueful smile.

She found herself in front of an antique mirror she'd bought in Capetown, and stood there looking at her face for a while. Not so bad-looking, even at fifty. She hadn't allowed herself to go downhill, even back in the days when she'd been selling herself in that house in Jackson. It had boiled down to a business decision, when all was said and done. If she had to be a prostitute, she was going to be a high-class prostitute; that way she could call all the shots, decide which men could touch her and which ones couldn't.

Knowing Chance had spoiled forever the notion of romantic love. All men were fools, and to make use of a woman's body for an hour they became bigger fools. She'd spent a lot of effort keeping herself youthful and attractive so she could exploit that foolishness to the farthest limit.

No man would ever again use her the way Chance had. She'd been young then, young and passionate, and reckless enough in her love to hold nothing back. But in giving herself to Chance she'd gambled on a rigged wheel. Just when the little ball should have dropped into the red, it had popped over into the black. Chance had been a perfect name, because she'd risked it all on him.

It was 5:00 A.M., and the waiting was getting worse. She hadn't smoked in more than eight years, but she felt the need for solace grow strong in her now. She went to Sandra's desk and rummaged in the middle drawer until she found an un-opened package of Lucky Strikes. Good name, Lucky Strike. Chance would have liked it. The taste was awful after so many years, but as she drew the smoke into her lungs, the nicotine eventually began to work its magic.

The sky was beginning to brighten through the big picture window, and she sat down to watch it, leaning back and drawing in the calming smoke. The German clock on the wall began to chime, tolling five times. It was a little slow, like she was getting to be.

Coming back here had been a mistake. Of that, she was completely certain. Coming back had made her play the wheel again, when she already had everything and didn't need to take stupid risks.

There was supposed to be wisdom in old age, but there was always a small piece of reckless youth hiding in the back, waiting for the opportunity to rush out. Helen was wise now, in ways she'd never wished, and suddenly older than she'd ever wanted. As she watched the sun creep higher in the sky, Helen had a chilly premonition that the waiting would soon be over.

Chapter 30

At 9:00 A.M. Wednesday morning Wesley Farrell crossed Tulane Avenue and merged with the crowd entering New Orleans Charity Hospital. The halls inside rang with the sound of many footsteps echoing off the marble floors. He found the information desk and bent down to speak to one of the women there. The woman was shuffling through some papers while she spoke into a telephone receiver caught between her shoulder and chin.

"Can you tell me where Savanna Beaulieu is?" he asked.

The woman said something into the telephone, then hung it up. "What name was that?" she asked.

"Beaulieu, B-e-a-u-l-i-e-u, first name Savanna," he answered. "She should be listed as a new patient. She might be in intensive care."

"With an aristocratic-sounding name like that, she oughta own the place," the woman said, turning up one corner of her mouth in a smart-aleck grin. Farrell said nothing while she checked her directory.

"Can't seem to find her," the woman said, frowning a little.

"Maybe you'll find her listed in the Negro female ward," Farrell said.

The woman cocked a sharp eye at Farrell and looked at him intermittently as she checked another directory. "Yes. A gunshot wound. She's out of intensive care now, sir, and in Ward 10C. Take the elevator over there to the tenth floor, then go left down the corridor."

Farrell touched his hat with two fingers of his right hand and walked quietly away from her curious stare.

The elevator was slow, and it took Farrell another five minutes to get on it and eventually reach the tenth floor. He found the ward easily enough, and walked to the nurses' station. A fresh, bright-eyed young nurse looked up from a chart she was marking and smiled at him.

"Can I help you, sir?"

"I'm looking for Savanna Beaulieu," he answered. "They told me downstairs that she's on this ward."

"Yes," the young nurse said. "She's a very lucky woman. The doctor said that if the bullet had gone an inch in either direction, she might not be here now."

"She's expected to recover then?" Farrell asked.

"Oh, yes, sir," the nurse answered. "She'll be in the hospital for a couple of weeks, but she'll be right as rain by then. Are you her employer?"

"No," Farrell said. "I'm a friend."

"Oh," the young nurse said, flustered. She picked up a stack of charts and began straightening them energetically to cover her embarrassment. "Well, she can receive visitors; that is, if you . . ."

"Thanks, miss," Farrell said. "I'd like to."

"Yes, she . . . she's at the end of the ward, behind the screen."

Farrell gave the young woman a small smile, removed his hat, and entered the ward. There was little privacy, and he could see that a number of the patients were quite ill. He decided immediately to try to get Savanna into a private room. He finally reached the end of the ward and peeked behind the screen.

Savanna lay flat on her back with the head of the bed cranked up slightly. An intravenous infusion was going into the bend of her right arm, and her eyes were closed. Her chest rose and fell regularly. As Farrell quietly drew up a chair and sat down in it, he noticed that her skin had an unhealthy gray tinge to it. He felt a deep anger at seeing her this way, and a greater anger at himself when he remembered that she'd gotten hurt trying to help him.

He placed his hat on the floor, took her right hand in his own, and sat there watching the rise and fall of her chest as she slept. Some time later, he could not say how long, Savanna's eyelids began to flicker. Slowly, her eyes opened to narrow slits, and she blinked to clear them. "Mmmph," she said sleepily. "What the hell you doin' here?"

"I came to see you. I had to know how you were doing, Savanna." Farrell dropped his eyes and squeezed her hand gently.

Savanna sneered slightly, and a faint laugh escaped her dry lips. "Thought you'd be with your li'l white girlfriend."

"No. Not anymore," he answered.

"You don't have to worry about Savanna, white boy," she said. "I took care of myself long before I ever saw you." She turned her head away and pulled her hand from his grasp.

Farrell could think of nothing to say. Shame burned so deeply in his gut that he almost felt nauseated. He shifted uncomfortably in the wooden chair. "You don't understand . . ." he began.

Savanna's weak laugh came again. "Sure I do. You ofays is all alike. A black woman's good enough to have a few laughs with, but let a white chick come along and shake her little white ass in your faces, you burn up the road gettin' over to it."

"I've got that coming, I guess," Farrell said. "But you're wrong about the other thing."

"What's that?"

Farrell hesitated, licking his lips. This wasn't nearly as private as he wished it was, but as he made up his mind about what he was going to say, he knew he had to say it no matter where they were. "I never really told you much about myself. I didn't trust you; but then, I never trusted anybody else, either. I had my reasons—reasons I thought were iron-clad—but they don't seem so good anymore.''

Savanna waved her hand impatiently. "Gimme some water," she said in a harsh croak.

Farrell poured water into a thick tumbler with a glass straw in it, then held it so she could get the straw into her mouth. She sucked at it like an impatient baby at a mother's breast. Finally she stopped drinking, and her chest heaved from the effort. "Farrell, I don't know what you're talkin' about," she said finally. "If all you came for is to talk me the rest of the way to death, just get the hell on out of here."

Farrell flushed to the roots of his reddish hair, and dropped his gaze to the floor. "Wait," he began. "I . . . I've got to tell you something important. I've got to tell you who I really am."

"For Christ sake," Savanna said. "What're you talkin' about?"

"You can look at something, and think you're seeing all there is," he began, "but what's on the surface is only skin deep. What's underneath is what's real, what you have to live with. No matter what you look like, it's what's inside that you can't run away from." He leaned over and laced his fingers together as he stared at the floor. "You and everyone else look at me and you see a white man, but that's not all there is, Savanna. My father . . . he was white, but my mother's name was Delvaille. She was a colored Creole . . ." Farrell found he didn't know how to say what he wanted, and his shoulders slumped tiredly.

Savanna looked confused for a moment, then her eyes widened with a slow recognition. She began to laugh, a dry, nearly silent wheeze that rocked her entire body. Farrell looked on, a little afraid that she might hurt herself.

"Oh, my," she said finally. "Oh my, oh my, oh my." She laughed some more, loudly this time, and tears began to run out of her eyes, and make pale tracks across the dark skin of her face. "All this time . . . all this time I thought you were really something, and you . . . and you're just another nigger, like me." Savanna dissolved into more laughter.

Farrell leaned back in the chair, stunned, not knowing what

to say or do. He heard footsteps, and turned to see a young resident come past the privacy screen. His face was a study in outrage.

"What the devil's going on here?" the resident demanded. He moved quickly forward to check Savanna's pulse, and lay a hand on her brow.

"I was just talking to her, and she started to laugh, doctor," Farrell explained lamely.

"Good God, man," the young man huffed. "This woman was seriously injured. She doesn't need excitement, she needs rest. I'm going to have to ask you to leave right now."

Farrell picked up his hat, and got up to go, but Savanna waved a hand, and got her laughter under control.

"Wait a minute," she said to the doctor in a hoarse voice. "This man's a friend of mine. 'Sides, ain't laughter supposed to be the best medicine?"

"Well," the young man began. "I don't know . . ."

"Please, doctor, I'll be good, honest I will," Savanna said, smiling winningly at him.

The resident asked Farrell to move, went over to Savanna's side, and pulled the covers back. He checked the dressing on the wound, and after muttering to himself, pulled the covers back over her. "All right," he said. "You can stay for a few more minutes, but no more of this foolishness, understand?"

Farrell promised to be quiet, and the doctor left.

Savanna beckoned for him to draw his chair closer. "Why're you tellin' me all this?" she asked. "You've been covering this up all your life, so why're you tellin' me now, Farrell?"

Farrell took her hand again, and shook his head. "I don't know if I can explain it to you, because I don't understand it all myself. But some things have happened to me in the past few days, things that made me realize how alone I was. Maybe . . . maybe I've been locked up alone with myself for as long as I can stand it." He paused and ran his fingers through his hair again. "Maybe this was the only way I could think to tell you I want to trust you. For us to trust each other."

Savanna said nothing, but she examined Farrell's face with a look of frank appraisal, then she nodded her head gently a couple of times. Something wordless passed between them, and Farrell nodded back to her. She squeezed his hand with a strength so formidable, he knew she was a long way from dead. She pulled him closer.

"That kid you asked me about. Was he one of the ones who shot me?"

Farrell nodded. "He got away, but I killed one of the other two."

"Good," she said with relish. "I heard something the day I got shot about this kid. I don't know if the information's still good, but if you want it, it's yours."

"Talk, baby," Farrell said.

"There's a little brown-skin girl, a teaser named Thomasina Castanelle, has some rooms upstairs in a building at the corner of South Roman and Melpomene."

"Yeah," Farrell said, all interest.

"One of my girls heard this teaser braggin' in a bar that she'd snagged a good-lookin' light-skinned kid with fancy clothes and a lot of bread. He might be the one you're looking for."

Farrell's eyes got a hot, excited gleam in them, and he stood up quickly.

"Farrell," Savanna said. "Before you go, I got somethin' else to tell you."

"What's that, baby?" Farrell asked.

"I haven't been completely honest with you, either," she said with a smile. "Savanna Beaulieu ain't my real name. I was born Rosalee Ortique." She grinned up at him.

Farrell smiled, then leaned over and kissed her mouth. He was still smiling when he stopped outside to have them move Savanna to a private room.

Chapter 31

Frank Casey stood quietly to the side of the autopsy table while Dr. Jack Chehardy spoke for the benefit of the short, curly-haired man on the other side of the room who acted as his stenographer. Chehardy talked in a growl around the butt of a cigar he had clamped brutally in the corner of his mouth. Occasionally he would stop talking, remove the cigar, and expell a deep, phlegmy cough.

"Goddamn," Chehardy said feelingly. "I don't know what's worse on this cough, the chill in these rooms, or these cigars. Before it's all over, somebody's gonna have me on one of these tables, Frank."

"Why don't you give up the cigars?" Casey asked. "Think of the money you'd save. Besides, they smell like burning rope."

Chehardy began to laugh, but the laughter broke up more phlegm in his chest, and he coughed violently.

"If it wasn't for these ropes, I'd have dropped out of this work a long time ago," he said when the spasm ended. "This is a pretty good lookin' corpse we got here. You oughta see some of the others, like that guy they fished out of the river a couple of days ago. Jesus, God! He started to fall apart on the table before I even touched him.''

Casey said nothing, and Chehardy reached for his scalpel and began to cut.

"You knew this one, huh, Frank?" Chehardy asked as he worked.

"I used to bounce her on my knee, but that was almost thirty years ago," Casey answered in a toneless voice. He tried to blot out the sight of Sandra's nude body with the memory of the little girl, but was unsuccessful. His eyes were drawn inexorably to the surprised look on her face. It seemed to Casey that she must have learned some important, elemental secret of life in the split second before she ceased to exist.

"All right, Lenny," Chehardy said to the fat little stenographer. "Everything from now on is for the record, so get your pencil ready. Victim is a white female, five feet, four inches tall, weight one hundred five pounds. No noticeable marks or scars on the body. According to Inspector Casey she is about thirty-two years old, and is in good physical condition. She has a single large perforation just below the left breast." Chehardy paused and lifted the body slightly in order to see the back of the torso. "No exit wound."

The autopsy became mechanical, and Chehardy's voice droned on in a monotone that became a soothing buzz. Casey ceased to know, or care about the details of Sandra's physiology. He didn't want to hear the sickening sound of Chehardy opening the chest cavity, or see him sponging away the blood. Finally Chehardy called out and got his attention.

"Okay, Frank," Chehardy said, pausing to cough again. "Here's what you've been waiting for. The shot tore through the left ventricle, death was probably instantaneous. And the bullet . . ." He paused and grunted a little as he probed deeper into the body. ". . . the bullet lodged against the spinal column, cracking the eleventh vertebra. Could be some spinal cord damage, but it was the hole in the heart that did it for her." He pulled the lead slug from the body with a Kelly forceps, held it up, and dropped it with a loud clang into an enameled steel basin.

"Pretty big slug," Chehardy observed. "Looks like a .45. Not too much expansion, so you should be able to match it with a gun—if you find it."

"It's from a .44 Special," Casey said.

Chehardy looked up with an expression of mild curiosity. "Yeah, it could be. It's not copper-nickel, so that probably rules out an automatic. You seem pretty definite, Frank."

"Thanks for taking care of this so quickly, Jack," Casey said, straightening his hat on his head. "Tag and bag that slug, and let me have it, will you?"

Chehardy put down his bloody scalpel and stared at the red-haired cop. "Normally I don't do that, Frank. The slug and my report should go up to the coroner's office so he can schedule a hearing; you know that. We've done this together a hundred times."

"This is a special case," Casey said. "I'm dead certain I can prove who fired that bullet, and I'm equally certain the crime lab boys can identify it with a slug that's already on file. As soon as they do, I'm going over to the district attorney's office and get a warrant sworn out against the guy who fired it before he takes a notion to clear out of town."

Chehardy removed his cigar from his mouth, and looked intently into Casey's eyes. "You ain't gonna tell me what this is about, are you?"

"It's gotta have a hush on it," Casey admitted.

Chehardy turned his head and spoke over his shoulder. "Lenny. Make a note for the report that the slug we took from this dame was turned over to Inspector Frank Casey. Make sure you put the case number and everything on that. Okay?" he asked, turning back to Casey.

"Okay," Casey replied. "Where's your phone?"

"In my office," Chehardy answered.

Casey left the chilly autopsy room and went into Chehardy's office. He picked up the telephone and dialed, and waited impatiently as he listened to the whirring noises in the receiver. Finally he got an answer.

"This is Inspector Casey," he said. "I'm calling from the medical examiner's office. I need to speak to the chief and to somebody from the district attorney's office right away." He listened and checked his watch. "Fine, I'll be there in an hour. You might suggest to the chief that he have somebody from the Treasury Department present. Yeah, I know he hates federal badges, but they'll be grateful to him when they hear what I've got. Thanks." Casey hung up and left the office.

The neighborhood surrounding the corner of South Roman and Melpomene was as mean and shabby as New Orleans could get. Most of the clapboard shotgun houses and camel-back doubles were badly in need of paint, and had been since Teddy Roosevelt ran for his second term. Farrell pulled his Packard over about a half block down Melpomene, and looked the area over. A few old Negro men and women sat listlessly on their front porches fanning themselves, reading newspapers, or staring out into nothing.

The few automobiles lining the curbs were pocked with patches of rust, and showed ample evidence of the catastrophic combination of liquor and gasoline. Several had suffered the violent amputation of bumpers and fenders. Farrell's car belonged there like a diamond on a dish of field peas.

As he got out of the car, he saw a large, three-story clapboard building on the corner. He began walking slowly toward it.

Marcel was pushing against the brown-skinned teenaged prostitute for all he was worth. Noises like those from a steam engine toiling up a long, tall mountain exploded from his lips each time he pumped downward. The girl was giggling, whispering love talk into his ear, and pulling his head down between her round little breasts.

Soon Marcel's moans began to reach a crescendo and the girl, sensing an end to her labors, began to mimic him. All of a sudden, he let out a long, high-pitched cry, and, as she grinned to herself, she cried out, too. Their mingled cries went on for about fifteen seconds before Marcel finally ran out of gas, and collapsed on top of her.

"Oh, baby," she said feelingly. "You 'most too much man for me, know that?" She expertly pulled herself out from under his sweaty body, and propped herself up on a pillow. He laughed weakly, and she smiled to herself again, thinking about how much easier it was to make money on her back than it had been behind the counter at Woolworth's.

"Hey," Marcel panted. "Give me a few minutes, and we'll do it again, okay?"

"You ain't had enough yet, sugar?" the girl asked as she lit a cigarette. "Where you gettin' all that money you been spendin' on me, huh?"

"Just don't you worry, honey," Marcel said, turning on his left side in order to see her. "I got plenty, and I know where I can get more."

The door to the bedroom swung open quietly, and the girl looked over Marcel's shoulder to see a tall bronze-skinned man standing there. He held his finger to his lips, and winked. The girl froze, not daring to breathe.

"Money's just lyin' around out there, sugartit," Marcel said, warming to his subject. "All you gotta do is know where to look, is all."

"Let's have a little talk about where you've been looking lately, Marcel," Farrell said in a soft voice.

Marcel squeaked with fright, and threw himself out of the bed, but as he reached for his .38 on the nightstand, Farrell snapped the stiletto down sharply with his fingertips, barely missing Marcel's outstretched fingers. Marcel jerked back his hand, and Farrell threw a left into his stomach, then followed up with a right cross to the chin. The blows stunned Marcel, and he dropped like a stone.

The teenaged whore had crawled into the corner of the room, clutching a feather pillow against her nakedness. Her eyes were the size of saucers, and small, frightened whimpers came from between her chattering teeth.

"How much he owe you?" Farrell asked kindly.

"T—ten b-b—bucks," she stuttered.

Farrell found Marcel's coat draped over a chair, and he ransacked the pockets until he came up with a roll of money.

He peeled off two bills, and held them down to her. "Here's fifteen. Now get out of here, and keep your mouth shut."

The girl dropped the pillow, snatched her dress from the floor, and ran out without another word.

Marcel still lay on the floor, his half-closed eyes glazed and stupid. Farrell spotted a dirty washstand in the corner with an old, cracked pitcher on it. He picked up the pitcher, walked over to where Marcel lay, and emptied it on the boy's face. Marcel sputtered, and moved his head back and forth to escape the stinging stream of cold water.

Farrell retrieved his still-quivering knife out of the nightstand, grabbed the boy by the hair, and dragged him upright. "Where's the big man? Where's he hiding?"

Marcel looked up at Farrell's face, and into eyes as cold and bleak as a tax collector's heart. "I dunno what you're talkin' about," he gasped.

Farrell put the point of the blade against Marcel's neck. "Yes you do, you half-white sonofabitch." He began pressing the point of the knife inward until the skin broke, and a thin stream of blood began to trickle down the side of Marcel's neck. Marcel screamed a high, thin scream.

"You shot a friend of mine, you little bastard," he said. "I'm gonna give you a better chance than you gave her." He let go of Marcel's hair, and slapped his face, hard.

Marcel fell to his knees, and began to blubber like a lost, frightened child.

"Take your time, kid," Farrell said in a dry, soft, quiet voice. "I got all day."

Chapter 32

It was about 5:30 in the afternoon and getting dusk when Farrell reached the vicinity of O'Meara's rooming house on South Cortez Street. Marcel had told him a lot of what he'd wanted to know, but there were still questions to which he wanted answers.

Many of the houses in that part of town didn't seem to have house numbers, and he was on the point of getting out of the car to find O'Meara's address when he saw a man leave a house three doors down from where he sat with the Packard's motor idling. The man was big, and moved with the cat-footed grace of a much smaller man. His hair was covered by a dark cloth cap, but Farrell was almost certain it was O'Meara. As he watched, the big man walked across the street to an old Hudson sedan, and got inside. Farrell waited until O'Meara pulled away from the curb and started down the street.

Farrell put his car into gear as he saw O'Meara turn off to Canal Street. Farrell drove after him, and followed until the Irishman reached Jefferson Davis Parkway. The Hudson continued down Jeff Davis until it reached Toulouse Street. O'Meara turned there, and drove until he was about a block from South Broad, where he pulled to the curb, and shut off his engine.

Farrell, seeing this from a distance of two blocks, cut his own engine and coasted to a stop. As he watched, O'Meara got out of his car, and walked into a shabby building with three brass balls hanging over the entrance. Farrell got out and hurried after him.

Moise Fink was spending the last few quiet moments of the day as he often did, reading from the Talmud. It had been a long day that had impressed upon him how badly the Depression was affecting his clientele. Many of them had been in that day, pawning wedding rings, heavy nickel-plated watches, silver spoons, and an odd assortment of useless junk like box cameras, tools, even a hammer dulcimer.

Fink was not a particularly successful pawnbroker, because he did not have a ruthless heart. Today, as he had so many times before, he read the distress in the eyes of some of his customers, and gave several more than their pawned items had been worth when brand-new. How he sometimes wished he had the heart of a Shylock. He'd be living a good deal better than he was, that was for certain.

He had closed his book and was staring off into space, when he heard the jingle of the bells at the entrance. He turned and saw a large man, grinning at him over the barrel of an automatic pistol. Like most pawnshop owners, Fink wore a gun, but the short-barreled Smith & Wesson .32 on his belt seemed a million miles away from him at that moment.

"W-what do you want?" Fink asked querously.

"Well now," O'Meara said, waggling the pistol at him. "What else would an armed man want in a pawnshop but money. Now get it and put it into this bag," O'Meara said, throwing a cloth sack at the tall, slender man.

Fink caught the bag awkwardly, and shakily stood up from his chair. The Talmud slipped from his lap and fell to the floor unnoticed. Nervous sweat was already collecting under the arms of his shirt and in the crotch of his pants. He desperately wanted to pull them loose, but he feared that any movement he made contrary to the gunman's orders would be construed as an act of hostility.

"I—I don't have very much money here today," Fink said. "Business hasn't been good at all this week."

O'Meara laughed. "That's a good one, that is. A bad day for a kike pawnbroker would probably make for a nice holiday in the south of France for the rest of us. Get moving and fill that sack," he said in a menacing voice.

Fink knelt cautiously on the floor in front of his safe, and began to pull out drawers. Slowly and methodically he emptied each drawer into the sack. He was nearly finished when he heard a new voice.

"Don't even twitch, O'Meara," Wesley Farrell said.

But the big Irishman swung left, bringing his gun up at the same time. Casey's revolver exploded in Farrell's fist, and the slug took O'Meara high in the chest, knocking him flat on his back. He stared above him with shocked, unbelieving eyes, and he moved his right hand around on the floor, searching for his gun.

Farrell stepped forward and kicked an automatic away from O'Meara's questing right hand. He noted, somewhat absently, that it wasn't a Webley. "Are you all right?" Farrell asked the pawnbroker.

"Yes, yes, I am all right," Fink said in a rush. He wiped his face with a crumpled handkerchief, and looked at Farrell with a sickly smile. "I thought I was a dead man," he said.

"You damned nearly were," Farrell said. "He's killed three people that I know of."

"W—w—wrong," O'Meara managed to gasp. "Only—only two." He smiled at Farrell as blood leaked from the corners of his mouth and down his neck.

Farrell looked at him sharply. "Who put you up to killing Tartaglia, and why?" he demanded.

"N—not Tartaglia. Told—told her that was stupid."

Farrell knelt down and grabbed O'Meara by the collar and shook him roughly. "Who put you up to it, O'Meara? Answer me."

O'Meara laughed, but the laugh turned to a watery cough

as blood came up from his throat and out his mouth. "The Flynn woman. Her idea. Right bitch, that one. T—to—took me to bed, promised me m-money. Lied . . . liar. S-should've never . . ." O'Meara coughed, and several tablespoons of blood ran out of his mouth. "S-see you . . . in h-hell . . ." O'Meara's voice trailed off, and as Farrell looked down into his eyes, he saw them glaze over and gradually become opaque.

Farrell stood up slowly, rubbing his chin with his left hand. Fink slowly came from behind the counter and stopped at a discreet distance from him.

"S—should I call the p-police?" Fink asked in an apologetic voice.

Farrell's grim face snapped over to the pawnbroker, his eyes narrowed to slits. "What did you say?"

"The police," Fink said again, his eyes wide with shock. "Should I call them?"

As Farrell looked at the man, he noticed the revolver on his belt. "What's the caliber of that gun?"

"What?" Fink asked. "Oh, you mean this?" He drew the revolver from his holster with two fingers, as if it were a piece of rotting meat. "It is a .32."

Farrell took the gun from him and made a quick circuit of the room with his eyes. On the wall above their heads was a moth-eaten and badly mounted deer's head. One of the glass eyes had fallen out, giving the deer's face a lopsided, drunken appearance. Farrell pointed the .32 at the head and fired it once. A bit of dust flew, but the hole was too small to attract any attention.

Fink jumped a foot when the gun went off. Farrell turned, grabbing Fink and closing his hand over the butt of the revolver.

"Now call the police," Farrell said. "Your gun's caliber is close enough to mine that they won't ask any questions. Tell them you shot him. There's a reward, and they'll give it to you."

"B-b-but . . ." Fink began.

Farrell grabbed him by the collar and drew him close. "I wasn't here, you understand?"

Fink nodded his head and looked over at the dead man. He

was a bit unsure as to what had transpired in his shop, but he was completely certain he didn't want to know. If he had to lie to the police, that was a small price to pay to prevent his becoming embroiled in something that could only bring him grief.

When he looked up the door to his shop was slowly swinging shut, and Farrell was nowhere in sight.

Chapter 33

"I can't believe this, Frank," Chief of Police Sullivan said, shaking his head. "Gus Moroni's one of the most highly decorated officers on the force. You expect me to believe that he's involved in five different forms of corruption?" He bowed his head and shook it vigorously, like a dog shaking water from his fur.

"I know you don't like it, Chief," Casey said, "but I can back up everything in my report, especially the murder of Sandra Tartaglia. The bullet the ME dug out of her chest a little while ago is a perfect match to the one we've got on file down in the crime lab with his name on it. Besides, we've got an eyewitness to the kill."

"Your witness is far from the most credible, Inspector," a bald, thin, lugubrious man said from the corner of the office. "Farrell has been brought to the attention of the district attorney's office more than once. If sufficient proof had ever been available, he would now be in Angola breaking large rocks into smaller ones."

Casey lowered his eyes and laced his fingers across his middle. "I realize Farrell's past may be grounds for skepticism, Mr. Crockett, but I've seen quite a bit of the guy over the past week. He's shot straight with me all the way down the line.'' Casey paused and looked back up into District Attorney Crockett's eyes. ''I've been a cop for almost forty years, and I think he's okay. I trust him.''

The chief twisted his mouth and took on a reflective expression while he rolled a pencil around on the blotter of his desk. ''Okay, Frank,'' he said finally. ''I've known you a long time, and I know you don't stick your neck out unless you're pretty sure it won't get chopped off. I'll accept your report—until somebody comes along with something better.''

''What about these diamonds that've been smuggled into New Orleans?'' a third man asked. ''Can you show them to me?''

''Not at this minute, Mr. Ewell,'' Casey answered. ''But I've seen them with my own eyes, and I know how they got into the country. According to Farrell, Ganns and Moroni have them. They haven't had time to fence them yet, and I think if I can bag Ganns and Moroni, I can get the diamonds, too.''

''There're too many 'ifs, ands, and maybes' about this to suit me, Casey,'' Ewell said. ''I can't get a federal judge to issue any search warrants with no evidence, and I won't mix Treasury agents up in this—not yet, anyway.''

''I have to confess that I'm skeptical, too,'' District Attorney Crockett said, ''but I'll play ball on the murder warrant. I think Judge Garibaldi's still in his office. I'll call him now, if I may use your phone, Chief.''

''Help yourself,'' the chief said. Then he turned to Casey and said, ''I hope you know what you're doing, Frank. It's a damned hot potato you've picked up, and it'll burn the hell out of you if you don't watch out.''

''I know, Chief,'' Casey replied. ''It's gotten kind of personal, so I'll handle it myself. If there's any mud flying when this is over, I'll be the only one messed up with it.''

It was nearing 7:00 P.M. when Casey finally had the warrants and was on his way out to Emile Ganns's house. An autumn storm was brewing in the western sky, and the air was hot with

depressed air and discharges of lightning. Casey tried to listen
to the radio, but the galvanic atmosphere filled the airwaves
with static.

When he arrived at Ganns's house electric floodlights illuminated the yard, and the curtains in all the windows were drawn.
Two men were standing in the front yard, and they walked
toward Casey as he got out of his car.

"Sorry, pal. Mr. Ganns ain't seein' nobody this evening, so
you might as well shove off," the taller of the two said.

Casey held his left hand up; light reflected off his gold
detective's shield. "I'm not nobody," he said. "Mr. Ganns
better be home to me, or I'll get on the phone and have a
wagonload of harness bulls come down here to take the place
apart."

The taller man's eyes flicked from Casey's face to the badge,
and back again. "You got a warrant?" he asked.

"I got a pocketful of 'em," Casey said. "They're all blank,
and I can put anybody's name on 'em I want, even yours. Now
get out of the way before my patience wears out."

The tall man's eyes shifted to his partner as he said, "Wait
here, Sam. I'll go talk to the boss." He turned and stalked back
up to the house. Lightning flashed, and a sharp gust of wind
whistled through the trees, snatching at the tail of the man's
coat, and at the hat he held down with one hand.

When the wind slackened Casey casually reached inside his
coat. The other guard, a stocky, neckless thug, started, and his
right hand dove down to his right coat pocket.

Casey glanced at him with a knowing grin and said, "Nervous, pal? I don't blame you a bit. Here, have some gum." He
held out a package of spearmint to the stocky man, who looked
down on it with disdain.

Casey unwrapped a stick of gum and stuck it into his mouth.
"That the dirtiest look you got?" he asked. "If it is, you'd
better go down to Dillard's Department Store and look into a
job as a floor walker. You're not scary enough for this job."

The heavyset pug's face darkened with suffused blood, and
he was about to say something when his partner, still clutching
his hat against the wind, came back.

"Okay, copper, the boss says he'll see you. This way." He turned and led Casey up the walk to the porch. He opened the front door and, with a gesture of his chin, indicated that Casey should walk in.

The foyer was well lit, and Casey stood there admiring the paintings and a German grandfather clock as he removed his hat.

"Well, Inspector, this is a pleasant surprise," Ganns said.

Casey looked around for the source of the voice, walking farther into the house. "I don't think it'll be so pleasant once we get talking, Ganns," he said to the air. "You've had a pretty busy week. It's too bad everything you've done has been against the law."

Ganns's voice laughed mockingly from somewhere in the house. "Much of what I've done for the past forty-two years has been against the law, but laws are made by stuffy little men who get no joy out of life." Lights went up in the living room, and Ganns got up from a high-backed chair and walked toward Casey. "There is a great deal of joy to be derived from life, I've always found, but one has to have money to enjoy it."

"I know," Casey said with a wry smile. "I've been working for a living since 1899. You ever try it?"

Ganns went to a taboret table and poured calvados, then lowered his nose into the glass. He savored the smell for several seconds before he finally allowed himself a small taste. "You wound me deeply with that remark," he said when he'd swallowed. "You seem to believe that dishonest money is somehow easier to make than legitimate money. I can assure you it is not. I've always held the view that money made through vice, gambling, and larceny is harder to make, requiring a higher degree of intellectual skill than the ponderous, plodding kind exhibited by your average Wall Street broker." He gave Casey a small smile and sipped the calvados again.

There was silence in the room for a brief time, broken only by the faraway boom of thunder. Casey reached inside his coat and brought out a folded piece of paper. "I hate to cut into your enjoyment of life, Ganns, but I've got a warrant here for your arrest. Finish your drink and get your coat. I wouldn't want you to get caught in the rain on your way to jail.''

Ganns smiled again, and sat back down. "On what charge?" he asked.

"For starts, accessory to murder," Casey said. "I think we can also pull enough together to have you tried on a federal smuggling charge. And I expect there'll be some others as we go along the way." He tapped the folded warrant against his open left palm.

"Whom am I supposed to have participated in killing?" Ganns asked. "I haven't left the house for two days, except to go to my office downtown."

"For starts, Sandra Flynn," Casey said, holding up one finger. "For seconds, Marie Turnage, both killed early this morning down on Soraparu Street."

Ganns's smile wavered for a second, and he brought the small glass to his mouth in an attempt to hide it. When he had made a show of tasting the apple brandy again he looked back up at Casey, his eyes hard and opaque. "I don't see how you can accuse me of killing people I don't even know. I've never heard of either of them."

Casey removed his hat and dropped it on the coffee table. He sat down across from Ganns, leaned forward on his knees, and smiled into the other man's face. "That isn't the way Farrell will tell it in court. I expect he'll be willing to tell the jury about how you tried to kill him, too."

Ganns's face might have been set in stone. His normally placid brow was bent over his eyes, and his ordinarily smooth complexion was now a topography of anger and struggle. "I very much doubt I have anything to fear from Farrell's testimony in court. The word of a nightclub owner and gambler will mean little against that of a man with the kind of friends I have."

Casey leaned back in his chair with his hands folded in his lap. His easy smile was that of a man at complete peace. "You know," Casey said, ignoring Ganns's remark, "you might have gotten through all this if you'd left Farrell out of it. You'd probably have even gotten away with killing Tartaglia if you hadn't tried to get so cute. You set Farrell up to be killed, then you started to kill his friends. That was a pretty stupid thing for a smart man like you to do.''

"There is one problem with your analysis of this situation,'' Ganns replied. "I did not kill Tartaglia, nor did I attempt to have him killed.''

Casey chuckled and waved a hand. "That won't wash in court, Ganns. Farrell and I found out that Tartaglia was skimming profits from the things he fenced for you. He'd been doing it for a long time, so Paul Markowitz says, and he ought to know. He was getting some of the take.'' Casey reached up and ran his fingers through his hair. "It won't take much more than that to convince a jury that you put out the contract. My guess is that Moroni pulled the trigger for you.''

The storm outside had increased in intensity while the two men had talked, and the wind was lashing the house with sheets of rain that sounded like birdshot hitting a bucket. A huge bolt of lightning came to earth somewhere nearby, and the reverberation of thunder shook the house to its foundation.

Casey got out his handcuffs and threw them on the coffee table in front of Ganns. "I told you if we didn't get going you were gonna get wet. Better put those on and we'll go on downtown. It's only a matter of time before they pick Gus up, and I figure he'll sing a long, sweet song in order to shift most of the blame on to you.''

Another report of thunder shook the house, and the lights flickered. In the silence that followed, Casey heard the sound of a hammer rolling back on a gun.

"They ain't got me yet, Frank,'' Moroni's voice said. "And they ain't gonna.''

"Don't be stupid, Gus,'' Casey said without turning around. "I left a meeting with the chief, the DA, and the chief resident Treasury agent before I came here. I got a warrant for murder in my pocket with your name on it. What do you think's gonna happen if I don't report back pretty soon?''

"The storm'll buy us some time, I figure,'' Moroni said as he came up behind Casey, reached into his coat, and removed the .38 from his shoulder holster. "After I take care of you I'm gettin' the hell away from here."

Moroni came around in front of him and laid Casey's .38 on a table. "You better run hard and far, Gus," he said with a tight smile. "Farrell's on the loose, and he's gonna chop you into fish bait for what you did to Sandra Flynn. If you do anything to me, he'll burn you alive."

Moroni's brutal lips parted in a hideous grin. "Farrell's a tough baby," he said, "but he ain't bulletproof. Besides, you're just another cop. Why should he care if you get knocked off?"

Casey knew things were getting out of his control; he had to think of something that might buy him a little time. Only one thing came to mind, a wild gamble that might end up a disaster if it didn't work. "Because he's my son," Casey said.

When Farrell left the pawnshop the storm was just beginning to break. O'Meara's final words had done more to confuse him than provide any enlightenment. He wanted to talk to Casey, to try to figure out what to do next. Technically he was still a fugitive from justice, a target for any trigger-happy cop he might meet. He should have made some plans with Casey before he left him at Soraparu Street early that morning, but he was too used to doing things his own way. He hadn't even said good-bye, and he felt a little ashamed about it now.

Farrell felt great confusion over having a father who was a cop. It was hard to trust him, even after all he knew. But the one thing that made it impossible for Farrell to write him off was the commonality of the love the two men shared for Marie Delvaille. That meant a great deal.

Farrell saw the lights in a corner drugstore and pulled his car to the curb just as gale-force winds tore the store's green canvas awning from its supports like a cheap paper doily. Rain as hard and sharp as metal followed, and Farrell was soaked to the skin in the three seconds it took him to leave the car and get inside.

He saw two telephone booths at the far end of the store and walked quickly into one of them. Before he had any more time to think, he had reached police headquarters and asked for the detective squad.

"Detective Squad, Officer Parker speakin'," a voice said.

"I need to speak to Inspector Casey," Farrell said. "It's urgent."

Storm-bred static cut through the transmission, but Farrell could make out Parker saying that Casey wasn't there.

"Listen, do you have any idea where he went, or when he's supposed to be back?" Farrell shouted into the transmitter.

". . . arrest Emile Ganns" was all he caught of what Parker said before the line went dead. As if on cue, the lights in the drugstore went out, plunging everything into impenetrable darkness.

Ganns and Moroni stared openmouthed at Casey.

"Your son? Hah!" Ganns said. "That is priceless. Wesley Farrell the son of a policeman." He chuckled merrily. "I know now that God truly has a sense of the ironic."

"It's true, though," Casey said. "And he wants the two of you pretty badly. The best thing you can do is give me those guns and come along down to the calaboose with me. The accommodations aren't what you're used to, but you'll be safer there, believe me."

"I ain't goin' to jail, Frank," Moroni said. "You know what happens to cops on the inside. I wouldn't last a month."

"Tough break, Gus," Casey said. "I never liked you much, but it's hard to understand how you could stoop to something as low as protection and loan-sharking, much less smuggling and murder."

"Your captain made a small mistake a number of years ago," Ganns said, refilling his glass. "He is immune to most vices, but he occasionally indulges in rough sports with women. Women who offer such services, I hasten to say; well-paid women." Ganns tasted the brandy, rolling it around on his tongue luxuriously. "Unfortunately, one time he'd had a little too much to drink, and he slipped. A woman died. A woman, I may add, who was employed in an establishment I owned."

Casey shook his head and smiled appreciatively. "I bet you thought *you'd* died and gone to heaven."

Ganns gave his small smile again. "It has proven to be helpful, having the chief of detectives on the payroll. It made my operations in New Orleans much less hazardous. And since my continued silence about his moral lapse was imperative to his well-being, I had less to worry about with him than I sometimes did with Tartaglia. I shall miss having Captain Moroni around," he said, flicking his deep-set little eyes up at the big policeman.

"So you admit knowing that Tartaglia was dealing from the bottom of the deck with you," Casey said.

"Of course, Inspector," Ganns replied, raising his eyebrows. "One always suspects the help of cheating a little. It's important to their morale."

"He wasn't just cheating, according to Markowitz," Casey said. "He was about to steal the entire case of diamonds, sell them to Luc Bergeron, and skip out on you. Like I said, it's enough to burn you for his murder."

Ganns shook his head. "Well, that is interesting news. I knew Tartaglia was a miscreant, but it surprises me to learn just how bad he was." Ganns chuckled again. "But I did not know, and I did not have Moroni kill him, although I might have if I had known."

Casey frowned. "You're just splitting linguistic hairs now. If you didn't have Moroni do it, you probably had O'Meara do it."

"O'Meara?" Ganns asked, raising his eyebrows. "I know of no such person."

Rain pelted the house with such intensity that it was beginning to be difficult to talk and be heard. The lights flickered, went out, then came back, though they were less intense now.

"I've had enough talk, Frank," Moroni said, raising his large nickel-plated revolver. "I know I'm washed up here, so I may as well buy myself as much time as I can. Stand up."

"Don't be a fool, Gus," Casey said. He could feel sweat gathering under his arms and trickling down through the hair on the back of his neck. He had a short-barreled Detective

Special in his hip pocket, but it might as well have been an oasis in the desert and him a hundred miles away on foot. "If you kill me, they'll never stop looking for you. You've been a cop; they won't even try to take you alive, and you know it." He was talking fast now, fear lending a speed to his tongue that he wished was going to his feet.

Casey saw Ganns watching, his dark little eyes gleaming with something unrecognizable. Moroni had laid Casey's Police Positive on the table nearest Ganns, and the little man's hand had closed over the butt and was slowly picking it up. Casey saw that Ganns wasn't looking at him, but up at Moroni.

"Look out, Gus," Casey shouted. "He's got my gun."

As Moroni turned, there was the sound of a window breaking somewhere in the house, followed by a high-pitched scream. Another bolt of lightning exploded nearby, and the house went dark as the first shots were fired.

The tropical storm had hit without much warning, and low-lying streets were flooded in many parts of the city. Farrell had made it as far as City Park and was creeping the Packard through flood waters that had overflowed from Bayou St. John over Wisner Boulevard. Farrell had the powerful engine racing, trying desperately to keep it going as long as he could. He was still a couple of miles from Ganns's home, and wanted to get as close as he could before he had to abandon the car.

New Orleans had seldom seen such violent discharges of lightning, or winds of such magnitude. Farrell heard it tearing at the canvas top of his car, and water leaked in steady streams in several places. The water had a nasty chill to it, but Farrell felt himself sweating in spite of it.

Finally he saw the grounds of the Agricultural Research Station and knew he'd reached Robert E. Lee Drive. He turned left and began looking for Foliage Park Road, the street that would lead him to Ganns's house. From the few houses he passed Farrell could tell that power had failed in this part of town. It was a handicap now, but it might be useful if he could just reach Ganns's place.

As he eased the Packard into yet another wind-whipped pool of water, he quickly discovered it was something worse. He'd lost the road in the storm and had driven into a deep ditch. Cursing, he threw his shoulder into the door, forced it open, and bailed out.

He found himself thigh-deep in a thundering hell of water that cut into him like a million small daggers. His hat was torn from his head and his clothes immediately became plastered to his skin. Bringing up his forearm to protect his eyes, he bent into the storm. He'd never felt so puny, so diminished by anything before.

He lost track of time as he fought to bring each leg up out of the water and put it in front of the other. Then he saw something; a dark shape was suddenly illuminated by a bolt of lightning as thick as Farrell's arm, and he saw it was Ganns's house. Pausing for a moment, he made a sudden decision to go around to the back.

The house and yard were in complete blackness, and it was difficult even to distinguish the windows from the brick walls. In another flash of light he saw a set of French doors that opened onto a raised brick patio. Some white wrought-iron patio furniture sat there, unperturbed by the savagery of the wind. Farrell wrenched up one of the metal chairs and flung it into the doors.

The glass exploded inward, and Farrell threw himself after it. When he came up the knife was in his hand. A body backed into him, and he spun it around, plunging the stiletto deep into the man's chest. The man let out a high, thin, tearing scream that seemed to go on forever before it finally ended. Shots were exploding in the front of the house, and Farrell flattened himself against the nearest wall.

He patted his hip and found, to his relief, that he still had Casey's gun, and he drew it.

"Frank," he called. "Frank, it's Farrell. Are you all right?" Two shots whined in his direction, and he flinched away from plaster dust as one struck the wall near his head.

"Look out, kid," Casey's voice spoke hollowly from the darkness. "There's four of 'em in here." Another shot sounded, then another; then there was the sound of a deep sigh, and a body falling, knocking furniture about.

Farrell froze. He felt a moment's blind panic at the thought that those last bullets had found Casey's heart. He forced himself to stay quiet and began inching toward the sound of the shooting.

Now the only noises were those of wind and rain. The violence of the storm had not abated but, rather, seemed stronger still. Farrell crept along the edge of the room, the .32-20 up and cocked in his hand. The sounds of the storm assaulting the house blotted out all other noises. He wondered nervously about Casey but knew it could be worth his life to call out again.

Then he felt, rather than heard, a presence near him. He moved toward it, a millimeter at a time. His breathing was so shallow it was almost like not breathing at all. He still had the open knife in his left hand, and he shifted it to attack, but it quickly occurred to him that the presence he felt might be Casey. He placed the handle of the knife between his teeth, then gently let down the hammer on his gun. He could hear the other man breathing now, the rapid panting of a man gripped by unreasoned terror. He put out his left hand, and as soon as his fingers met cloth, he whipped the butt of the pistol down, feeling it connect with bone. As the man slumped, he caught him by the collar and gently let him down to the floor. He felt the man's face with his free hand; the absence of facial hair told him he hadn't slugged the red-haired detective. He half wished it had been, knowing that Casey was still in as much danger from his gun as from those of the other men in the house.

There was a bigger room ahead, with a window in it. Occasional distant flashes briefly brightened the gloom, but never for long enough to enable him to see anything. He moved painstakingly ahead, the gun reversed in his hand again, its single dark eye hungering for a target.

Farrell was now at the opening to the room, and he prayed for enough lightning to help him see something. But no flashes came, and the passing seconds seemed like hours. His hand was sweating on the butt of the gun, and the chill of the storm on his skin was gone now. He felt as if he was in the grip of a fever as he waited for the moment that could make or break this game of chance.

He couldn't tell how long he had stood there, but it was long enough for the darkness to begin playing tricks on his eyes. He felt blind, and panic tugged at the edges of his consciousness. He knew he couldn't stand here all night, that sooner or later he would have to force some action.

He was gathering his legs under him to charge the room when it happened: Lightning struck a tree in the yard outside the window, bathing the room in fiery light. For one brief second Farrell saw Gus Moroni standing behind Casey, the big revolver moving inexorably toward the back of Casey's head. Farrell shouted a warning, and his gun swept up, throwing long lances of flame across the room. Even as the light died, he kept squeezing the trigger, sending bullet after bullet at the place where Moroni's body had been. In the darkness he heard deep grunts of pain, and the sound of lamps being knocked over.

"Frank," Farrell cried in a shaky voice. "Frank, are you all right?"

"Yeah," Casey's voice spoke. It was the voice of a man who knew a new definition of fear. "Yeah, I'm here. There were two guards; did you see 'em?"

"I got both of them," Farrell said. "What about Ganns?"

"I think he's dead. Somebody stood too near the window a few minutes ago, and I fired at him," Casey said. "C'mon in. I've found a candle."

A match flared, and Farrell moved toward it. He found Casey, his red hair disheveled, leaning against the wall. His face was chalk white in the glow of the candelabrum he held, and Farrell saw that a bullet had grazed his head, just above his left ear.

Over in front of the window lay the small, perfect body of Emile Ganns. His left hand was folded over his breast, and Casey's .38 was cradled in his outstretched hand. The starched white bosom of his shirt was decorated by two large rosettes that were slowly growing toward each other.

Moroni lay on the floor; Farrell could see where three of the powerful .32-20 slugs had entered his massive trunk. He took the candelabrum from Casey and stood over him. Moroni's questing right hand still sought his pistol, and Farrell could see the iron of struggle yet in his eyes.

"You . . . lousy . . . b-bastard," Moroni gasped through the blood on his lips. "I'll . . ."

As his fingers touched the butt of his large revolver, Farrell placed his foot on the hand and bore his weight down on it. "You'll die," Farrell said through his teeth. He cocked his revolver and pointed it at Moroni's head, but Casey's hand closed over the pistol and stayed him.

"He's gone already," Casey said. "You can't kill him any deader than he is now."

Farrell stared down at the large body at his feet and saw that the eyes were staring fixedly past him. "If I'd killed him sooner . . ." His voice quivered and almost broke.

Casey took the gun from Farrell's yielding fingers and laid a hand on his shoulder. "Yeah, I know."

The two men were silent for a moment, each lost in his own thoughts. Then Casey noticed the howling of the wind again, and took back the candelabrum. "We can't do much until the storm passes," he said finally. "Let's find a couple of blankets and drink some of that apple brandy. The way Ganns played with it, it must be pretty good stuff."

"Yeah," Farrell said softly. "I . . . I'm feeling kind of cold and tired right now." Then he sat down heavily in a chair and was silent.

Chapter 34

Thursday morning dawned pale and gray as cloudy remnants of the previous night's gale drifted eastward over the water-logged city. Farrell and Casey, both drawn and tired-looking, rolled uptown on St. Charles Avenue, taking silent stock of the ruined gardens and splintered trees left in the storm's wake. Farrell's Packard convertible was dented in several places, and the interior already smelled of mildew, but it handled well under Farrell's guidance.

Both men were tired, their faces grainy with sorrow and lack of sleep. They'd spent several tough hours with Chief of Police Sullivan, Assistant District Attorney Crockett, and Treasury Agent Paul Ewell, explaining everything they knew about the time leading up to the murder of Chance Tartaglia, and the hectic, blood-spattered week that followed it. Farrell and Casey each had sticking plaster over minor wounds on their faces and heads. Casey held the russet leather suitcase of diamonds on his lap.

"It's been a hell of a week," Casey said as they made the dogleg that turned St. Charles to Carrollton Avenue.

"It's had some moments," Farrell agreed laconically. He turned off Carrollton to Sycamore Place and drove slowly down

the three blocks to Helen Tartaglia's house. Already there was
black crepe on the front door. The two men walked up the
gently spiraling stairs to the door, where Casey pushed the
doorbell. After a moment Helen appeared at the beveled glass
door and opened it to them.

Casey took off his hat and smiled wanly at Helen. "Hello,
Helen," he said. "I thought we'd see each other again under
better circumstances. You remember Mr. Farrell, don't you?"

"Hello, Frank," Helen replied. "Yes, of course. Both of
you please come in." She stood aside to allow them entry, and
shut the door behind them. She led them to the sofa and chairs
in front of the fireplace, and invited them with a gesture to sit
down.

"Helen, I don't quite know how to tell you how sorry I am
about Sandy," Casey said as he sat down. He placed the little
suitcase on the floor, beside the chair. "She was as sweet a
little girl as I've ever known."

Helen made a smile that threatened to break into tears, but
she lowered her eyes, patted her hair absently, and fought them
back. "I guess coming back here wasn't a very good idea,"
she said in a broken voice. "I thought we were coming back
home, but it's just been . . . a horror."

Farrell leaned his elbows on his knees, looking at the floor
between his feet as he clasped his hands in a furious grip. He'd
hardly had time to get used to Sandra's death himself, and
Helen's barely suppressed anguish brought feelings of his own
rushing to the surface, feelings he knew he couldn't let out
here.

"I know she'd become fond of you, Mr. Farrell," Helen
said, seeming to sense his unspoken grief. "I hope this hasn't
been too difficult for you."

Farrell looked up at her but could do no more than nod.

"If it means anything to you," Casey said, to break the
uncomfortable silence, "we got the man who did it. He was a
corrupt police officer in the employ of the same gangster Chance
worked for. Both men were killed resisting arrest last night."

Helen nodded, her eyes cast down to the floor. "Thank you,
Frank. It isn't worth much, but it's something, at least."

There was silence again for several seconds; then Casey said, "You might also be interested to know that Griffin O'Meara was shot yesterday evening during the attempted robbery of a pawnshop. The shop owner killed him."

Helen had picked up a throw pillow from the sofa and hugged it tightly to her stomach. "Griffin O'Meara?" she asked. "Am I supposed to know him?"

Casey looked at her sadly, thinking, *This isn't the woman I knew thirty years ago. That woman must have died somewhere along the way.* "I think you know him," he said, "just as you probably know why I brought this suitcase."

For the first time in several minutes Farrell looked up and addressed Helen Tartaglia. "Sandy told me that her father hadn't recognized her when he came to get the diamonds last Thursday morning. She was calling herself Flynn, so nobody— not Ganns, or Moroni, or Tartaglia, himself—had any idea who she was."

"We didn't know that diamonds had anything to do with this case until we started checking on Chance's movements on the day he died," Casey said. "We found out that he'd spent his last hours with a high-class hooker named Holly Ballou. When Holly was killed, too, by O'Meara, our first thought was that O'Meara was an enforcer, sent to knock off Chance for trying to steal the diamonds from Ganns." Casey paused to bring the suitcase around. He lay it flat on the floor in front of him.

"It figured that when he discovered Chance didn't have the diamonds, O'Meara must have believed that he had left the ice with Holly," Casey continued. "What nobody knew was that Chance regularly left stolen material with the building superintendent, a punch-drunk ex-fighter named Leo Terranova. Terranova was a perfect go-between because he never knew what he was holding for the fence, and was too empty-headed to even think of asking."

Casey leaned forward, unsnapped the latches of the case, and opened the lid. He turned it around so Helen could see the little glassine envelopes still stacked in perfect, orderly rows.

"Things began to come unglued for everybody when

O'Meara went to Holly Ballou's," Casey said. "If he hadn't run into Farrell on the stairs, we might never have known anything about his involvement at all."

"I don't see why you're bothering me with all this police business, Frank," Helen said, pushing the throw pillow away from her. "Sandy's loss has been a terrible blow to me, and I'm not up to much conversation right now." She turned a haggard face to Casey, and he could see that her eyes were bloodshot, with dark circles under them.

"There's a reason for all this, Helen," Casey said. "Just bear with us for a few minutes more."

Farrell spoke again. "After I saw O'Meara on the stairs at Holly's he tried twice to kill me." He spread the fingers on one hand and ticked off the numbers. "The first time was across the street from Paul Markowitz's house. Markowitz worked for Chance, so once again I believed somebody thought I was getting too close to the diamonds." He paused and ran his fingers through his hair.

"The second time was behind my club a couple of nights ago," Farrell went on. "O'Meara had two others with him that time, and they shot a friend of mine."

Helen pushed back a few errant strands of hair and patted them into place. "I'm terribly sorry for your friend, Mr. Farrell, but I still don't know what you're talking about."

Farrell placed a Camel in the corner of his mouth, lit it, and drew smoke deeply into his lungs. "All the time this was going on," Farrell continued, letting smoke feather out of his nose, "I thought this was about two gangs of crooks fighting over the diamonds. Ganns brought me into this to find Tartaglia's killer, hoping I'd find the diamonds in the process. I figured that O'Meara was working for the other side, trying to take me out before I lucked onto the ice.

"The thing that tripped up O'Meara was the fact that he was playing two different games at once," Farrell continued. "Whoever he was working for either didn't know he was going all over town pulling penny-ante heists, or knew and didn't care. We know, for example, that he and two other men knocked over a small hardware store last Saturday and killed the owner with the same gun that killed Chance.'' Farrell took a last drag on the cigarette, then crushed it out in a small silver ashtray. ''I was lucky enough to trace O'Meara to a rooming house where he was holed up, then followed him into a pawnshop he was planning to rob. He didn't live long after that, but he hung on long enough to tell me that he wasn't the one to kill Tartaglia. He said that 'the Flynn woman' was responsible for it. I thought at the time he meant Sandy.''

Now Casey leaned forward and pointed a finger at Helen. ''While Farrell was tracking down O'Meara, I spent my time trying to locate Emile Ganns. I found him at home just before the big storm broke. I'd believed that O'Meara was working for him, and that he'd had Chance killed because he was skimming money from jewelry and other things he was fencing for Ganns. Only Ganns didn't know Chance was stealing from him. He also said he didn't know O'Meara.''

Casey leaned back in his chair, a look of complete weariness on his face. ''So now we have a deathbed statement from a known killer, and a statement from two crooks who had no reason to lie, since they were talking to a man they planned to kill within seconds. I think that's what the district attorney might call 'incontrovertible evidence.' ''

Helen sat quietly on the sofa, her arms folded in a protective gesture in front of her. She no longer looked at either Farrell or Casey, almost in a world of her own.

Casey stood up, walked over to the window, and looked out at the gradually brightening sky. ''The thing that confused me for so long was how to connect the diamonds with a killer who used a .455 Webley navy automatic.'' He paused and turned back to Helen again. ''While I was trying to figure out how the diamonds got into the country past the Customs and Treasury people, I remembered seeing a Fox newsreel about the diamond mines in South Africa, which happens to be part of the British Commonwealth.''

Helen got up and walked over to the bar. She opened a bottle of Peter Dawson scotch and poured about three fingers into a tall, slim glass. She didn't offer any to Farrell and Casey, and drank from the glass without turning back to them.

"I began looking for ships with British registry that had docked here over the past couple of weeks," Casey went on. "There were only a couple from South Africa here during the time in question. I found one ship, the S. S. *Broor Mickkelson,* which brought Sandra in last Wednesday, probably with the diamonds. The Treasury people are looking into that part."

Helen finished her drink, then poured another and turned back to Casey. The skin had tightened across the planes of her face, giving it the look of dried-out flesh on a skull. Her eyes glowed from deep inside that ravaged face like something unmentionable.

"I found another ship that docked three weeks ago, Helen," Casey said. "The S. S. *Roark's Drift.* There was a Helen Flynn listed among the passengers. I must have looked at that name ten times before I remembered that Flynn was your maiden name. There was also an Irish sailor on that ship. One Griffin O'Meara, who stole a .455 Webley automatic pistol before he jumped ship."

Casey slowly walked over to where Helen stood and put his hands in his pockets. "In the years I've been a cop I've seen a lot of smart crooks end up dead, or in jail, because they took a simple crime and complicated it with something stupid. I figure that you and Sandra cooked up an idea to smuggle some diamonds into the country. My guess is that O'Meara was a hooligan you hired to help you with any strong-arm stuff." He paused and scratched his stubbled chin. "You made contact with Ganns before the diamonds arrived, and he sent Tartaglia to meet Sandra and collect the diamonds. Sandy recognized her father and told you about it, and you decided to pay off a long-standing grudge. You found out where he lived and, probably together with O'Meara, waited until your opportunity came. When it did, you took O'Meara's gun and shot Tartaglia twice, at point-blank range." Something that sounded like a sigh escaped Casey, and his shoulders slumped with fatigue.

"Do you know what happened to me after I left Chance?" Helen asked after a long silence. Her voice was dry and cracked, like an old woman's.

"No," Casey replied.

"I became a whore," she said. "I found out pretty quickly that I could only make money on my knees, scrubbing somebody's floor, or on my back." She poured more scotch in her glass and walked slowly back to the sofa. "I figured that if I worked as a maid, I'd probably age fast and die young. I had Sandra to think about, and I didn't want her to be left alone in the world, like I'd been."

"No matter what had happened between you and Chance," Casey said, "I'm certain he wouldn't have wanted that to happen."

"Oh, it was my decision," Helen said. "I wanted to be independent of him, free of him and every other man. I was scared at first," she said with a nervous little laugh. "I thought what I was doing was a sin. You see, I still had illusions then." She laughed again, but it was brittle, without humor. "But like everything else, the more I did it, the easier it got. I learned how to pretend I was having a good time." She paused as a single tear ran from the corner of her right eye down her hollow cheek and dropped onto the collar of her blouse.

"I'm sorry," Casey said. "I didn't know. If I had . . ."

"Don't try to take any of this on yourself," Helen said. "I did what I did, and I ask no pity because of it. I was disillusioned in love and decided to make every man I met pay for my disillusionment." She placed her elbow on the arm of the sofa and lowered her face into her hand. "I reinvented myself, remade myself every night, and every time I was different, better than the last time. By the time Sandra was twelve I had my own apartment and regular clients. By the time she was fifteen I was able to send her away to school. When she graduated I had a lot of money in the bank and owed nothing to anybody. I retired then, and she and I moved abroad for a number of years."

"What made you get into smuggling?" Farrell asked. "That was a pretty dumb move for such a smart woman."

"Sandra was ambitious," Helen replied. "I suppose I made her that way. My ambitions were always for her, and as she grew up, she adopted them for her own. We ended up in

Capetown several years ago, and she began a business exporting
antiquities to the United States.''

Helen got up again and walked to the window. The sun was
beginning to break through the clouds, and dust motes swirled
in the beams of light filtering into the room. Both men watched
her with the rapt attentiveness of an audience caught up in
some tragedy by Eugene O'Neill.

''I think now that she must have had some of her father in
her, even though she never knew him,'' she said after a brief
silence. ''The earned money wasn't very exciting to her. She
was a child who liked thrills. A Chinese trader introduced her
to the idea of smuggling diamonds and other precious stones
to America, and she fell completely in love with the romance
of it. I begged her not to do it, but she was running the business
completely on her own by then and was doing it well. She had
no time to pay attention to the fears of an old woman.''

''What made you come back to New Orleans?'' Farrell asked.

''I guess I was homesick,'' she answered. ''If you are born
here, as I was, no place else is ever quite as good as New
Orleans. Besides, I still had some friends here from my days
as a joy girl, and through them I was gradually put into contact
with Emile Ganns. By way of personal messengers who visited
us in Capetown, he promised to fence anything Sandra could
acquire. With that assurance in place, she eventually decided
to move her entire operation here, planning to continue to
import antiquities as a cover for the smuggling. She was really
doing quite well, but then she met Chance.''

''And you decided to kill him,'' Casey said.

She glanced over at him and smiled thinly. ''You make it
sound so calculated. I was really feeling very happy. I'd met
O'Meara aboard ship and become quite friendly with him. He
had a sense of humor, something I've found in few other men.
I hadn't had any interest in men for years, but he sparked
something in me with that blarney he spouted. I took him for
a lover.'' She smiled, looking almost young for a brief moment.

''I received a wire from London this morning,'' Casey said
quietly. ''O'Meara may have been funny, but his record isn't.
His real name was Sean Deegan, and he's wanted over there

for several murders in the name of the Irish Republican Army. He's been on the run for five years.''

"He was quite candid about his past," she said. "But who was I to judge him? Oh, he was no good, and he was always after me for money, but I enjoyed having him around—while it lasted."

"About Chance . . ." Farrell said. "You were going to explain about the killing."

Helen took another small drink and leaned against the windowsill. Sunlight was pouring in, dispelling the gloom from the corners of the room.

"I'd asked Griff to find out where he lived," she said. "We drove over there, and I decided to wait until he showed up. When he finally arrived I could see he was drunk by the way the car weaved around. He was staggering a little when he got out. I think that when I saw him leaning there, drinking from that stupid flask, and mooning up at the stars like some lovesick boy, I realized that he hadn't changed at all. He was having one more night with one more woman, just like when we were married. I made Griff give me the gun and I walked up to him. He'd dropped his flask in the street and bent over to pick it up. When he stood up he found me standing across the hood of the car."

She drank again, and Casey relaxed for the first time in days. It was almost over now.

Helen began to giggle. "You should have seen the stupid look on his face when he saw me. You should have seen how . . ." She began to laugh again, but the laughter began to take on a sick, strangled sound that turned into a moan of anguish. She dropped the glass on the floor, and Casey went over to her. He sat next to her, patting her shoulder until the sobbing began to lessen. He took her hand, then, and spoke softly to her.

"Who put O'Meara up to killing Holly?" he asked.

Helen wiped her eyes and nose with a scrap of lace handkerchief and looked at Casey with red-rimmed eyes. "After I killed Chance I thought . . . I thought to check his car to see if he still had the diamonds. We'd risked a lot to get them here, and I didn't want them to fall into the hands of the police. When I didn't find them I got Griff to snoop around until he found out some of Chance's habits. I don't know how he traced Chance's movements to the Ballou woman's apartment, but he did. Instead of just forcing his way into the apartment and making her tell him where the diamonds were, the fool killed her.''

She stopped to wipe her nose and look over at Farrell. "Griff described you to me with great care after he collided with you on the stairs. When I saw you at the funeral I recognized you instantly. I was so shocked to see you that for days I thought I'd tipped my hand to you. It was Sandra's idea to track you down, cozy up to you, and find out what you knew. We both believed you would eventually find the diamonds.''

She leaned back on the sofa, a look of total exhaustion on her face. "That turned out to be a fatal assumption. Sandra liked you immediately. I warned her not to get involved with you, that you were a danger to everything we'd put together.'' She paused and looked down at her hands. "I decided to have Griff kill you, too, before you figured out too much. But he wasn't good enough. After he failed the second time I told him to get out of town before you, or the police, found him. I promised him some money, but he said he needed more before he left town. He had some scheme to send money back to his associates in Ireland. If the rest of the Irish are anything like him, they'll be under England's thumb for eternity.''

"Where's the gun, Helen?" Casey asked.

"The drawer in that writing table over there,'' she answered, pointing to a small mahogany table.

Farrell got up and walked to the table. When he opened the drawer he found the blunt, bulky British automatic. He took it out, snapped out the magazine, and saw it still had two cartridges left.

"I made him leave it with me in case he was caught,'' Helen said. "I was afraid he'd lead the police back to me if they suspected he was involved in Chance's death.''

Casey stood up, picked up the case of diamonds, and put on

his hat. "Well, I guess that does it, Helen. Sorry we had to bother you today."

Helen raised her eyes, a look of complete surprise on her face. "You—you're not taking me in?"

Casey reached up and tugged at his earlobe, smiling slightly. "I don't think there's any need. We've got the gun that killed Chance, and we know that O'Meara stole it from the ship. If that isn't enough to close the file, I might be able to hang it on Ganns, or Moroni. Since they're both already dead it won't hurt them any." He walked over and put his hand on Helen's shoulder. "Sometimes people get dealt a bad hand, Helen. I know that better than most, I guess. Besides, the law can't punish you any more than you've been punished already. C'mon, Farrell. Let's go home."

Farrell followed Casey out of the room. They didn't speak until they were back in the car and headed downtown on Claiborne Avenue.

"I want you to know I couldn't have cracked this without you, Wes," Casey said. "You'd make some detective a good partner."

"Thanks," Farrell replied. "I'll remember that if times ever get tough."

"They won't get any tougher than the past week," Casey said, laughing a little.

The men fell silent, each feeling the tension building between them.

"I—I don't know how to say this exactly," Casey finally began. "For thirty-five years I've wondered what happened to you, and to your mother. If I'd known, I'd have gone to you, no matter how far away it was, or what sacrifice it took. When I lost her I grieved for years. Finding you after all these years . . . it's like a miracle to me. It's like finding a piece of her still alive. I don't want to lose you again . . . son."

The last word in Casey's declaration echoed in Farrell's ears like the peal of a bell, and as much as he wanted to, he felt helpless to respond to it. He stared out the windshield for a long time before he spoke.

"Look . . . Frank . . . you don't know me very well. If you

did . . . I've been skating along the edge of the law most of my life. I don't make any apologies for what I am, but you're a cop, and sooner or later it would come up between us. It's the way things are, and you know it.''

Casey turned to Farrell, resisting the impulse to lay a hand on his arm, knowing it was too soon for that. "Don't be too quick to judge me, or yourself. I'm no saint. I might have done some of the same things you've done in the same spot. You were a kid, alone, and I guess you had to make up the rules as you went along.''

Farrell shook his head for want of the words he could not find.

Casey, seeing the confusion, sank back against the seat and looked out the window. "I don't care what you did, or who you did it to, Wes. All that matters to me is that we not lose each other again. I'm not asking you to call me father or anything. I just want to be your friend. There are people out there who'll tell you I'm good at it.''

Farrell rounded the corner and pulled to a gentle stop outside police headquarters. He couldn't bring himself to look at Casey. "I'll keep it in mind . . . Frank," he said as he flexed his hands on the steering wheel.

Farrell felt Casey shift his weight in the other seat and looked down to see the older man's hand held out to him. Without a word he took the hand, and felt his own caught in a warm, firm grip. Then Casey was out of the car and standing on the sidewalk with the valise of diamonds.

"See you around, kid," Casey said.

Farrell hesitated, then held up his hand in farewell and drove quickly away. Casey watched him until the cream-and-red Packard was out of sight.

Epilogue

It was Saturday night, and the Cafe Tristesse was pulsing with the sound of a new orchestra. Up in his office, Farrell was sitting at his desk, tapping his foot to the sounds of Louis Prima's "Sing, Sing, Sing," coming through a special speaker box mounted on the wall behind him. He smiled appreciatively as the drum soloist perfectly duplicated Gene Krupa's frantic African rhythms on the skins.

Just as the drum and the horns were building to the final crescendo, Farrell heard a short knock at the door.

"Yeah," he called above the sound of the music.

The door opened, and Mickey, the big Negro handyman, stuck his head inside. "Miz Willie Mae Gautier's here, boss. You said show her right up."

Farrell reached under the edge of his desktop and silenced the speaker with a hidden switch. "Show her in, Mickey," he said.

Mickey's head disappeared, and the door swung wide to admit the little old woman. She was dressed in a subdued print dress but still wore the silver watch on her bodice, and the silver pince-nez on the bridge of her nose. She swept into the room, holding her shawl over one arm, and sat down without waiting for Farrell to invite her.

"I hope you've got news," she said in a brusque, impatient tone. "I've not seen or heard from Marcel in several days." Her face was set in hard lines, and her small, dark eyes were angry. "I was laboring under the impression that you intended to help me."

Farrell rocked back in his chair and placed the tips of his fingers together in a pensive pose. "Yes, Aunt Willie," he said. "But I'm afraid all my news isn't good." Farrell allowed a faint smile to touch his lips when he saw the look of uncertainty leap into the old woman's eyes.

"Let's start with the bad news first," Farrell said in a bland voice. "Marcel got hooked up with a couple of pretty wrong gees a couple of weeks ago. Apparently they've been going around the city casing small businesses until they knew the layout, then staging early morning robberies. A few days back they shot and killed an old guy in a hardware store. Later they almost killed a woman behind my club, here."

The old woman gasped, and her right hand leaped to her throat.

"Now that you've heard the bad news, let's go on to the good," Farrell continued. "So far I'm the only one who knows about Marcel's involvement in the robberies and shootings. His partners have both met with unfortunate . . . and fatal . . . accidents."

Willie Mae's brusque haughtiness was completely gone now, and the hand at her throat trembled. "What . . . what do you intend to do?" she asked in a quavering voice.

Farrell lit a Camel and blew smoke into the air across his right shoulder. "Aunt Willie, does the name Frank Casey mean anything to you?"

Willie Mae's olive complexion paled, and she sucked in her breath quickly. She began to cough uncontrollably, seemingly unable to get her breath. Farrell got up, went over to his taboret table, and poured a healthy measure of Hennessy's cognac into a glass. He took it over to the old woman and held the glass to her lips. She took in the whole measure in a single bite, and

Farrell smiled as he remembered her long-ago fulminations against the evils of drink.

As her coughing spasm died, Farrell sat back in his chair and regarded the old woman with an amused smile. "I have to give you credit, Aunt Willie; you're a tough adversary. You destroyed my parents' marriage and convinced me that my father had run away from my mother because he didn't want us anymore. I've spent a lot of years hating you." He paused as he walked back to his desk and rested a haunch on one corner.

Willie Mae's eyes were round with fear, and her hands, resting on the arms of the chair, trembled. She moved her lips but seemed unable to form any words with them.

Farrell smiled at her kindly and shook his head. "Once I'd have probably killed you for what you did, but I've decided to give you the benefit of the doubt."

"W—why?" Willie Mae asked in a quavering voice.

"Maybe because I've learned something about forgiveness in the past few days," Farrell said, shaking his head. "You and I are quite alike, really."

Willie Mae stopped shaking and threw a questioning glance at Farrell.

"It's true," Farrell said. "Both of us have spent years trying to keep control of our own lives by controlling everything and everybody around us." Farrell paused to brush lightly at a lock of his hair that had fallen over his eyebrow. "The trouble is, you can't always control everything, no matter how hard you try. I guess the bad part is that when you try that hard to control everything, you end up alone, without a friend when you might need one the most." He paused and looked down at the floor. "I'm luckier than most, I guess. A couple of weeks ago I was alone, too. Then, when everything fell apart, and it looked like I was going down, I found out I wasn't alone after all. Do you understand what I'm trying to say?"

The old woman looked mystified, and a little relieved that he wasn't going to punish her for her duplicity. When she said nothing Farrell smiled at her in a gentle way and shook his head, then pushed another button under the edge of his desk.

Three seconds later Marcel walked into the room. He was dressed in his expensive suit, with every pleat and press exactly as it should have been, but his face was badly bruised, and he had strips of sticking plaster over one eye and on his neck.

"Marcel," Willie Mae said with some surprise. "What happened to you? What are you doing here?"

Marcel stood still, indecision on his face and a touch of fear in his eyes. After a few seconds of silence Farrell began to speak again.

"I've had a little while to talk to Marcel, Aunt Willie, and we've discovered we have a lot in common, too," he said. "Both of us lost our fathers and mothers when we were young, and each of us ended up living with you." Farrell paused and looked at Marcel's battered face. "He says he still has nightmares about the leather strap, too."

"Wh—what are you going to do?" Willie Mae asked. Her voice cracked, and she looked every bit the tired old woman she really was.

Farrell turned back to face her. "I'm going to give Marcel the break I never had. He belongs to me now; he's going to move out of your house."

"But . . . but he's all I have," Willie Mae wailed. "He's all I have left of my daughter." Her face was twisted in pain, and her eyes were brimming with tears.

"Yeah," Farrell said, nodding. "I know. But I think I can do more for him than you can. Do you remember telling me I had to help him because he was family?" Farrell asked, pointing a finger at her. "Well, I realized you were right. Color is only skin deep, but his blood and mine are the same. Even more than the blood tie, he and I share a common experience. Like you said the other night, wherever Marcel is now, I've been there first. Now I'm going to see he gets started off on the right foot."

Willie Mae was sobbing now, and she held her face in her hands. Farrell gave her his handkerchief and patted her shoulder.

"Don't take on so, Aunt Willie," he said quietly. "You may not like what I'm going to teach Marcel, but when I get through with him, he'll be a man, standing on his own two feet. Marcel," he said to the boy, "take your grandmother downstairs and whistle up a taxi for her. Tell the cabbie to make certain she gets inside her house all right." He reached into his pocket, pulled out a money clip, and gave Marcel a ten-dollar bill for the cab. The youngster nodded, took the bill, and then helped his crying grandmother out of the office.

Alone in his office again, Farrell switched his speaker back on and heard the boy and girl duet downstairs softly singing "Stardust" to each other while muted clarinets chirped like songbirds behind them. Farrell went to the window and looked at the parade of cars gliding down the rain-slicked streets.

Farrell thought about the last few days, and how they'd changed him. They'd been difficult days for him, but for some reason he felt curiously uplifted by the experience. He'd been totally alone at the beginning, a man unto himself and no other. He'd been that way since his mother's death. But now he wasn't alone anymore. He had a family of sorts—a father, if he could find it in himself to accept him, a cousin to whom he could play mentor, and a woman who had gone beyond the role of casual lover into that of trusted confidante. Farrell had spent years making himself completely self-sufficient, but that was over now, and he was glad.

He heard the door open and close behind him, and he turned to see Marcel standing respectfully in front of the desk.

"I, uh, I got Grandma a cab. She's on her way home now," he said. "Is—is there anything you'd like me to do now, Mr. Farrell?"

Farrell walked over to his bar and poured rye whiskey into two glasses. Then he handed one to Marcel.

"I think we've done all the work for today we need to," he said to the younger man. "Let's just talk about what your life's going to be like from now on." He lifted his glass and gave Marcel a wink. "And by the way, I'm your cousin. Just call me Wes from now on, okay?"

THE SEVENTH CARRIER SERIES
BY PETER ALBANO

THE SEVENTH CARRIER   (0-8217-3612-4, $4.50)
The original novel of this exciting, best-selling series. Imprisoned in a cave of ice since 1941, the great carrier *Yonaga* finally breaks free in 1983, her maddened crew of samurai determined to carry out their orders to destroy Pearl Harbor.

RETURN OF THE SEVENTH CARRIER
                         (0-8217-2093-7, $3.95)
With the war technology of the former superpowers still crippled by Red China's orbital defense system, a terrorist beast runs rampant across the planet. Outarmed and outnumbered, the target of crack saboteurs and fanatical assassins, only the *Yonaga* and its brave samurai crew stand between a Libyan madman and his fiendish goal of global domination.

ASSAULT OF THE SUPER CARRIER
                         (0-8217-5314-2, $4.99)
A Libyan madman, the world's single most dangerous and fanatical despot, controls the fate of the free world. The brave samurai crew of the *Yonaga* are ready for the ultimate kamikaze mission.